Haunting Stories
of ghosts and ghouls

Haunting Stories

of ghosts and ghouls

Geoffrey Palmer
and Noel Lloyd

Illustrated by Ivan Lapper

Hamlyn
London · New York · Sydney · Toronto

Published 1982
The Hamlyn Publishing Group Limited
London · New York · Sydney · Toronto
Astronaut House, Feltham, Middlesex, England.

ISBN 0 600 36676 6

Printed in Yugoslavia

Contents

The stories in this book previously appeared in *The Obstinate Ghost and other ghostly tales*, *Ghosts Go Haunting*, and *Ghost Stories Round the World* all published by Odhams Books Limited.

Huw

IF YOU HAD ASKED ME a couple of months ago whether or not I believed in ghosts I could not have given you a straight answer. I would probably have said, 'Well, yes and no . . .' and gone on to explain that I could not answer one way or another because I had never actually seen such a thing, and though lots of odd things undoubtedly happen from time to time most of them surely have a rational explanation.

But that would have been a couple of months ago. Ask me the same question today and I would not hesitate to answer, 'Yes, I *do* believe in ghosts, and what's more, I'm not a bit frightened of them.' If you are wondering what happened to make me so definite I'd like to tell you all about it. I still find the whole thing very hard to accept, but I must accept it because it was real – it did happen.

It all began when my young brother Bryn invited me to spend a few days with him at Aberystwyth in Wales, where he was studying at the University. As I was between jobs my time was my own; and as a Welshman compelled to live in London the chance of spending some time in my home country was too good to miss. I accepted my brother's offer and decided to drive leisurely up through Shropshire and enter Wales by Snowdonia National Park instead of taking the quickest route.

The weather was good and I enjoyed the journey to the north-west. The Shropshire hills and valleys brought me into touch with that special, unassuming loveliness that is one of the charming features of the English countryside. I even went out of my way to visit Clunton, Clunbury, Clungunford and Clun, just to discover whether they are, as Housman claims, 'the quietest places under the sun'. They were pretty quiet.

At last I headed west into Wales, keeping well away from the major roads, choosing instead any road that looked barely wide enough to take a car, hoping to reach Dolgellau, the friendly little town in a valley that is protected by Cader Idris. The trouble with driving aimlessly, enjoying the scenery and refusing to hurry, is that it is very easy to lose track of the time – which is what happened to me. Daylight began to fade and the sky filled up with smoky clouds. There was a spatter of rain on the windscreen. The road was little more than a cart track and the country was very hilly. I thought I had better get on to a decent road as quickly as possible and head for Bala, leaving Dolgellau until the next day. At that point I realized I was running out of petrol.

It was quite dark by the time I had reached the main road and the petrol situation was serious. My map did not show any villages for several kilometres and I thought it quite likely that I would have to spend the night huddled up in the car in the middle of the Welsh mountains. Fortunately, this unpleasant vision faded when my lights picked out a solitary petrol pump by the side of a grey stone cottage. Of course, this little wayside petrol station was closed, but I was able to drag the owner away from his television set and persuade him to fill my tank.

I had only travelled a few kilometres farther when I saw the boy. By now the rain was very heavy and visibility was poor, but I saw him perfectly clearly as he stood by the side of the road, hands in pockets, looking towards the car. I pulled up and opened the passenger door.

'Missed your bus?' I called, taking it for granted that buses did run along this road. He didn't answer, but with a slight movement shook his head. He looked to be about thirteen or fourteen years old; he was tall and dressed in jeans and a black jacket buttoned up to his neck. His face was startling in its pallor.

'Do you want a lift?' I went on. 'If so, jump in.' This was no time to indulge in aimless conversation and the boy's lack of interest rather irritated me. I pushed the door open a little more, wondering whether he was going to accept my offer, but he slid into the passenger seat without hesitation. I reached across him, closed the door and snapped the safety lock.

'What a night!' I said. 'Have you missed your bus?' I asked him again – I could think of no other reason why a lad of his age should be standing in such a lonely spot on such a night.

He said nothing and I had to bite my lips to prevent myself making a sarcastic remark about the cat having bitten his tongue. I'll try once more, I thought. 'Where are you going? Where can I drop you?'

This time he did answer me – in Welsh, and I mentally apologized to him for misunderstanding his silence. Perhaps he did not speak English very well, although clearly he understood it. 'I'm afraid I know only a few words of Welsh,' I said, 'though I recognized the word "trees" – something trees – can you translate?'

'Stricken,' he answered in a husky adolescent's voice.

'Stricken Trees – that's an odd name. I can't remember anything like that on the map, either in English or Welsh. Is it a local name?'

'Yes,' he said.

'And is it far?'

'No.'

What marvellous dialogue, I thought, hoping that Stricken Trees was *very* near. I couldn't stand much more yes-ing and no-ing. Still, he was company of a sort, and talking to someone made a change from listening to the tyres swishing over the wet road.

'Well, you'd better tell me when we get there,' I said, 'otherwise you'll find yourself in Bala.' At that he twisted a little in his seat and turned to look at me. Ah, the first sign of life, I thought. Perhaps he's got a girl-friend in Bala and wouldn't mind being taken on there.

But the boy was showing agitation, not pleasure.

'What's the matter?' I asked.

'Don't go to Bala, Mister,' he said, with a sort of quivering urgency in his tone. 'Not tonight. . . .'

I could not help laughing at the intensity of his entreaty and my laugh was accompanied by a long roll of thunder. 'Why not? There's nowhere to stay before Bala, and I am so tired and my joints ache with the damp that I don't feel like driving the extra thirty kilometres or so to Dolgellau.'

'Don't go to Bala, Mister,' he repeated.

'It's not as bad as that,' I said jokingly. 'Haven't you ever been there?'

'Not the last time,' he said. 'I never got there, you see.'

I didn't see, but I let the subject drop. Frankly, I was beginning to feel a bit uneasy. I wondered if the boy was perhaps a bit simple – he was very unlike any fourteen-year-old I had ever met. 'What's your name?' I asked, mainly for something to say.

'Huw,' he replied. As he made no further contribution to the conversation I gave up and drove on in silence.

About ten minutes later, during which time I had, as I thought, been concentrating on the road, I remembered my passenger. 'Huw, this place – Stricken Trees – are we anywhere near it?' My eyes were glued to the winding road and I could not tell whether he had heard me. 'Huw!' I said, raising my voice. 'Are you asleep? Are we anywhere near Stricken Trees?' Then the back of my neck tightened as though suddenly gripped in a vice, and without turning my head I knew. . . . . I pulled the car into the side of the road to make absolutely sure. Huw was no longer sitting by my side.

I remember my feelings as if it had all taken place an hour ago. First, a quick stab of fear, then puzzlement as I tried the door and found it still locked, then an amused relief when I decided what had happened. Obviously Huw had told me where to stop, had got out and left me to continue alone. I had been guilty of falling asleep at the wheel – a constant fear of those who drive long distances alone. I had been driving by instinct . . . and could thank my guardian angel that the absence of any other vehicle had prevented an accident. 'Let this be a lesson to you,' I told myself. 'You'd better stop at the next village for a rest and a snack.' I let in the clutch and drove on, and within five minutes had reached a tiny village.

There was an inn among the collection of houses, and I parked the car and went in. An elderly lady sat behind the high counter, knitting. The small bar, hot and smoke-filled, was crowded with men puffing at pipes and talking in Welsh. But the landlady spoke to me in English with a musical lilt that seemed to embrace the whole scale. 'Good evening, sir, *terr*ible weather, and what can I get you?' She slid off her stool and put down the knitting.

'A pint of bitter, please,' I said. 'And could you possibly make me a sandwich? I haven't eaten for hours.'

The landlady disappeared into the back room and soon returned with the thickest, juiciest roast beef sandwich I have ever eaten. It was a most welcome sight and I tucked into it eagerly. The other customers took little notice of me after their first casual glances, but Mrs. Cadwallader, as the landlady was called, and I got on famously. As it turned out I bought my milk from her brother's dairy at the corner of my road in London, and she had heard about my aged Auntie Blodwen who lived at the top of a hill in Flintshire and made lace that was known throughout North Wales. When I told her that I intended to spend the night in Bala she was delighted. 'Beautiful town,' she said, 'and if you want a *lovely* place to stay, Morgan Llyfnant Arms is my brother-in-law. The rooms overlook some fine gardens and on good days you can see the lake, and the linen is as crisp and clean as Snowdon's white cap!'

'The Llyfnant Arms it shall be,' I promised. Talk of Bala had brought back vividly to my mind my strange passenger from Stricken Trees. Mrs. Cadwallader had turned to do something at the back of the bar and I raised my voice slightly. 'By the way,' I asked, 'do you know a young lad from these parts named Huw?'

Every sound in the room suddenly faded. Mrs. Cadwallader, her back still turned to me, seemed to freeze. I could feel every eye swivel round and fix on the back of my head. I felt as though I had committed a crime – though what it was I had no idea. I blundered on. 'And where is the place called Stricken Trees?'

When Mrs. Cadwallader turned round her eyes were full of sympathy, though not for me, as I soon realized, for she was looking past me into the room. 'It's all right now, Mr. Griffiths,' she said softly. 'Don't you worry.'

I shifted my position to see who Mr. Griffiths was and to guess why he shouldn't worry. From a solid group at the back there came forward a tiny wizened man with a skull-like face. Dark mournful eyes were the only living feature in it. When he spoke his voice was rich and deep, like an orator's. It was odd hearing it emerge from his spare frame.

'You have seen Huw tonight.'

I didn't know whether he had made a statement or asked a question, but I felt like a schoolboy before a stern headmaster. 'Yes, I gave him a lift about twenty kilometres back, to a place called Stricken Trees. To be honest, I don't remember dropping him.'

'No, you wouldn't,' Mr. Griffiths said, smiling grimly.

'I think I was overtired and dropped off to sleep for a few seconds.'

'What did he say?'

'Not a lot,' I replied. 'He was a silent lad – at the awkward age, I suppose. Oh, he did tell me not to go to Bala tonight.' I expected smiles when I said that, but the only smile in the room was my own. There was another silent spell before Mr. Griffiths spoke again. 'Then don't go to Bala tonight. . . .' He gave a curious sound like a strangled sob and with shoulders bowed he moved slowly across the room and went out into the night.

One man from the group got up as if to follow him, but another clutched his sleeve. 'No, Dai, let him be. Nobody can help.'

The others muttered agreement, so Dai sat down again. From that moment the atmosphere changed. No longer distant and clannish, the men crowded round me, asked me my name, where I came from, my profession, my taste in music and books, as if they were all trainee television interviewers, but never a word did they utter about Huw or Stricken Trees. I soon understood that they were deliberately avoiding those two topics, so I tried to probe the mystery. But every question was met by a chorus of false laughs.

'Huw? Only Ted Griffiths's boy.'

'Worries about him, see?'

'Very close, that family.'

'Have another drink?'

'No, thank you,' I said. 'Only one pint when I'm driving. But what have the Griffiths family got against Bala? I'm looking forward to seeing Morgan Llyfnant Arms.'

More false laughter – even from Mrs. Cadwallader too. 'Have another beer,' was all I could get out of them. I had to get away. There was a mystery, but obviously I wasn't going to be let into the secret. I thanked the landlady, said goodnight to the men and promised I'd call again when I was in that part of the country. I was relieved to get back to my car, even though the rain was still tumbling down and the dark clouds were scurrying across the sky like crowds going to a football match.

Away from the village lights it was pitch-dark again. I tried to quell my uneasiness by humming *Men of Harlech*, but before I had got to the end there was an ominous splutter from the engine. Please don't break down, I willed – not here; but the car stopped decisively, with a final spiteful chuckle. I was just about to get out and peer beneath the bonnet when the truth dawned on me. I was quite out of petrol! The needle registered an empty tank. It was impossible, but a fact.

Bristling with anger I went to the back of the car. The cap of the petrol tank was missing. Somebody had siphoned out all the six gallons I had bought at the wayside pump. I wished that I was not too old to burst into tears. As it was I had to clench my fists to contain my feelings. Then I caught a glimpse of someone standing by a wooden pole at the side of the road. It was Huw, peering at me, his white face caught in the headlights.

I dashed towards him. 'Huw!' I cried. 'What's going on? Who stole my petrol? Was it you or that strange father of yours? Huw – where are you? Don't play tricks on me, for heaven's sake!'

But it was useless to keep on. He had disappeared. All that remained of Huw was a voice whispering in my ear, 'Don't go to Bala tonight, Mister. . . .'

I'm not going anywhere tonight, I thought despairingly, except to a makeshift bed in the back of the car. Idly I looked at the spot where Huw had been standing and noticed a painted board at the top of the wooden pole. Out of curiosity

*Then I caught a glimpse of someone standing by a wooden pole
at the side of the road.*

I got a torch from the car and shone it on to the board. I gave a gasp when the words on it were visible.

DAFYDD FARM
BED & BREAKFAST
DAIRY PRODUCE

Well, if not a silver lining, this was at least a slightly less leaden one. I grabbed my case from the back seat, locked the car and trudged up the lane to Dafydd Farm, heedless of the rain and the ankle-deep mud.

Mrs. Jenkinson did not seem at all surprised to receive a visitor at such a late hour and welcomed me warmly. The farmhouse kitchen was scrubbed and spotless, and soon I was sitting down to a meal of ham and eggs that tasted better than anything the best four-star hotel could provide.

Mrs. Jenkinson hovered around me as I ate, making sure that I had everything I needed, and I found myself telling her the story of Huw, his father, my empty petrol tank and the strange behaviour of the men in the inn. She nodded knowingly several times, and when she had put a huge dish of apple tart and clotted cream in front of me she sat down at the opposite side of the table.

'I dare say it all seems very mysterious to you, sir,' she began, 'but I think I can make things a bit clearer. Huw is a ghost. . . .' She uttered the words in a matter-of-fact way as though she might have been saying, 'Huw is a boy. . . .' She smiled at my start of surprise and went on, 'The people in the village delude themselves that he only exists in the mind of his father, but he's a real ghost. I've seen him myself, and spoken to him, and I'm not one to imagine things, I can tell you.'

'I'm sure you're not,' I said. 'Where does Stricken Trees come into the story?'

'That is where the Griffiths family lives. Years ago the trees outside their cottage were struck by lightning. Not a leaf has grown on them since, but the skeletons still stand there, bent and withered like rheumaticky old men. As for Huw – three years ago it happened – when the boy was thirteen. Ted Griffiths always maintained that he was delicate and wouldn't allow him to play out with the other boys, though when Huw got the chance to climb trees and kick a football it was clear that he was as strong as the rest of them. One day the travelling circus came to Bala. Huw wanted to go with his pals, but his father wouldn't hear of it. Said the night air might affect his chest and a lot of foolish things like that. I remember seeing the party set off in Wyn Evans's old bus, excited as only children can be at the thought of seeing clowns and tight-rope walkers, lions and elephants. Huw waved them off and went back sadly to Stricken Trees. But he never arrived home because little Billy Price Top-shop had left his new bicycle leaning against his front wall, and as Huw passed by, looking both ways – it suddenly seemed as though the temptation was too much for him. He took the bike and rode off after the bus like the wind.

'If he had stopped to think he would have realized that there was no chance of getting to Bala in time for the circus as it's over thirty kilometres away and up and down hill all the way. But Huw *didn't* think. He just went on pedalling for all he was worth. He was about half-way to Bala when the tragedy happened – a chance in a thousand, it was. A huge boulder rolled down from the hill and knocked him off the bike into the path of a car coming towards him.

'He was hurt very badly. The people in the car were frantic with worry. They wrapped him up in a blanket, put him in the car and drove him to Stricken Trees as fast as they could – Huw was conscious at first and able to tell them where he lived. But by the time they had got there he was dead.

'His father nearly went out of his mind with grief and since then has shrunk away almost to nothing. Huw was the apple of his eye and he had little else to live for. Nowadays the only sign of life he shows is when he thinks Huw's ghost is about. Then he walks the roads seeking the boy, calling his name and asking forgiveness for not letting him go in the bus.'

'Does Huw always warn people away from Bala, as he did me?' I asked.

'Now there's funny,' said Mrs. Jenkinson. 'I haven't heard of him doing that before. I wonder why he didn't want you to go there. . . .'

Even with so much to think about I slept well that night between sheets as Snowdon-white as those at Morgan Llyfnant Arms. Before I finally sank into sleep I wished I could give Huw a lift again. I would have been more understanding.

The next morning, after a wonderful breakfast, I set off early. Mr. Jenkinson, fortunately, was able to replace the missing petrol. The aimless wanderings of the mountain sheep kept my mind on the serious business of driving, though I was able to marvel at the beauty of the towering mountains on one side of the road and the deep rich valleys on the other. When I saw the policeman ahead of me he seemed strangely out of place – directing traffic in that lonely spot surely wasn't necessary, I thought. He waved me to a halt and it was almost like being back in London.

'Sorry, sir,' he said when I poked my head out of the window. 'I'm afraid you can't go any farther. Road to Bala's closed.'

'But I must get there,' I protested. 'When will it be open again?'

'Couldn't say exactly, sir, but it'll be some time, I reckon.'

'Has there been an accident?' For some reason my thoughts flew to Huw sprawled on the road with a car coming towards him.

'More an act of God, I'd say, sir.'

'What *has* happened then?'

The policeman jerked a thumb behind him to the corner I had been approaching. 'Landslide last night in all that rain. Near on half a mountain came down on the road and slid over into the valley. Thank your lucky stars you didn't start out any earlier yesterday and weren't anywhere near here last night, sir, or you'd never have got to Bala – *never*.'

Huw, I thought, you can siphon the petrol out of my tank any time you like if your motive is always as good as it was last night. I reversed the car and drove back to find Stricken Trees. When Mr. Griffiths knew that Huw's ghost had saved my life his pride in his son would surely lighten his grief and give him the courage to face his loss.

So, you see, that is why I believe in ghosts and why, if they are at all like Huw, there's no need to be afraid of them.

The Bag of Ghosts

MANY YEARS AGO a barber and his wife lived in a small town in the Indian Province of Bengal. He was a quiet, friendly, popular man, but he was always short of money and often neither he nor his wife had enough to eat.

There was no shortage of beards to trim but the barber was so kind-hearted that time and time again he refused money for his services. He was often moved to tears by the hard-luck stories that his customers told him, and they, quick to take advantage of his kindness, invented more and more heart-breaking stories to avoid paying for their haircuts.

The barber accepted his poverty as the price he had to pay for helping those less fortunate than himself – but not so his wife. She called him foolish, selfish, and a weakling, and complained bitterly both night and day.

'Why did you marry me if you are unable to support me?' she whined. 'There was always enough to eat when I lived with my father, but life with you is one long fast!'

'But, wife, we have our health,' said the barber, 'and we must be grateful for that. The wife of one of my customers has lost both her legs. Think of that!'

'And *your* wife has lost her temper, think of that!'

'The children of another customer are dying from a terrible wasting disease,' added the barber, tears starting from his eyes.

'And your wife is wasting too,' said his wife. 'I hope *that* will bring tears to your eyes. Don't you know that only widows fast? When I married you I didn't think I would have to become a widow in your life-time, but that is just what I am with so much fasting!'

One day the barber returned home with no money at all. He tried to explain to his wife how moved he had been listening to the anguished tales of his customers' troubles, but she would not listen.

'You don't deserve to have a wife,' she interrupted. 'Go away from me and don't come back until you have earned enough money to enable us to live in comfort.' She picked up a broom, hit her husband over the head and drove him out of the house. She threw his bag containing the tools of his trade after him.

The barber rubbed his sore head but told himself that he deserved such harsh treatment. 'I won't come back until I'm rich,' he vowed to himself. With a last wistful look at his house he picked up his bag and set off on his travels.

He trudged from village to village looking for beards to trim, but with very little success. Other barbers were jealous and turned him away from their territory, and when he did find customers the merest hint of misfortune in their lives was enough to make him refuse to take payment.

One night he found himself at the edge of a thick forest. He knew that it was useless to travel further until daybreak so he settled down for the night under a tree. He lay there for hours, brooding about his bad luck and racking his brains for an answer to his problems.

The barber was so wrapped up in his troubles that he had quite forgotten that ghosts rested at night in forests and that it was dangerous to venture far into them after dark.

It so happened that the tree which the barber had chosen to shelter under was the home of a particularly mean and cruel ghost whose chief pleasure was to destroy human beings. When at last the barber fell asleep his snores broke the silence of the night-shrouded forest and disturbed the ghost. It looked down from the topmost branches to see what was making such a raucous noise; on seeing a human under the tree, the ghost was filled with a wicked pleasure.

With a whoosh like a gust of wind the ghost slid down the tree and confronted the barber with arms outstretched, mouth wide open, and feet spread out like roots, so that it looked like a huge gnarled tree itself. The barber, feeling an eerie presence, woke up with a start. When he saw what he thought was an ugly tree in front of him, which he knew had not been there earlier, he gave a gasp of surprise, and when the 'tree' spoke he yelped with fright.

'You are right to be frightened, barber,' the ghost said with a snarl, 'for I am going to destroy you, slowly, bit by bit – and you need not shout, for nobody will hear you!'

Although by now he was shaking with fear, his teeth chattering, and his scalp pricking as though it were on fire, the barber did not completely lose control of himself. He thought hard, and a way of outwitting the ghost suddenly came to him. Instead of cringing away when the ghost made a movement towards him he said boldly, 'How glad I am to see you, ghost!'

The ghost stopped. '*Glad* to see me?' it roared. 'No human being has ever been glad to see *me*! How dare you say such a thing!' Its eyes flashed green with rage.

'I do dare to say such a thing,' the barber said confidently, 'for a very good reason. I hoped that you would threaten to destroy me when I sat down to rest under your tree.'

'It's not only a threat,' screeched the angry ghost, 'I *will* destroy you!'

The barber shook his head and sighed. 'That is what they all said, but still they ended up in my bag. You have no idea the number of ghosts I've captured tonight and packed into my bag. And now I'm going to have another.'

The ghost slid down the tree and confronted the barber with arms outstretched.

'What are you talking about, you stupid human?' There was a slight note of unease in the ghost's voice. 'Do you expect me to believe that you have already captured some ghosts?' It tried to reassure itself by giving a horrible, doom-laden laugh.

'It's a pity you don't believe me,' the barber said. 'I had hoped that you would not be troublesome. Just to convince you – would you like to see one of my captives?'

The ghost did not reply. It had never met a human being like this, and was at a loss what to say next.

The barber picked up his bag, pretended to open it very carefully, and thrust his hand inside. He rummaged around and withdrew the small mirror he gave his customers to inspect his handiwork. He stood up and placed it in front of the ghost's face. 'There,' he said. 'See for yourself. This is one of the ghosts I've caught and put in my bag. Hurry up, though, because I mean to put you there too so that you can keep the others company.'

The ghost did not realize that it was looking at its own face. It was overcome with terror at the prospect of being confined in the small bag, and filled with awe at this strange human being who had such an unheard-of power over ghosts. It fell to the ground in supplication. 'O, barber, sir, please do not put me in your bag. I will be your servant and do whatever you command, but, *please*, do not put me in your bag!'

The barber frowned and scratched his head, pretending to consider the ghost's plea. 'How can I tell whether you are to be trusted?' he asked. 'Ghosts are known to be terrible liars and hardly ever keep their promises.'

'I will, I will,' cried the ghost.

'That is what you say now, but suppose I let you go free and you don't obey my commands?'

'But I will, I will,' the ghost repeated. 'Please give me a chance.'

'Very well,' said the barber, 'I will put you to the test. My first command is that you bring me one thousand gold pieces.'

'I will do so,' the ghost said, eager to get away from this man who spoke with such authority.

'Wait!' commanded the barber, before the ghost could make a move. 'By tomorrow night you must build a granary at my house and fill it with paddy!' He smiled at the thought of so much rice in the husk: why, his wife need not go hungry for a long, long time. 'Now, fetch me the gold, and if you bring back one piece less than a thousand into my bag you will go!'

The ghost bowed low and was off like a hurricane, leaving the barber to resume his rest under the tree. He had barely closed his eyes when a rustling told him that the ghost had returned. It placed a large bag in front of him.

'One thousand gold pieces, barber, sir,' the ghost said, bowing even lower than before.

The barber was delighted and decided to return to his wife at once to tell her of the good news. Before leaving the forest he waved his bag of tools in front of the ghost's nose. 'Don't forget my second command!'

'No, barber, sir,' said the ghost. 'A granary filled with paddy.'

'By tomorrow,' the barber added sternly, and turned his back on the quivering creature.

During the barber's absence his wife had begun to regret her harsh treatment, slowly beginning to feel that shortage of food was a small price to pay for a husband with such a kind heart. When, just before dawn, the barber hammered on the door calling, 'Good wife, let me in and see what I have brought for you,' she welcomed her husband with cries of joy and tears of remorse.

She could hardly believe her eyes when she saw the

thousand gold coins and, feeling that the barber had obtained them dishonestly, begged him to tell her where he had come by so much money. The barber could hardly tell his story for laughing, but bit by bit his wife heard all about the ghost who was afraid of being put in a bag.

'But wait till you see what the ghost will bring us tomorrow,' chuckled the barber. 'It will be an even greater surprise!'

Meanwhile, the ghost was waiting for nightfall. Every time it thought of the barber's bag it gave a shudder and resolved to build the strongest granary ever seen in the province of Bengal. As soon as it was dark it started to work, and carried on all through the night. When the building was completed the ghost laboured hour after hour to fill it with bag after bag of paddy. The barber looked through his window, saw the weary ghost toiling away and rubbed his hands with satisfaction.

When it was nearly at the end of its task the ghost was joined by another, an even more hideous ghost, who entered the granary like an icy blast and surveyed the paddy bags. The first ghost straightened its tired back and saw that the newcomer was its uncle.

'Why are you toiling so, nephew-ghost?' said the uncle-ghost, angry to see a relative forced to work so hard.

'You may well ask, uncle-ghost,' it answered, and told the newcomer the full story. The uncle-ghost gave a horrible laugh that sounded like the death shrieks of a hundred devils.

'You fool!' it bellowed. 'You are unworthy to bear the dishonourable name of ghost! Can't you see that the barber is a cunning man and has tricked you? How could he put such a huge and terrifying ghost as you into a small bag? Why didn't you destroy him at once, instead of allowing yourself to be fooled?'

'It's all very well talking like that, uncle,' said the first ghost. 'You are older than I am, and much wiser, but if you doubt the barber's ability to bag me, come and see for yourself.'

Still disbelieving, the uncle-ghost followed its nephew out of the granary and up to the barber's house. They peered in through the window. The barber suddenly felt a lowering of the temperature and knew that the ghost was near. He turned his head slightly and saw from the corner of his eye that there were two ghosts with their faces pressed against the glass. 'Something is amiss,' he said to himself. 'They're up to something. But they shan't get the better of me.'

Without saying a word to his wife he picked up his bag and went to the window and opened it. 'Ah,' he said to the crouching creatures, 'another ghost for my collection! You have obeyed my orders,' he said to the nephew-ghost, 'but there's plenty of room in my bag for your ugly companion.' He reached in his bag, took out the mirror and placed it so that the uncle-ghost saw the reflection of its startled face. It shrank away from the window as it heard the barber say, 'I shall put you in the bag to keep the other ghosts company.'

The uncle-ghost fell to the ground. 'Please don't, barber, sir,' it gasped. 'I couldn't bear to be put in a bag! I'll do anything if you won't shut me up with that awful creature whose face you just showed me! I'll – I'll build you another granary, and I'll fill it with the finest rice. And I'll bring you *two* thousand gold pieces! Will you spare me if I do all that?'

The barber, inwardly shaking with laughter, pretended to consider. 'Very well,' he said. 'Do all that and you shall go free.'

The uncle-ghost kept its promise as faithfully as its nephew had done. A second granary appeared, next to the first, bulging with sacks of the finest rice. A second bag of money, twice as big as the first, was left on the barber's doorstep. Then the two ghosts gratefully took leave of their dreaded master and returned to the forest, where they spent their time hunting and destroying less wily travellers than the barber.

The barber was now a very rich man and his wife was well content with such a clever husband who had provided her with an abundance of food and money to buy dresses and jewels. She became very fat and good-natured, and the happy barber spent his days trimming his friends' beards and asking for no payment.

The Beggar Woman of Locarno

THE RUINS of an old castle which can be seen at the foot of the Alps, near Locarno in Switzerland, have caused many a traveller to shiver with apprehension. Even those who do not know its story feel the presence of a spirit from its tragic past. The town of Locarno, situated at the north of Lake Maggiore, is a famous health resort. It is in the Italian-speaking canton of Ticino and is reached from the north by way of the famous St. Gotthard Pass.

In the early part of the 18th century the now charred and desolate ruin was a proud citadel.

It belonged to a wealthy and powerful marquess who spent a large part of his time hunting in the thick, dark forests which surrounded it. He was proud of his fine castle with its lofty, beautifully proportioned rooms, its high towers and narrow windows; but he was a selfish man too, and lived only for himself and his family, with little thought for the poor and unfortunate.

One day, the marquess was out hunting while his wife, the marchioness, was busy in her own room. The elderly housekeeper, attracted by the brilliance of the spring sunshine, left the castle to walk through the picturesque grounds. As she passed by the main gates she was puzzled to see a bundle of dirty rags lying just outside.

'Tch,' she muttered, 'the master would flare into a fine rage if he saw those.' She knew only too well that the

29

marquess' pride demanded that his beloved castle should be spotless both inside and out. She was about to pick up the bundle when, to her amazement, it stirred, and from the dirt-encrusted folds a hand appeared, held with palm upwards as though begging.

The housekeeper felt a kind of outraged disgust as the rags slowly revealed an old woman, hollow-cheeked with hunger; then, as the creature rose unsteadily to her feet, her disgust turned to pity. The old woman was lame and used a crude wooden crutch to hold herself erect.

She tried to speak but could only manage a low moan. She looked at the housekeeper with pleading eyes.

The housekeeper knew that she could not turn the woman away. 'I would gladly give you money,' she said, 'but you need more than that. Warmth and food and a refuge from the hazards of the forest, that's what you need. Come with me!'

The beggar woman hobbled after the housekeeper, who was wondering where to take her. She knew that no one else in the castle would share her feelings of sympathy, and she could not risk anyone meeting the old cripple. At last she decided that the safest place would be a room on the second floor which was used as a store-room for the marquess' guns and hunting equipment. Apart from these weapons the room contained only some bundles of straw that had come from packing cases.

Once inside the musty-smelling room, the beggar woman sank down gratefully on the straw and began to eat the food which the housekeeper had fetched from the kitchens.

'Rest here, poor soul,' the housekeeper said, 'and remain silent so that no one will discover you. You need not leave until you feel stronger, then I will give you some money to help you on your way.'

The beggar woman stretched her cracked lips into a smile as the housekeeper left the room.

When the marquess returned from hunting he was in one of his worst tempers. Everything had gone wrong. He and his friends had searched for wild boar all day long, but not one had been sighted. Then, just as they had decided to give up, a bristly, long-tusked monster was seen in the distance. The marquess rode after it triumphantly, but at the crucial moment of firing he found that his gun had jammed and was useless. . . .

So now he kicked open the door of the armoury next to the stables where he kept his favourite guns and made as if to throw the offending weapon on the floor. Then, suddenly changing his mind, he decided to put it with the cast-off guns in the upper store-room.

The housekeeper was horrified when she saw her master stamping up the stairs, shaking the gun as though he were trying to strangle it, and in a state of nerves she fled to her own quarters and locked the door behind her.

The marquess entered the store-room and flung the gun away from him. The crash, as it hit the floor, frightened the dozing old woman and she made a movement which caught the marquess' eye. He stalked across to the bundle of rags and looked down at it with distaste. 'Who are you? What are you doing here?'

The old woman could only make a croaking noise in reply, and the marquess prodded her roughly with his foot.

'Get up from that corner, you miserable wretch, and be gone!'

There was no movement so he prodded her again. 'Do you hear?' he shouted, 'Get out, *now!*'

The beggar woman, shaking with fear, took her crutch and struggled painfully to her feet. She stood, breathing heavily, and would have fallen had she not been able to support herself against the wall. The marquess, further irritated by her slowness, turned abruptly and left the room.

'If you won't go of your own accord I'll get two of my men to throw you out!' he shouted over his shoulder.

The beggar woman tried to hobble to the door but she was so weak that the effort made her lose her balance, her crutch slipped from her grasp and she tumbled to the floor. Spurred on by her fear, she managed to reach the fireplace before collapsing for the last time.

The housekeeper had heard the marquess clattering down the stairs and ventured to creep up to the store-room when he had disappeared. She saw at once that the beggar woman was dead, a look of peace on her worn face. The housekeeper sighed once, then had to decide on a plan of action.

She hurried from the room and intercepted the two servants who were on their way up to the store-room. She told them what had happened and begged them to agree to her request. The men put on a show of reluctance, but she won them over with a bribe.

At her request they carried the dead woman to a quiet corner of the castle grounds and there they buried her.

Afterwards they told their master that they had done his bidding and turned the old woman out of the gates.

'The last we saw of the old hag,' one of them said, 'she was clip-clopping down the drive like a drunken fishwife!'

The marquess was well pleased; and for him the unpleasant incident was over.

Years went by, the housekeeper died, and the fortunes of the marquess declined. Wars and the failure of crops brought him almost to bankruptcy, and the time came when he realized that his beautiful castle would have to be sold to pay his debts. In order to get a better price, he decided to make it as attractive as possible. Among the changes made to the interior was the renovation of the second floor armoury, because of the magnificent view a prospective buyer would have of the distant mountains.

So everything was cleared from the store-room; then it was papered, painted and furnished in splendid fashion. A four-poster bed was installed and hung with rich crimson draperies, and the moulded head and tail boards were covered with gold leaf. It was a room fit for a king, and it was with great pride that the marquess himself showed the first enquirer round.

The guest, an Italian from Florence, was duly impressed, and the marquess and his wife were delighted. When they retired for the night they were in the highest of spirits, convinced that they would succeed in selling the castle at a high price.

It was in the middle of the night, at the dead time when dawn seems an age away, that the marquess was jerked from an easy sleep by a commotion outside the room. A voice, half speaking, half shouting, sounded from the corridor, and there were vigorous thumps on the bedroom door. The marquess spoke a calming word to his startled wife, lit the lamp and opened the door. The figure of the Italian rushed past him into the room, pushed him aside rudely and crouched against a screen in a corner, shivering uncontrollably.

'Signor, tell me, please, what is the matter?' the marquess gasped.

'What evil trick are you playing on me?' the Italian shouted. His eyes were wild, his face distorted with fear. 'Have you brought me here to send me mad? Are you a black magician? What have I done that you should treat me so?'

The marquess felt his temper rising. He had, after all, given his guest the best and most beautiful room in the castle. 'I do not understand you, signor,' he said. 'I should be obliged if you would return to your room at once. You are annoying my wife by your presence here.'

The Italian rushed over to him and fell to his knees. His

The Italian crouched against a screen in the corner, shivering uncontrollably.

manner changed, his voice pleaded. 'No, no, please, I beg of you, do not ask me to return – not to that terrible, evil room!'

The marquess threw off the clutching hands. 'Evil?' he exclaimed unbelievingly. 'What do you mean, sir? I am fast running out of patience, I warn you. What do you mean by an evil room?'

'Do you not know?' The Italian seemed to realize that the marquess was genuinely puzzled. 'Are you ignorant then?' He looked across at the marchioness who was sitting up in bed, a cloak round her shoulders. 'Forgive me, my lady, but I must speak. That room is haunted!'

'Haunted?' The marquess, even in his state of puzzled anger, could hardly suppress a smile. 'Really, signor, you are blessed with an active imagination, made more so by your long journey and by sleeping in a strange bed.'

'I tell you – it is *haunted*,' the Italian repeated emphatically.

The marquess shrugged and asked his guest with a show of patience to explain his charge.

'I was lying in bed half asleep, watching the firelight on the wall, when I heard a strange noise,' the Italian went on. 'At first I thought it was the crackling of the fire, but then I realized that it was something very different. It was as though something were moving on – straw. That was it – *straw*.

'I thought perhaps a dog or cat had entered the room without my noticing, so I sat up in bed to get a clearer view. As I did so, the noise changed, and there was a shuffling, uneven step such as would be made by someone walking with a crutch. . . .'

The marquess started. Surely there had been an incident with an old woman many years before – he remembered vaguely that he had found her in the store-room and had ordered the servants to turn her out. She had used a crutch and had shuffled through the straw on the floor. For the first time he wondered who she was and what had become of her.

This was an amazing coincidence, but only a coincidence, of course. He now gave all his attention to his guest.

'The shuffling seemed to be moving towards the bed,' the man continued, 'and all at once I felt an inexplicable coldness surrounding me – like the coldness of the tomb. Then the footsteps seemed to turn towards the fireplace; they stopped, there was a crash as if the crutch had fallen, followed by the thud of a body and a most piteous groaning. Then everything was quiet again, except for the crackle of burning logs. I dared not look at the floor by the fireplace. Hardly realizing what I was doing, I flung myself out of bed and came in search of you. Tell me, was it some sort of trick?'

'It was no trick,' the marquess said quietly, 'but I am equally sure that it was no ghost. I can only repeat what I said before – that you were overtired and the strangeness of new surroundings has preyed upon your imagination. I will stay with you for the rest of the night, signor. Let us go to your room and –'

The Italian cut him short. 'No, no! I will not return to that room! Give me another, no matter where. I will sleep on a couch or a chair, or the floor even, but I will not go back *there*.'

The marquess saw that it was useless to try any further persuasion. He took his trembling guest into the room next to his own and left him to sleep there with all the lamps burning and the door wide open.

Early the next day the Italian, with hardly a word to anyone, saddled his horse and departed with all possible speed. To the marquess, the worst aspect of the affair was not the presence of a ghost but his failure to sell the castle. After the Italian's hurried departure people's tongues began to wag, and before long it was common knowledge that something was amiss in the castle. As soon as prospective buyers heard of the rumours they cried off.

The stories grew wilder and wilder in the telling, and there seemed to be no end to the horrific tales of screaming phantoms and hideous spectres haunting every corner of every room of the castle.

Things became desperate for the marquess. Unless he sold the castle within a short time he would be ruined. To make matters worse, most of his servants left, driven away by fear of the unknown. At last he determined to lay the story of the ghost once and for all by spending a night himself in the haunted room. If nothing happened he would be able to convince people that they were being taken in by superstitious nonsense.

Accordingly, he retired to the one-time store-room early, lit the lamps and prepared to stay there all night if necessary. But something happened long before the faint grey light of dawn filtered through the narrow windows.

On the stroke of midnight the marquess sat up in bed with a jerk, the skin tightening on his forehead. A cold, light wind blew about him, though he noticed that it had no effect on the steady flames of the fire. Then he heard the noises, just as the Italian had described – the rustling straw, the shuffling, limping steps which stopped at the fireplace, the final bump and collapse, the groaning sobs. Then there was a profound silence, almost as frightening as the mysterious sounds. The marquess fell back, half fainting, and lay for a long time in a terrified stupor. Finally he sank into a heavy sleep that was racked with nightmares.

The next morning, white-faced and heavy-eyed, he joined his wife at breakfast and told her what had happened. The marchioness grew pale and thoughtful. 'Are you sure you did not dream the whole thing?' she asked. 'Perhaps you were expecting something to happen and the noises came out of your inner mind.'

'Nonsense, woman!' the marquess exploded. 'I tell you I heard the things I have described just as clearly as I am hearing my own voice. We are going to be ruined, I tell you. Nobody will ever buy this castle. If you don't believe me you had better spend a night in that room yourself!'

The marchioness drew her lips together. 'I will!' she said decisively. 'This very night you and I will sit up together and discover what is going on. Two judgements are better than one. If there *is* a ghost we will confront it and put an end to its tricks. Two humans are surely more powerful than one ghost!'

'Brave words,' her husband muttered. He was reluctant to spend another night in the haunted room, but in the face of his wife's determination he could hardly admit his fear. But I'll be armed, he told himself. The old woman will be sorry she ever came back here. . . .

That night, as the marquess and his wife approached the room to keep their vigil, they saw the house dog lying on a rug outside the door, and they decided to take the dog with them. 'She won't fancy her ankles being nipped!' the marquess chuckled, pretending to put on a brave front. Then they sat down on a couch, the dog at their feet, and a sword and pistol between them.

The marquess and his lady spoke little to each other, both occupied with their own thoughts. Bells announced the slow passage of time. Their desultory conversation ceased altogether as midnight drew near. The only sound in the room was the heavy breathing of the sleeping dog.

One, two, three, four – the sombre bells tolled twelve times, each stroke increasing the tension. Suddenly the dog gave a low growl. It got to its feet and began to whine, all its hairs bristling as the sound of rustling straw came from a corner of the room.

When the lopsided shuffling started, the dog ran frantically to the door and clawed at it, trying to get out, whimpering with terror. The marchioness felt as though she were rivetted to the couch. She wanted to shriek, but no sound would come. With a tremendous effort she forced herself to her feet and extended a trembling hand. 'I – I can see her – ' she gasped faintly. 'An old bent woman – with a crutch – she's coming to me –' She shuddered violently and covered her face with her hands.

A desperate courage surged into the marquess. Hatred for whatever it was that was tormenting them drove his fear away. He grabbed his sword and called out harshly, 'Who is there? Who are you? Answer me!' His eyes raked the room but he could see nothing out of the ordinary. The invisible crutch clumped menacingly nearer.

The marchioness moaned. 'Help – help me – I can't bear it – her eyes –'

The marquess gave a great bellow of rage and the sound broke the spell which bound the marchioness. She threw herself towards the door and quickly unlocked it. The dog scuttled out and she followed it, running blindly down the stairs, along the corridors, across the great hall and out into the open.

Her husband, nearly berserk with frustrated anger at not being able to see what had caused her panic, thrashed around him with his sword, lunging about in every direction, leaping over the furniture, cutting and slashing through the air, shouting hoarsely as he heard a faint sobbing from the fireplace. 'So I've got you at last, have I, you old hag? Take that –'

The marchioness reached the courtyard and stumbled through the gates. With thumping heart and exhausted limbs she sank down on the ground, gasping and sobbing. Behind her the darkness lessened. The sky became suffused with red. It is the dawn, she thought dully, seeing the rosy outline of familiar things. Perhaps the morning will bring back normality and sanity. The morning is no time for ghosts. . . .

She turned her head, expecting to see the horizon lit with the golden glow of the rising sun, but to her horror she saw, not the sun, but bright tongues of flames leaping out of the windows of the room in which she had left her husband and licking at the stone walls with a roaring glee.

She cried out and struggled to her feet. Her legs seemed weighted with iron bands as she tried to hurry, and with every step she took she saw that the flames were gaining a greater hold. She was helpless, nothing could stop the progress of the fire. It was the end of the castle and – the thought pierced her dazed mind – the end of her husband. She gave up the struggle to go forward and fell unconscious to the ground.

The remains of the marquess were never found despite the valiant efforts of his few remaining servants to rescue him. In his wild attempts to kill the ghost he had overturned lamps and candles. The tapestries had caught fire, then the curtains and furniture. The room was a blazing inferno before the realization of what he had done reached his maddened brain.

Encircled by the greedy, hissing flames he dropped his sword and fell to his knees by the fireplace. His hands groped around him. His eyes, blinded by smoke, could just make out what he was touching – a bundle of old clothes lying on a bed of straw. . . .

The old beggar woman of Locarno had waited a long time for her revenge, and when it came she extracted a high price for it.

Ghost in Distress

LOFTUS HALL, IN COUNTY WEXFORD, in southern Ireland, has been rebuilt since the days when the Tottenham family lived there, and the ghost of Anne Tottenham has long been silent. But from the middle of the 18th century to the middle of the 19th she was seen and heard by many different people at different times. It is likely that she ceased to haunt her ancestral home because she was so angry at the alterations that had been made to the room in which she died that she could not bear to be associated with it any longer. At any rate, in 1868 she just gave up. . . .

Anne Tottenham was the younger of the two daughters of Charles Tottenham, a rich landowner and master of Loftus Hall. Her own mother was dead and her father had married again, to a woman who did not care for Anne and had little to do with her. Anne's sister Elizabeth was married and lived away from home, and since her departure Anne had led a lonely life. She had no friends, her stepmother was distant, and her father was so wrapped up in the affairs of his estate that he had little time for her. His nature, too, was cold and unfeeling, and Anne was left alone most of the time to amuse herself.

One winter's night Anne and her parents were sitting in the large drawing-room. While she did her embroidery she listened to the howling of the wind outside and the rain beating against the curtained windows. Suddenly they were all startled by a loud knocking at the front door. Loftus Hall was very much off the beaten track and they were not expecting any visitor at that time of night.

'Who can it be?' asked Mrs. Tottenham.

Her husband shook his head. 'I can hear Joseph going to the door. We will wait to see what he says.'

They listened to the servant's footsteps approaching the drawing-room. He knocked and entered. 'Sir,' he began, 'there is a young gentleman outside. He has lost his way, his horse has gone lame, and he begs for shelter for the night.'

A gust of wind from the open front door swept into the room and made them all shiver, and the sound of the rain was like the hiss of escaping steam.

'I suppose he had better come in,' Mrs. Tottenham said. 'We can't very well send him away on a night like this. Show him in, Joseph.'

'Very good, Madam,' said the servant and withdrew. He returned in a moment with the unexpected guest, and Mr. Tottenham stood up to receive him.

When Anne saw the stranger her heart missed a beat. He was so handsome, dark and wild-looking, with intensely blue eyes. He looked down at her from his great height and smiled straight into her eyes. In that moment Anne fell in love with the man who had come in out of the night.

Mr. and Mrs. Tottenham listened to his story and invited him to stay until his horse was fit again. A room was prepared for him, and then they all sat down to supper. As he ate the young man told them stories of his gay life in Dublin, and Anne listened as though he were from another world. She had never been to Dublin and knew nothing of big cities, balls and parties, and as she drank in every word she knew that life would never be the same for her again.

The handsome stranger stayed for several days, and with each hour that passed Anne fell deeper and deeper in love. The young man appeared to enjoy her company. They went walking in the grounds; he persuaded her to play the piano for him; asked her about her life, and when she told him of her loneliness a grave look came into his eyes.

'That will have to be changed,' he said quietly.

Then one day the groom announced that the horse was well. There was nothing to keep the attractive stranger at Loftus Hall any longer, and soon he was taking his farewell of Anne's parents and thanking them for their hospitality. As he pressed Anne's hand, he murmured, 'We shall meet again. . . .'

The girl watched him ride away, sad at his going yet happy in the knowledge that she would see him again, and next time he came she was sure that she would be riding away with him into the gay life of Dublin.

Days, weeks, months passed. There was no sign, no letter, no news. The stranger might have been part of a dream. Every day Anne stood by her window looking along the long road that disappeared into the world beyond, yearning for the sight of a galloping horseman coming to claim the girl he had left behind. She waited in vain.

In the end the strain of frustrated waiting destroyed her mind. The shy, gentle girl became a storming, shrieking maniac. No one dared go near her, and the servants refused to attend her. Her parents were in despair. Doctors could do nothing. She was confined to the most inaccessible room in the house, a room at the end of a long corridor away from the main living quarters, whose walls were panelled and hung with great tapestries, dingy and discoloured with age. In one corner there was a huge cupboard, almost as big as a small room itself. In that place Anne spent the rest of her days. Food was put through the door. No one visited her. No one cared what happened to her. She grew wilder, dirtier, more like an animal than a human being.

When poor Anne died at last she was buried without

In one corner there was a huge cupboard. In that place Anne
spent the rest of her days.

ceremony, and her family tried to forget all about her as quickly as possible. The tapestry room was never entered, its doors kept locked, and the name of Anne Tottenham was not mentioned in Loftus Hall for as long as her father and stepmother lived.

Years went by, and the Tottenhams grew old. Towards the end of the 18th century they held one of their infrequent parties and a large number of people were invited to Loftus Hall. One of them was the father of a well-known clergyman and was also a Justice of the Peace. When he arrived, somewhat after the other guests, Mrs. Tottenham apologized for the room she was forced to give him. All the other rooms, she explained, were already allocated to their guests. The room she led him to was at the end of a long corridor and its panelled walls were hung with tapestries. It had a strange musty smell as though it had not been occupied for a long time, and it seemed to have been hurriedly prepared.

The guest retired to bed, tired after his long ride. He put the pistols, that travellers always carried in Ireland in those days, on the table near the bed, and within minutes he was asleep.

Suddenly he woke up. Surely something had jumped on the bed? It felt like a large dog – it was certainly growling like an animal. But how could a dog have got through the door which he himself had most carefully locked. No, it must be some of his friends playing a stupid practical joke! Perhaps they had found a key and wanted to frighten him.

'Stop it, whoever you are!' he cried. 'If you don't, I'll fire my pistol!'

The tugging at the bedclothes grew more urgent, the growling was low and menacing, the weight on his body grew heavier. He heaved himself up with an effort and managed to grab one of the pistols from the table. Aiming it in the direction of the great wide fireplace, he fired, and the explosion in that confined space was deafening. When the reverberations had died down the visitor found that the growling had stopped and that whatever had been lying on the bed had withdrawn. He leapt out of bed, lit a candle and searched the room. It was completely empty. So was the great cupboard. The door was locked just as it had been when he retired to bed. There was just no human explanation for the peculiar experience he had undergone, and it was a very puzzled man who finally fell asleep in the early hours of the morning.

At breakfast he sought out Mrs. Tottenham and told her how he had been disturbed. She pursed her lips and did not try to give an explanation. All she said was, 'I am very sorry I had to put you in that room. I would not have done so if there had been another one to offer you . . .' and with that her guest had to be content.

Many years later the Marquess of Ely was staying at the Hall, and his valet, Michael Shannon, was given the tapestry room. In the middle of the night dreadful screams were heard. Shannon rushed out of the room in his night clothes, white-faced and shaking. 'I cannot spend another minute in there!' he spluttered out to his master and the other guests who had been aroused by the noise.

'Whatever is the matter?' the marquess asked him.

But it was some minutes before Shannon was recovered enough to reply.

'I was in bed,' he said at last, giving frequent nervous glances over his shoulder as he told his story, 'the room was dark and I was almost asleep. Then I heard the rattle of curtains being drawn back and the moon shone brightly on my bed. There, by the bedside, stood a woman. She was tall, her hair was tangled and there was a wild look in her eye. I heard the swish of her stiff silken dress as she moved towards me. I sat up and screamed, putting my hands over my eyes.

When I took them away she had gone . . . disappeared in a locked room. . . . Sir, do not ask me to go back to that room!'

After that, Anne Tottenham was seen frequently by visitors to Loftus Hall. Every person had the same tale. She appeared in a shaft of moonlight and moved towards the bed. She was wearing a dress of stiff flowered silk which rustled as she moved. Some of those who saw her buried their heads under the bedclothes. Others jumped out of bed and made for the door. Those who lay still and watched saw her walk round the bed, enter the great cupboard and disappear. One man, braver than the others, quietly got out of bed and then rushed at her. He threw his arm out, crying, 'Now I've got you!' But his arm went right through her and hit against the bedpost. The figure neither spoke nor turned her head. She quickened her step slightly and glided, as usual, into the cupboard. The astonished visitor immediately followed her. The cupboard door was closed and it took him some time to force it open, so stiff it was from disuse. When at last he peered inside he saw nothing but dust and cobwebs. . . .

In the middle of the 19th century Loftus Hall was owned by the Marquess of Ely and used only as a summer residence. One year the Marchioness of Ely, who later told the story to Queen Victoria, arrived there with her young son and his tutor, a clergyman named Charles Dale. The tutor was a sober-minded and unimaginative man. He had never heard of Anne Tottenham so when he was given the tapestry room as his bedroom he thought nothing of it and went to bed in the ordinary way.

For three weeks nothing happened. Then one night, when the family had retired later than usual, Mr. Dale had an experience similar to the one undergone by the Tottenham's guest sixty years before. He locked the door, fastened the shutters over the windows, drew the curtains, got into bed and blew out the candle.

He had not been there for more than a few minutes when he felt something jump on the bed, and make a growling sound like a very angry animal. The bedclothes were tugged off him and though he grabbed them and pulled hard, they slipped from his grasp as though the person or thing who had invaded the locked room were stronger than he. Mr. Dale let the clothes go, sprang out of bed and lit his candle. The room was empty. He looked under the bed and in the cupboard. There was nothing to be seen. Nervous, for perhaps the first time in his life, he made up his mind that he would not spend another night in that room. He refused to tell the Marchioness what had happened in the tapestry room, resigned his post and returned to England. He told his story years later.

The last recorded appearance of Anne Tottenham was in 1868, when extensive alterations were being done to Loftus Hall. The tapestries were taken from the walls of Anne's room, the cupboard into which she disappeared was dismantled. Additional windows were let into the walls and the room became a billiard room. A large billiard table stood just where the bed had been.

The changes evidently made poor Anne angrier than ever. After the builders had gone her room was unrecognizable. When the cover had been taken off the billiard table and the balls laid out ready for play, she came again, and for the last time. The housekeeper, Mrs. Neal, walking along the corridor late at night, heard strange noises coming from behind the door. She tiptoed to it and opened it a crack. She drew her breath sharply and blinked her eyes as though she could not believe what they were seeing.

'There was Miss Anne,' she told her mistress the next morning, 'and she was that angry! She was banging the billiard balls all over the table! Then she stalked to the corner where the cupboard had been, gave a last furious look at the room and disappeared into thin air!'

The Withered Bush

WILLIAM SUTOR, a farmer of Middle Mause, near Blairgowrie in Scotland, was returning from Drumlochy market on the last Monday of November, 1730.

It was dusk, and the road was deserted. He walked quickly, thinking of his warm fireside and the hot rum toddy that would be waiting for him. High hedges, broken only by gates leading into fields, rose on either side of him. Leafless trees loomed up at intervals. A light wind drove the dead leaves before his feet, and the last dying light of day drew weird shapes and shadows on the road and the banks at the roadside. The night gave promise of becoming wild for there were storm clouds piling up in the west. The burly farmer glanced round him and unconsciously quickened his pace.

'Don't want to be caught in a storm,' he muttered.

Suddenly he thought he heard a rustling behind him, as though an animal were padding through the leaves. He turned his head but saw nothing. Shrugging his shoulders, he decided that the wind was playing queer tricks on the lonely road, and he started to whistle, not to keep up his courage, for he was used to the menace of the lonely countryside, but for company. He wished he had been able to take his dog, Samson, along with him, so that he would have had him to talk to, but Samson had cut his paw badly, and was at home by the fire being nursed by Mrs. Sutor.

The strange rustling started again. There must be something – it couldn't be the wind, and once again the farmer turned, this time stopping dead in his tracks.

There *was* an animal – a dog, as far as he could see. Or was it a fox? A creature grey as the night, with eyes as red and shining as rubies, was about ten metres behind him, trotting purposefully forward, soundless except for the movement of its feet among the leaves. For one moment William Sutor thought that it was Samson who had somehow managed to get out of the house and in spite of his bad foot had come to meet him. But he soon realized that it was not so. Samson would have been barking with friendliness, and leaping up to lick his hand.

The creature drew nearer, not lifting its head as it approached. It seemed quite unaware of his presence on the road. It had the shape and appearance of a dog, but somehow William Sutor felt that it was not an animal of this world. It did not give out any warmth or feeling of life and solidity. It was as though a dead dog were moving forward, a wraith passing through the night. A strange feeling of unease possessed him. He felt suddenly cold and unsure of himself. He wanted to get out of the creature's way but his feet were rooted to the spot. It was coming straight at him. . . .

The dog brushed past his legs and touched his trousers. Immediately he felt a fierce burning pain in his leg, and an agonized cry escaped from him. The pain died away at once, leaving a numbing ache, and he wiped the sweat from his brow with a trembling hand. The dog passed on, and as it slowly disappeared into the gloom the farmer distinctly heard it speak. 'Within eight or ten days do or die,' it said, neither turning its head nor giving any indication that it had seen the farmer.

William Sutor gazed after it, his thoughts wildly churning in his mind. 'Within eight or ten days do or die. . . .' Whatever did it mean? How could he have heard a dog speak? But was it a dog? What had happened – what had he

The dog brushed past his legs and touched his trousers.
Immediately he felt a fierce pain.

seen – what did it all mean?

Slowly, thoughtfully, he set off again. The growing blackness ahead of him was empty of both man and beast. He was as alone as he had ever been. The gaunt trees bent their talons over him. The wind blew leaves into his face with a mocking chuckle. He found himself shivering with impatience to be home and among familiar things.

The next five kilometres seemed endless, but at last he saw the lights of the farmhouse ahead, and opening the gate he stumbled down the drive to the front door. He stood for a moment, trying to steady his breathing and bring himself to normality.

'No one shall know of this,' he told himself grimly, 'or they will think I am mad. . . .' As he opened the door he heard the welcoming bark of Samson coming from the kitchen quarters.

A week later William Sutor and his brother James visited a sick sister at Glanballow. On their way back in the evening they had to travel along part of the road that William had tramped the week before. As they neared the spot where the dog had appeared William experienced a feeling of great nervousness. He glanced behind him so frequently that his brother looked at him curiously, asking finally, 'What's the matter?'

'Nothing – nothing at all,' William replied quickly, but his voice was far from steady.

Then he saw the dog again, moving silently, steadily, with no flicker of tail or twitch of ear – just two red eyes glaring into the darkness.

'James!' he gasped, clutching at his brother's arm. 'Do you see it?'

James looked round him. 'See what?' he asked.

'The dog – if dog it is –'

'I see no dog,' James said shortly. 'Are you playing a trick on me?'

The dog passed close, touching William's leg with its grey body. Again he felt the searing pain, followed by the aching numbness. Again the dog spoke as it passed by. This time it said, 'Come to this spot within three days,' before it went ahead and was swallowed up in the darkness.

'Did you hear that?' William said. 'It spoke – that's the second time it has spoken to me.'

James jerked his arm away impatiently. 'I heard nothing, I saw nothing. I don't know what you are talking about. You had better see a doctor.'

William sighed and said no more, and they walked the rest of the way to the farmhouse in silence. James left him then to go to his own home with a brief goodnight.

Two days passed. During that time William had regained his courage and had determined to get to the bottom of the mysterious affair.

'I will not be scared by a dog, whether real or ghostly,' he told himself. 'If it can speak, it can answer questions. If it is all in my imagination, then I must know for sure. I will go to that same spot tonight, and take a stout stick with me.'

At midnight he set out. It was very dark and very still, and his footsteps ringing on the road seemed twice as loud as they normally did. As he approached what he called to himself 'the ghost spot', tremors of nervous excitement tingled inside him, and he grasped his stick more firmly. There was an elm tree near the roadside and he waited beneath it, remembering gratefully that evil spirits were supposed to steer clear of elms.

He did not have to wait long. Two pin points of light shone in the distance and grew larger as the creature advanced as stealthily as before. When it drew level with the farmer it stopped. Slowly the head turned and William Sutor found himself gazing deep into a glare as fierce as the hot glowing coals in the heart of a fire.

He flinched and drew back. His fingers tightened on his stick. He tried to speak but his throat closed up. For what seemed an eternity the man and the beast looked at each other, the one in horror, the other with a fixed inhuman gaze. At last William managed to jerk out a few strangled words. 'What are you? In the name of God, what are you?'

A voice came from the animal, though there was no movement of its jaws. 'I am David Sutor.'

'David Sutor – my grandfather's brother? But – but that is impossible!'

'I am David Sutor,' the creature repeated. 'I killed a man more than thirty-five years ago, and buried the body not far from here.'

The farmer put a hand to his head as though to steady the thoughts that were whirling around inside. 'But David Sutor was a man. You appear as a dog – I do not understand –'

The deep voice continued in the same passionless way. 'I killed a man. I killed him with a dog. I set my mastiff on to a poacher and made him bite the man to death. Now I am forced to appear as a dog and speak out of a dog's mouth.'

'Thirty-five years ago!' William cried. 'Then why have you just appeared? I remember the story of my grandfather's brother – how he disappeared from the village and how it was rumoured that he had enlisted in the army. How is it that you have never been seen before as a dog?'

'Because,' said the creature, 'I, David Sutor, died only a few days ago, on the last Monday of November. I died in a foreign land, killed in battle. Now I have returned to my native land and to the place where I killed a man. . . .'

William Sutor found some of his strength returning. The dog was a ghost. He was a human being of solid flesh – how could it harm him? His voice grew more confident. 'Then why have you returned – and to me? My brother did not see you the other night.'

'I have returned to you because you are a good man and you will do what I ask. I want you to find the bones of the man I killed and bury them in holy ground. Only then will I be free of my punishment.'

'But where are the bones? Where did you bury the body? Where am I to look?' William took a step forward. His generous heart had felt immediate concern for the ghost's plight, and he decided then and there that he would try to do what it had asked. From that moment the dog was no longer an object of terror but of pity. 'David Sutor, tell me, where are the bones?'

There came from the throat of the ghostly dog a sound that could have been a sigh. 'Under the bush – the withered bush – that is all I can tell you – under the withered bush. . . .' The dog turned its fiery eyes away from the farmer, sighed again and moved off down the road. Soon its grey shape was lost in the enveloping darkness.

William Sutor felt as though he had been released from a spell. A great burden of fear had dropped from him. Now he was himself again, free to think and act. He returned home with determination in his tread and a plan in his mind.

The next morning he went to see the minister of Blairgowrie and told him the whole story, half expecting that the old man would pooh-pooh any idea of ghosts and a dog that could speak, but this did not happen. Instead, the minister nodded thoughtfully. 'I remember David Sutor leaving the village,' he said, 'though I had but newly come to Blairgowrie. There were rumours too that his departure was caused by his wicked conduct, but nothing was ever brought out into the open, and the matter was never pursued. The story you tell is strange indeed, but it might well be true.'

'The only way we can find out, sir, is to dig,' said William eagerly.

'Yes, but where? There are so many withered bushes in the fields on either side of that road.'

'We must dig,' William repeated doggedly. 'We shall find the bones under one of them, I feel sure. I will collect all the men from my farm and we will start today.'

'I will come with you,' said the minister.

The late autumn sun shone thinly on a strange scene later that day. Men were digging around and under every withered bush in the fields close to the spot where the ghost dog had appeared. Some of them grumbled at their task, not believing the story their master had told them. Some dug fearfully, wondering what their spades might uncover. William Sutor and the minister wandered from bush to bush, from hole to hole, inspecting progress, hoping that the next spadeful would reveal the bones of the murdered poacher. But the sun went in, the day grew cold and nothing was found. When dusk fell they gathered their spades and returned to the farm, tired and dispirited.

'What now?' said the minister.

'I don't know,' the farmer replied. 'There's no other bush in any field. It couldn't have been a hoax. The dog's appearance was not an hallucination. Something has gone wrong. There is something we do not yet know.'

What that something was was shown to William Sutor that night as he lay in bed, restless and worried. What *had* gone wrong? The dog had said the bones would be found under a withered bush – then why hadn't they been? He tossed and turned, going over in his mind all that had happened. Suddenly, though the door was closed and the curtains drawn over the windows, the dog was in the room, its glowing eyes turned on him, its body misty and insubstantial in the faint glimmer of light that came from under the door.

William Sutor felt no fear. It was with reproach in his voice that he said, 'You did not tell me the truth. There are no bones beneath any of the withered bushes. Why did you lie to me?'

The dog lifted up its huge head so that the light from its eyes fell straight upon the farmer. 'You forget that I have been away for thirty-five years. The bush under which I buried the bones is there no longer. It must have been uprooted by a storm many years ago and carried away. You did not dig in the right place.'

'It's all right telling me that now!' spluttered William indignantly. 'You said there was a bush. . . .'

'I was mistaken.' The dog's voice was as expressionless as ever. 'But now I will give you another sign. Go to the field behind the elm tree and look for a cross on the ground, a cross in the grass that I have flattened with my feet. There was the bush, and under that cross you will find what you are looking for. Dig there and this time there will be no mistake.'

'How do I know –' William began, but the red eyes were no longer glowing. The dog had disappeared. William fell asleep wondering whether he had had a waking dream and whether to ignore the whole business and put ghosts out of his mind.

But the next morning he realized that the dog's words had left a deep impression on him. I must satisfy myself once and for all, he thought. I'll get the minister and the two of us will go. We'll tell no one, so that if our quest is unsuccessful no one will be any the wiser, and we can forget the matter for good and all.

The two men stood in the field behind the elm tree. Around them was the evidence of the previous day's digging. It looked as though an army of moles had been throwing up the earth in all directions. William Sutor shaded his eyes with his hand and looked round him. 'I can't see anything,' he said.

The minister moved forward a few paces. 'Keep moving and be careful where you tread,' he said. 'The cross may not be easily visible . . . why, here it is!' he added excitedly.

'Look!'

The farmer joined him. At their feet they could just make out in the short grass the rough shape of a cross about a metre long. It was not a natural formation – the grass had been pressed down deliberately. William sucked in his breath. 'Yes, that's it!' he exclaimed. 'Right, now I'll get busy.'

He thrust his spade into the ground and started to dig. The minister stood by, his white hair stirring in the breeze, his black gown billowing round him. It was not long before William felt his spade strike against something hard. He threw the spade to one side, knelt down and began to lift the earth away gently with his hands.

When all the bones of the man David Sutor had killed had been exposed William stood up. Together the farmer and the minister stood looking into the crude grave. The minister lifted up his hand. 'Later we will bury him in the church-yard,' he said, 'but first I must say a prayer over these poor remains, the sad ending to a tragedy of long ago.'

As the minister began to pray a sound was heard. It started as a low moan quivering in the air around them. It rose higher and higher till it became the high-pitched howl of an animal in dire distress. For what seemed minutes the unearthly sound filled their ears, beating in their heads, until the whole world seemed to be a physical expression of anguish, remorse and pain. Gradually the pressure lessened, as though release from pain was taking over. Before it died away altogether it had dissolved into a gentle sobbing, a human sound, not the voice of an animal.

'That's no dog,' muttered William Sutor.

The minister finished his prayer. 'David Sutor's soul has found the peace it was searching for,' he said. 'Come, let us go to the churchyard. You will never see the dog again.'

Appointment with Death

WHETHER THE APPARITION that came to Thomas, Lord Lyttelton in the night and gave him a grim warning was a ghost or a dream we shall never know. Much has been written about it. Some people believed in the ghost, some did not, and when the warning came there were explanations to prove that the whole affair could have been quite natural. Even Lord Lyttelton himself, in the half-hour before his death, joyfully convinced himself that the ghostly visitor had been a mere dream. But had it?

One evening in the November of 1779, Lord Lyttelton called for his servant and announced that he was going to bed. The servant raised an eyebrow. His master was not in the habit of retiring at such an early hour. Usually it was long after midnight, and sometimes, when he was entertaining guests, they would sit talking until dawn. The servant halted discreetly before leaving the room.

'I hope you are not ill, my lord,' he said.

'No, no, William,' Lord Lyttelton answered. 'I am quite well but I think that for once I will retire at a reasonable hour. I feel restless. Perhaps it is the atmosphere, heavy and dank as though a storm is on its way.'

Shortly afterwards Lord Lyttelton was lying comfortably in his vast four-poster bed, having drunk a glass of medicine to calm his nerves. William drew the curtains round the bed, quietly put out the lights and tiptoed out of the room. The minutes went by. Outside the heavy stillness gave way to a gusty wind which rustled through the trees in the garden and caused the branches to tap at the window, preventing Lord Lyttelton from dropping off to sleep. He tossed and turned, trying to make himself comfortable, but his thoughts raced after each other, and the noise of heavy rain and the periodic striking of the parish church clock kept him awake.

What seemed hours later, just as he was on the edge of sleep, a different sound jerked him right back into wakefulness. As though pulled by a string he sat up in bed and peered into the darkness. The sound seemed to be the flapping wings of a huge bird, and it came from inside the room. Strange, he thought, no bird could possibly get in, and he felt his heartbeat quicken. What could it be? Dare he climb out of bed to investigate? Should he call William?

Then the flapping stopped, making the silence that followed even more frightening. It was a wary silence, as though a waiting, listening presence were in the room with him. He felt an urge to cry out for help. He tried, but no sound would come. . . .

Sitting bolt upright, Lord Lyttelton found his eyes focussed on the curtain at the foot of the bed. As he gazed at it, to his horror, it began to move. Slowly it fell back and there, in an unearthly light, stood his visitor. It was the most beautiful, the most angelic woman he had ever seen in his life. Whatever horrifying spectre he had thought to see was far removed from this. Again he tried to speak, and again no sound came. All he could do was sit there, a slightly ridiculous figure, and stare at the tall, stately, unknown woman.

Then she spoke. 'Thomas, Lord Lyttelton, take note of my words.' It was a wonderful voice, commanding and yet strangely beautiful, but it was not human. It sounded like the wind and the waves, yet it had an echo of the tomb. It came from all places at once, a voice he could almost feel as well as hear.

*Slowly the curtain fell back and there, in an unearthly light,
stood his visitor.*

'Take note of my words and prepare yourself. In three days' time, at the hour of twelve, prepare yourself for death. In three days' time, you will die. Prepare yourself. . . .'

Terror overcame Lord Lyttelton. Sweat trickled down his face as he tried to force his voice to ask questions of the vision, but all the noise he made was an ugly croaking.

'Prepare yourself . . . prepare yourself . . . prepare yourself. . . .' Gradually the voice of the mysterious woman faded, she herself began to fade. The curtains dropped back into place and all was silent again. Exhausted with fear and anguish, Lord Lyttelton fell back in a dead faint.

When William came in the morning to wake his master he thought he had had a stroke or seizure during the night, and when at last he succeeded in waking him, the noble lord was far from normal. William did not know what to do. Should he go at once for a doctor? Ought he to leave the wretched man who lay on his bed, eyes staring, shivering as though he had a fever? To the servant's anxious questions Lord Lyttelton was unable to give coherent answers. No, he was not ill, yes, he was unwell, search the room, close the windows, open the windows, get the doctor, do not get the doctor, send for a parson, stay here, go away.

Eventually Lord Lyttelton showed signs of recovery. The relieved valet suggested that he should fetch a bowl of beef broth, which was about the most soothing thing he could think of. Pale and exhausted, Lord Lyttelton agreed. 'Yes, I should like that,' he said in a more normal voice.

'And the doctor, my lord, shall I send for him?'

'No, I shall be all right presently. I must have had a bad dream – a nightmare. I doubt if the doctor has any pills against that! But there are some friends I must see during the day. Send messages to them – Mr. Andrews, Mr. Ayscough, Mr. Pigou – I will give you a full list later. Fetch the broth and then I will leave my bed.'

When he was alone Lord Lyttelton went over and over in his mind the events of the night. Could it have been a dream? It seemed real at the time, but dreams could seem real too. He got out of bed and carefully examined the curtains. There was nothing to suggest that the mysterious woman had stood there and addressed him. Yet she was still so vivid in his mind – her features, her voice, and above all, her words!

He shuddered at the memory of them. He did not want to die. He enjoyed life; still fairly young, he had everything to live for. The only thing to do now was to talk it over with his friends, Miles Andrews and the others. Perhaps they would reassure him. . . .

During the day a steady stream of callers came to the house in Hill Street. To each of his friends Lord Lyttelton told the story of his dreadful night, and as the day wore on he found the reassurance he was seeking. Without exception, his friends found his story amusing.

'Was she pretty, Thomas?' asked Miles Andrews.

'Not pretty exactly,' Lord Lyttelton replied, 'but beautiful!'

His friend laughed. 'Beautiful? Dreaming of beautiful women, eh, Thomas? More likely you'll be married in three days, not dead. Of course it was a dream. I wish you weren't so superstitious!'

The weight of his friends' views finally convinced Lord Lyttelton that they were right. He began to feel less worried, less haunted. Although when he was alone the face of the woman and her warning words returned to his memory, he decided that he must keep his mind off the whole affair, at least until after the three days were up. So he filled his house with company, for breakfast, lunch and dinner.

The plan succeeded, thanks to the good nature of Lord Lyttelton's friends. They had jolly parties with witty talk. Lord Lyttelton entered into it all with eagerness and everybody agreed that he was himself again. When Miles Andrews explained to his host that he would not be present in the evening, having to go to Dartford for a few days, he remarked afterwards to one of the other guests, 'He seems to have forgotten all about the wretched dream. I doubt if he can even remember when it is that he is supposed to die!'

On the morning of the third day, Lord Lyttelton came slowly into the breakfast room at ten-thirty, advancing in rather a subdued way, and greeting his friends who were already there very quietly. When asked after his health he simply shrugged. He seemed content to listen to their talk without contributing anything himself. Jonathan Graves, a popular musician and church organist, who had been invited to entertain the others with his latest compositions, was particularly worried. His playing and singing seemed to have no effect on Lord Lyttelton's sudden melancholy. Miles Andrews had been wrong – he had not forgotten when he was due to die. . . .

By dinner-time, however, Lord Lyttelton seemed to have shaken off his gloom. After the meal he rose from the table, smiled at them all and said, 'Gentlemen, I am myself again! Thank you!'

The guests were dismayed when, shortly afterwards, their host slipped back into his former mood of depression, and when he was out of the room Jonathan Graves remarked, 'Friends, we can do no more to cheer him up with talking and joking. It is obvious to me that we must practise a little deception.'

'Deception?' said Mr. Ayscough. 'How do you mean?'

Graves looked towards the door to ensure that there was no danger of his host overhearing. 'It is simple,' he said in a low voice. 'Thomas is sad because he expects to die at midnight. Every watch and clock must seem to stare at him as if to say, "We will fetch you at midnight . . . in four hours, three hours, two hours," and so on. By the time midnight comes the poor fellow will probably die from sheer relief. But if, when midnight comes, he is safely asleep in bed, then the danger will be over.'

'But how can we cause him to retire before midnight?' asked Mr. Ayscough.

Graves leaned towards the others. 'By altering every time-piece in this house – by putting them forward half an hour.' To illustrate his point he took his own watch from his pocket and carefully put it forward half an hour. After a discussion it was generally agreed to be a good idea and each man altered his own watch. Jonathan Graves rang for the valet. He explained the plan to him and asked him if he could arrange to have the clocks altered.

'Yes, sir,' answered William, 'and I will be responsible for altering his lordship's watch which lies at this moment on his dressing-table.'

Then Lord Lyttelton returned. The party continued, and it was half past eleven by the clock when he got up and announced that he wished to retire. He bade them all goodnight, received their thanks for the pleasant evening, and left the room with perfect calmness.

His departure brought a certain relief to his friends, and they were able to talk openly about the subject that was in everybody's mind. None of them was prepared to accept that it was a ghost who had brought the warning to Lord Lyttelton, but no one had a better explanation than the dream theory.

'I think we can put our watches right now,' Jonathan Graves remarked later. 'Good heavens, it's time I went home,' he added, realizing that the actual time was nearly midnight.

'I too,' said Mr. Ayscough, 'and I shall leave happy in the knowledge that our friend is soundly asleep.'

'Let us hope so,' said another guest, as they made for the

cloakroom to collect their coats.

Suddenly, out of the blue, came the sound of a bell. The men fell silent, looking at each other in consternation. Another bell rang out.

'That is one clock we could not alter,' Graves whispered hoarsely. 'I had forgotten the parish church. . . .'

Three, four, the bell clanged, five, six, seven . . . and from above there came a shout.

'Come quickly, my lord is dying. . . .'

Eight, nine, rang the bell. The men dashed up the stairs to where William, pale as death, stood outside the door of Lord Lyttelton's bedroom. Ten, eleven. . . . Inside the room, Graves, Ayscough and some others saw Lord Lyttelton twisting in agony. Twelve! The last bell of midnight sounded and they saw their friend collapse in death.

Later, with all the guests gathered together in the library, the valet told them what had happened.

'When my master came into his room,' he said, 'he made his usual preparations for bed. While I was putting away his clothes I noticed that he was taking frequent glances at his watch. I had the impression that he wished me to stay as long as possible because he did everything very slowly. When he got into bed he ordered the curtains at the foot to be closed. Then he looked at his watch again and saw that it was a few minutes to twelve. He asked me to look at my watch and was much relieved when it agreed with his. He then put both watches to his ear, making sure that they were both going. He stared at them until the hands had passed midnight. Then he handed mine back to me and told me to prepare his medicine. When I returned with the glass it was turned a quarter after twelve. His lordship gave a wry smile:

'The mysterious lady is not a true prophetess, I find. Come, I will wait no longer. Let me drink my medicine and then I'll try to sleep.'

'He drank it and bade me goodnight, but as he settled down to sleep the parish church clock began to strike. At that moment his lordship gave a sort of choking gasp and tried to say something to me. I could not tell what he was saying, and I rushed to the door to call you gentlemen . . . his friends.'

'So the mysterious lady *was* a prophetess,' said Jonathan Graves sombrely, 'and she kept her appointment. . . .'

The Message

VINCENT SHADWELL was a successful portrait painter in the early years of this century. He was so much in demand by wealthy people who wanted to sit for him that he scarcely ever left his studio in Kensington, and rarely finished working until late evening.

One year, as a balmy spring gave notice that summer was near, he decided that he could not bear to spend the hot summer months in London. He did not want to paint another portrait of a stout alderman or bejewelled hostess. He longed instead for simple things – landscapes, village scenes, the flowers that starred the country hedgerows. So he made no more appointments for sittings, finished the portraits he had already started, and asked friends for their ideas as to where he should go for his rest.

In the end he chose to stay with the family of a rector in Kent. The rectory was very large and the rector was glad to have a paying guest for a few months to help towards its upkeep. Vincent Shadwell at once took a great liking to the gentle, unworldly rector, his pleasant, bustling wife and their large family, and also to the low, rambling house which stood at the far end of the village next to the square stone church.

Almost at once the artist's days fell into a regular pattern. For most of the time he was in the woods and fields with his paints and easel, and only returned to the rectory when the light failed. When he wanted company he would join the family after supper, but usually he sat in his room, writing letters, or reading, or planning what he would do the following day. To add to his contentment he knew that his landscapes were as good, in their different way, as his portraits.

Day after day the sun shone, but at last the weather broke and a cool, rainy period set in. Cooped up in his sitting-room, Shadwell grew bored with inactivity. One evening he was sitting in front of the fire dozing over a dull book. After a while his head began to nod and the book slipped from his hand. Suddenly something made him spring into wakefulness. He experienced a momentary fear and his skin began to tingle. Then he realized what had awakened him and he chuckled at his foolishness. It was nothing more sinister than the door opening with a creak.

He turned in his chair, expecting to see the rector's wife bringing him his evening drink, but to his surprise a little girl about eight years old was standing in the doorway. She had a thin, pale face, her dark hair was in ringlets, and she wore a crimson dress covered by a white pinafore.

'Hello, my dear,' he said, smiling. 'How nice of you to visit me. But who are you? Have I seen you before?'

The child gazed at him with mournful eyes but did not answer.

'Have you lost your tongue?' Shadwell laughed. 'Very well, I'll have to guess your name! Let's see – I'd better start with who you're *not*! You're not Lorna, because she's only five. And you can't be Emily, for she's a baby.'

The little girl continued to regard him gravely, and Shadwell felt a twinge of uneasiness. 'Well, you're certainly not Edward or Henry,' he went on, 'and they wouldn't thank me for suggesting it! So who have I left out? Barbara, of course – but she's barely three.' A surprised note entered his voice. 'Surely I've mentioned all the rector's children? Then who are you? A cousin? A friend?'

The little girl remained silent. Then, very deliberately, she averted her eyes from his face and gracefully, almost as though she were gliding, moved across the room. She passed the window, the bookcase, the fireplace and the desk, and made for the opposite wall. For a moment she stood quite still in front of it, then she raised her arm and pressed her hand lightly on the wallpaper. She turned again and looked pleadingly at the artist. Shadwell saw the small furrows in her brow. 'She wants to say something,' he told himself, 'but she can't. What is it, I wonder. . . .?'

Once more her eyes dropped. She left the room as slowly, yet as purposefully, as she had entered it.

'Odd,' thought Shadwell, 'very odd indeed. What an extraordinary child. Not a single word nor' – and the thought brought back his unease – 'nor the slightest sound.'

He shrugged his shoulders and picked up his book again. He decided that the little girl *must* be one of the rector's children. Perhaps she had only just returned from visiting relations – but it was strange that the rector had not at least mentioned her – and he was puzzled as to why she should be so solemn when the other children were gay and mischievous. It was unlikely that she was deaf and dumb. . . .

He settled down to his book and tried to forget the incident. But he found it impossible to get the child's face out of his mind, and her indifference to his questions left him vaguely uncomfortable. The striking of the church clock jerked him out of his thoughts and he realized with a shock that it was half an hour after midnight.

He intended to bring up the subject of his strange visitor at breakfast the next morning, but neither the rector nor his wife was present at the meal. The rector was taking an early service and his wife was busy with the children. The sun was shining again and Shadwell gathered his painting materials together and was about to set off when he met the rector in

She turned again and looked pleadingly at the artist.

the hall.

'Good morning,' Shadwell said, and before the rector could return his greeting blurted out, 'A little girl paid me a visit last night, Rector, a thin, dark child about eight years old. I didn't know you had another daughter. I've been wondering why you have never mentioned her.'

The rector's face turned white and he made an odd choking noise. 'So you have seen her,' he whispered huskily.

Shadwell found it difficult to suppress his astonishment at such a strong reaction. 'I'm sorry if I have upset you –' he began, but the rector cut him short, grabbing his arm.

'Please – not here – come to my study and I'll try to explain.'

Shadwell put down his equipment and followed the rector into the book-lined room. The rector made sure that no one was in the hall outside before he closed the door, in an almost stealthy way, Shadwell thought.

'I apologize for behaving so mysteriously,' the rector said, motioning Shadwell to a chair, 'but I think you will understand when I tell you that your visitor was Mary – my eldest daughter.'

Shadwell still looked puzzled. 'But why are you so upset?'

'Mr. Shadwell, Mary died – five years ago.'

'Died?' Shadwell shivered as though icy fingers had touched him. 'Then –'

'What you saw was no living child, but the spirit of a very unhappy little girl. She has been seen before, but not by me or my wife. That explains why I hustled you into this room. My wife must not know about Mary's visits – it would be too upsetting for her – and I beg you not to mention your experience to her.'

'Of course I won't,' said Shadwell, relieved now not to have seen the rector's wife at breakfast. 'But – a ghost! I can hardly believe that that is what I saw last night.'

'Let me tell you the full story, Mr. Shadwell, and then you can make up your own mind. Five years ago we had workmen in, trying to cure a dampness that was affecting the north side of the house. One of the rooms they were working in was your room. One day my wife, who finds it hard to refuse pedlars who come to the door, wished to pay for some trifling articles she had bought. Although she is inclined to be soft-hearted, she is sensible enough not to leave the kitchen unattended, so she told Mary, who was eight at the time, to run upstairs and fetch a half-crown piece which she knew was on the dressing-table in our bedroom. Mary was gone for some time and when she returned it was without the money. She said she could not find it, that there was no money on the dressing-table. My wife knew beyond doubt that it *had* been there, and she was both angry and exasperated that Mary had failed to bring it. She remembered that there were a few shillings put by for the milkman in an old pewter mug in the kitchen, so she paid the pedlar at the door and as soon as he had gone she began to scold Mary, accusing her of either stealing the half-crown or of hiding it for a joke.

'The child hotly denied the accusations but my wife found it difficult to believe her, and in desperation said that when I came home I would get the truth from her. . . .'

The rector paused and stared into space.

'And did you?' Shadwell asked gently.

The rector sighed. 'I wish I knew. Mary persisted in declaring that she had not been able to find the money. It seemed as though it were a question of believing either Mary or my wife, that both of them could not be telling the truth. In the end my wife, in a very upset state, sent the child to bed in disgrace. During the night – I remember it so vividly – we could hear her sobbing. I wanted to go and comfort her but my wife dissuaded me. She had convinced herself that Mary needed punishment, and that solitude was the best method.

'The next morning she went to Mary's bedroom, expecting to find her tear-stained and repentant. Instead – she found her dead. Her sobbing had brought on convulsions which led to unconsciousness – and death.'

The rector put his hand over his eyes to conceal his falling tears. Shadwell longed to say something that would comfort him, but no words would come.

The rector continued. 'As you can imagine, our grief was mixed with remorse. Suppose the child had been innocent? Suppose another person had taken the money – one of the workmen, perhaps? The missing half-crown was never found. . . . My wife and I have never ceased to reproach ourselves. We were both to blame for Mary's death. . . .' His voice trailed away to silence. He took out his handkerchief and put it to his eyes.

'And Mary still visits you?' Shadwell asked when the rector had recovered a little.

'Not us,' he replied sadly. 'Not us – that is what makes it harder to bear. My wife knows nothing about Mary's visits to the room you are occupying. But other visitors who have had that room have seen her. She never speaks. She just goes to the wall, touches it and goes away again.'

'I wonder –' The artist got up and paced about the study. 'I wonder – may I have your permission to make an experiment?'

'I would prefer you to forget the whole thing,' the rector said.

'I appreciate your feelings,' Shadwell said, 'but do you think that Mary will visit me again?'

'No. She has never been known to appear twice to the same person. I don't know why – it seems as though she is seeking help, and when it is not given she does not try again.'

'If you will agree to my experiment,' Shadwell said, a growing excitement in his voice, 'it may give Mary's spirit the very help she is looking for. It won't take long – please come with me to my sitting-room.'

Without waiting for an answer Shadwell strode out of the study and went up the stairs two at a time. The rector followed reluctantly, shaking his head.

Shadwell went straight to the wall on which Mary's ghost had pressed her thin little hand. He took a large penknife from his pocket and opened out one of the blades. 'May I?' he asked.

The rector nodded, a glint of understanding in his eye. Shadwell felt around the wall with his fingers, muttered 'Ah!' and began to dig into the plaster with his knife. Little showers of white dust fell on the carpet as the knife worked around a growing hole. The rector began to share some of the artist's excitement.

At last Shadwell had finished probing. He inserted his fingers into the hole and drew something from it. In silence he passed it to the rector, who gazed with amazement at a tarnished half-crown. . . .

'That spot was exactly where the child placed her hand last night,' Shadwell said. 'Do you see now why she has visited everybody who has occupied this room?'

'Of course,' said the rector. 'She came to show us where to look.' He sat down suddenly as though his legs had given way. 'But I still don't understand – did she hide the coin in the wet plaster for mischief, or so that she could take it out afterwards when the incident had been forgotten?'

'Or did one of the workmen sneak into your bedroom and take it, and then hide it when he heard your wife scolding Mary?'

'Yes, that might be so,' the rector said thoughtfully. 'But in that case how did Mary know where it was?'

Shadwell made a gesture of uncertainty. 'Perhaps ghosts have the power to acquire knowledge – who can tell? It might have been only a coincidence. We shall never know. Death claimed your little daughter, but her spirit could find no rest until at least this much of the truth had been revealed. She came back to give her message in the only way she could. I have a feeling that she will never come again.'

'No, Mr. Shadwell, I don't think she will.' The rector looked pale but relaxed. 'I'm sure she would thank you if she could.'

Shadwell was staring dazedly down at his right hand as if he had never seen it before. It was his turn to be agitated. 'Thank me?' he gasped. 'Why, that is just what she *has* done – I have just felt the pressure of warm flesh against my fingers. . . .'

The Duke's Decision

DUKE CHRISTIAN OF EISENBURG sat in his study reading State
papers. It was a spring morning in 1705 and the Duke was in
a pleasant frame of mind. He enjoyed this time of day more
than any other, and it was a strict rule in the palace that no
one should disturb him on any pretext when he was busy with
his papers. It was not that he disliked people – far from it –
but his life was usually so full that he needed the luxury of
solitude for at least a small part of each day.

When he heard a gentle tapping at the study door his first
feeling was of annoyance. How dare anyone disturb him
during his private time! But there was no point in getting
upset, he decided, and called 'Come in.'

The Duke expected to see a servant or guard, and so was
somewhat taken aback when a lady entered the room. His
surprise was all the greater when he saw that she was dressed
in the style of a hundred years earlier. This must be a joke, the
Duke decided, and not a very funny one at that. However, he
put down the documents he had been studying and rose from
his chair. Before he could speak his strange visitor forestalled
him.

'Do not be alarmed,' she said quietly.

The Duke made a gesture of irritation. 'I am not in the least
alarmed, madam,' he said. 'I would very much like an
explanation of your presence here.'

'I need your help,' the woman said simply.

'Indeed? Before you state your business perhaps you will

kindly explain how you contrived to get past my guards. And why you wear fancy dress?'

'Your guards did not see me,' the woman replied, 'and these clothes are of my time. I am a spirit.'

'A spirit?' echoed the Duke. 'You mean you are a ghost?'

'Do not be alarmed,' the woman said again. 'I am no evil spirit and I wish you no harm. I am Princess Anna, the wife of Duke John Casimir of Saxe-Coburg.'

The Duke dropped back into his chair, bewildered. The Duke Casimir was one of his ancestors . . . he had died a hundred years ago . . . could this – this woman – ghost – be speaking the truth? He had never met a ghost before although he had heard stories about such creatures. Usually they were said to be hideous and frightening – but this apparition was so ordinary – it was like talking to his own daughter. Was some hoax being played on him? He straightened himself as the stranger repeated, 'Do not be alarmed.'

The repetition of the words spurred the Duke into coherent speech. 'I am *not* alarmed,' he said, a bit shakily, 'but I am puzzled. Pray tell me what you want from me.'

'I wish you to bring my husband and me together again.'

'I do not understand.' The Duke looked and sounded helpless.

'We are not together in death, and although I am happy, he is not. He is wandering about in cold and darkness between time and eternity. You, only you, can bring us together.'

The Duke pondered her words. 'You mean that Duke Casimir is in some kind of hell? But why? I have seen no records nor heard tales of any wickedness connected with his name.'

'He was cruel to me towards the end of his earthly life,' the ghostly visitor answered. 'At the time of our deaths we had been on bad terms for some time. A madness had got into

78

him. He believed that I was deceiving him. His terrible suspicions turned to hatred. Many times I begged and prayed him to clear his mind of these false thoughts, but in vain.'

'How can I bring you together?' the Duke asked, after a considerable pause.

'I have known for a long time that one of our descendants would reconcile us. The time for reconciliation has now arrived. I beg you to listen to my plea.'

Duke Christian's mind grew more confused than ever. He felt himself in the middle of a fantastic situation. Was this really a spirit standing in front of his desk, this small, old-fashioned figure with her quiet voice and sad face? What should he do? What should he say?

'If you do not wish to decide now,' the quiet voice went on, 'I will give you eight days in which to consider my request. I will then come for your answer.' There was a faint rustle and she disappeared before the Duke's very eyes.

One moment she was there, the next she had gone. The Duke shook his head in baffled astonishment. Then he struggled to his feet, dashed to the door and hurried to the ante-room where he found two guards and one of his servants. They sprang to attention as he appeared and looked curiously at his white face and shaking hands.

'Have you – did you –?' he began, but as he spoke he realized that they had seen nothing and that they would think he was going out of his mind if he insisted that a woman had got past them. Wearily he returned to his study to think out the whole situation.

Eight days, the spirit had said. The Duke decided that his first move must be to get in touch with a clergyman in whom he had great confidence, a man who would not scoff at his tale of a ghostly visitation, and who, moreover, had a detailed knowledge of his family history. . . .

Together the Duke and the clergyman consulted all the

'Do not be alarmed,' the woman said again. 'I am no evil
spirit and I wish you no harm.'

family records, and as bit by bit they pieced the story together, they discovered that the spirit had told the truth. Duke Casimir and his wife had died within a short time of each other, and just before his death there had been rumours about his jealousy and cruel treatment of her. There was even a legend which foretold their final reconciliation by a descendant.

As the time for the ghost's reappearance drew near, the Duke decided to accept his clergyman friend's advice and to promise to do what he could for the two unfortunate ghosts. But still there was a doubt at the back of his mind. Was it all a dream, a practical joke, or was he really in touch with the inhabitants of a ghostly world? He took care to have his study door well watched and he gave special instructions to his guards as the eighth day arrived.

'Do not let your eyes stray from the door for a single second,' he warned, 'and raise the alarm at the slightest sign of anything out of the ordinary.'

But Casimir's wife appeared at the appointed time, unseen by the guards. . . .

Duke Christian felt almost relieved as she stood before him. At least he had not been dreaming the first time, and he waited for her to speak.

'What is your decision? Will you help us?'

'Yes,' answered the Duke, 'whatever it is in my power to do, I will do.'

'Then tomorrow night I will return with my husband. Although I can visit you by day, he can only come before you during the hours of darkness. Thank you, and farewell.'

Then once again she disappeared as though she had never been. The walls, floor and door of the room were of solid wood and stone and she had melted through them silently, effortlessly. . . .

'I'll double the guard,' he vowed. 'Somebody else *must* see her. It is impossible that she can come and go in this fashion.'

But his precautions were in vain, for the next night the small woman in her quaint clothes, accompanied by a man, appeared before him. Her escort was tall, handsome and richly dressed, though his eyes were tortured and his livid face had almost a greenish tinge. He held himself stiffly, and his words came out reluctantly, as though he were not used to talking.

'We will tell you our stories,' Casimir began, 'and when you have heard both sides, you will judge. We will abide by your judgement.'

'I understand,' said the Duke.

As if they were in a court of law, the two spirits related their grievances. Duke Christian listened to them carefully. First, the wife told of her misery at her husband's unjust suspicions, how she had pleaded with him to believe in her innocence, but he had dismissed all the evidence of this and had heaped insults upon her, and treated her with such contempt and cruelty that she had become ill.

Then Casimir told of how he had suspected his wife of plotting against him, of being unfaithful, of performing witchcraft to bring about his death. As a result he had become almost blinded by hatred of her. He admitted he had not had any proof of her alleged misdeeds, that she had always been an affectionate wife, that she had denied all his charges, but that in spite of all her protestations his jealousy and hatred had taken possession of him.

When he had finished, Casimir and his wife regarded Duke Christian with great seriousness, awaiting the judgement.

The Duke was overcome by a deep sadness as he began to understand how the two unhappy spirits had suffered over what clearly had been a terrible misunderstanding. It was a deep privilege, he felt, that it should be within his power to put an end to the trouble and unite his ancestors.

At last, smiling gently, he said, 'Dear, honoured ancestors, I have heard you both, and am moved to pity by your stories. Here is my judgement. Duke Casimir, I find in favour of your wife. She was cruelly misused by you. Will you accept my judgement?'

The ghost of Duke Casimir turned towards his wife and with a deep sigh said, 'I accept your judgement, and I ask my wife to forgive me.'

She moved a little towards him and stretched out her hand. 'I forgive you freely!'

The Duke wondered if he dared touch them. For a moment he hesitated, then left his desk and walked slowly towards the two ghosts. He lifted Duke Casimir's hand. It was as cold as a block of ice. He put it into the woman's hand and his own fingers covered the clasped hands. His warm blood did not flow to them. Their coldness struck into his body and he began to shiver violently. He withdrew his hand and backed away. During the short period of contact he had felt so strange, as though he had begun to move out of his own body. . . .

'Now my wife and I will be together for all eternity,' said Duke Casimir. 'My hell is over. Our thanks to you, good Christian, and farewell until we meet again.'

'When will that be?' the Duke demanded impetuously.

'We will meet ere long.' Duke Casimir's voice had thinned to the merest thread, and the Duke only just caught the words before he was alone in his study, gazing at the spot where, a moment before, two seemingly solid bodies had stood.

A great calm came over the kindly Duke, and a warm happiness grew inside him. 'I wonder when "ere long" will be,' he murmured, but felt no apprehension.

He died in 1707, two years after he had seen his visitors for the last time. He had spent the time in good works and was well loved by all his subjects. In his will he left instructions that his body should be buried in quicklime, for it was believed then that such a burial would prevent a person's ghost from haunting the living.

Duke Christian was determined that he would never give his descendants the experience that he himself had undergone.

The Staircase

ON A DARK JANUARY DAY in 1850 Joseph Hale's wife Isabel died after a short illness, and her sudden death so affected him that the house they had been so happy in for nearly ten years seemed ugly and unfriendly. The beautiful countryside of north Lancashire through which they had walked and taken pleasant drives appeared harsh and cold. Not even the appealing ways of his four children could console him. He knew that he would only regain his peace of mind by moving right away from all the places that had associations with Isabel and by starting life again in new surroundings.

After a long search Mr. Hale decided to buy a large Tudor mansion near the Midland town of Stafford, and lost no time in arranging to move his family, servants and belongings there.

The children arrived by coach soon after the task of moving in had started, and when they had clambered down they stared open-mouthed at the warm red-brick building with its twisted chimneys and mullioned windows. Clarissa, who was eight and the eldest, ran up to her father, who was supervising the unloading of the furniture, and pulled at his sleeve. 'Papa –' she began.

Mr. Hale gently disengaged himself from her eager grip. 'Not now, child,' he said. 'I'm very busy. You must keep out of everybody's way for a while.'

'May we explore the house?' she asked. 'Oh, Papa, may we?'

Mr. Hale smiled and patted her head. 'Certainly, as long as you take good care of the little ones. Don't be away too long!' he called after her, watching her skipping away with the seven-year-old John and with Edward and Emma, the twins who were nearly five.

'I promise!' Clarissa called back, and soon the four children, after examining with interest the huge wooden doors studded with nails and carved with leaves and flowers, had disappeared into the house.

The large hall was semi-circular. From the middle of the crescent a corridor led to the back of the house, and on either side an imposing staircase rose in an elegant curve to a wide gallery, and then to the upper floors.

For a moment the children gazed in awe at the unaccustomed grandeur. Then John ran ahead of the others. 'Come, Rissa, let's climb the stairs,' he called.

Clarissa, feeling very grown-up at having the younger children entirely in her charge, was about to protest that she must lead the way, but John was already half-way up so she had to follow, holding tightly on to the chubby hands of Edward and Emma.

John, who had already reached the gallery, was opening one door after another and peering into the rooms. 'Rissa, it's as big as a castle!' he exclaimed.

'It's more like a palace,' said Clarissa, remembering the fairy tales she had read. 'And it's empty – and all ours.'

Suddenly the children caught each other's excitement and caution went with the wind. John laughed. 'Follow me!' he demanded, pushing open another door and darting into the room. From that room a door led to another, and from that a staircase took them to another wing of the house. Along corridor after corridor they hurried, the twins having to trot to keep up with Clarissa and John, who behaved as if they had to enjoy their new house before it vanished. The rooms

Festoons of cobwebs hung before them, and mice scuttled away at their approach.

began to get smaller and the corridors narrower. Festoons of cobwebs hung before them, and mice scuttled away at their approach. Clarissa's eagerness to explore began to ebb. The twins were both tired and their feet were dragging, and it was only because John had plunged ahead determinedly, heedless of any request to turn back, that the others reluctantly carried on. 'What games of hide-and-seek we shall have!' he said, turning down yet another passage.

At the end of it the children stopped. John turned to his sister. 'It's a blank wall,' he declared. 'We can't go any farther.'

'Good!' Clarissa said feelingly. 'Now perhaps we can turn back.' She examined the panelling more thoroughly, curious in spite of having had enough of exploring, and suddenly pointed to a tiny knob of wood that did not seem to fit in with the pattern of the carving. 'I wonder what that is. . . .'

'Let me see!' John pushed her aside. 'It's rather strange, isn't it?' He poked at it with his forefinger, and gave a startled cry when a door in the panelling silently slid back to reveal a spiral staircase leading off a narrow stone landing, twisting upwards and downwards out of their sight. 'A secret staircase,' he breathed. 'We *must* explore this. Shall we go up or down?'

'Oh, no!' Clarissa wailed. 'John, don't! Let's go back!'

'We can't go back now – we might not find this again! I'm going up, whatever the rest of you do.' John stuck his hands on his hips and glared at his sister.

Clarissa sighed. There was no arguing with John when he was in one of his determined moods. He would go, whatever she said, and she did not relish the thought of telling her father that she had left him alone on a secret staircase and hearing him say, 'Clarissa, I'm disappointed in you – you were supposed to be in charge. . . .' So she gave a little gulp of apprehension. 'Very well, I suppose we'd better come with you. But I shall tell Father how naughty you've been!'

Stealthily they climbed the worn stone steps. There was no hand-rail and they had to feel their way by the rough surface of the wall. At intervals a narrow slit in the stonework let in a little light, and they realized that the staircase must be next to an outside wall.

Eventually they reached the top and stood on the landing. There was another door in front of them. John pushed it open and they entered the room, their feet echoing hollowly on the bare wooden floor. The only window, high in the wall, was all but boarded over, and in the gloom they did not at first notice that the room was round and that the ceiling rose to a point.

'It's a turret room,' Clarissa whispered. 'We're right at the top of the house.' She did not know why she felt so uneasy. The room contained no furniture, there was nothing in it to frighten them, yet there was something about it – something cold and eerie in the atmosphere – that made her wish with all her heart that they were back in the security of their father's presence.

Even John's high spirits had deserted him. White-faced, he sidled close to his sister, and the twins huddled together in the shelter of her arms.

In utter silence they stood, expecting they knew not what, staring around them at the perfectly ordinary walls and floor, yet aware that the room was not ordinary. It was empty now – but was it always empty? Had they disturbed a – a – Clarissa failed to put her thoughts into words and miserably wondered how they would ever break the spell that rooted them to the floor.

It was Edward who managed to bring them back to normality. 'I'm hungry!' he announced. 'I'm going back to Papa.'

Dear Edward, Clarissa thought – his stomach was always more important than anything else! She drew a deep breath and found that she was not afraid any more. 'What a good idea,' she said briskly. 'I'm sure we could all do with something to eat. I'll lead the way down and we'll soon be back with Papa.'

She felt her way down the steps of the secret staircase as quickly as she dared, the others laughing and chattering behind her now that the tension had gone. Down and down they went – the staircase seemed endless. Surely, Clarissa thought in a moment of panic, we didn't come *up* this number of stairs. The walls seemed to be closing in on them. It was quite dark now, and she realized that there were no more slits in the walls to provide the slivers of light that had helped them to find the way up to the turret room.

Suddenly she stopped dead in her tracks and behind her the others halted abruptly. 'Why have you stopped?' John complained. 'You should have warned us – I've trodden on Edward's foot –'

But Clarissa did not answer him. She was staring at a figure that had materialized out of the darkness and was standing there in front of her, just visible as a faint white glimmer. It moved slowly forward and she saw that it was a woman who was making an urgent gesture with one hand, as if she were trying to push the children away from her. It was not a threatening movement, more one of warning. 'Don't come any farther!' it seemed to say.

Clarissa's first thought was that one of the new servants had got as lost as they were, but there was something about the woman that was very familiar, and as Clarissa peered at her intently she knew that it was *not* a servant. She gave a wild cry. 'Mamma! It's – it's Mamma. . . .'

There was a moment of stunned silence, then the four children turned as one and began to stumble up the stairs as quickly as they could. Clarissa was the last, pushing out her hands blindly, grazing her shins and barking her elbows in a desperate effort to get away from the white figure. 'I've seen Mamma,' she whimpered. 'Mamma was there and was waving us back . . . oh, please hurry. . . .'

John reached the landing they had started out from and saw the sliding door they had missed on their way down from the turret room. 'Here it is,' he panted. 'This way. . . .'

They found their father still occupied with the workmen and rushed at him.

'Now, Clarissa, I told you not to interrupt our work –' he began, then saw their ashen faces. 'Whatever is the matter, my darlings?' he asked.

Clarissa hurled herself on him and burst into tears. 'I've seen Mamma – at the bottom of a dark staircase – but Mamma is dead – oh, Papa, what does it mean? Are we all going to die?'

Mr. Hale concealed the shock that Clarissa's words had given him though his eyes darkened with pain. 'Pull yourself together, my dear, and tell me exactly what happened.'

Clarissa faltered out her story. At the end of it she said wonderingly, 'Papa, she looked so kind and gentle – just as she used to do – but she was worried too – and she waved us back – she didn't want us to get any nearer to her – why did she want us to keep away, do you think?'

'I don't know,' Mr. Hale said, 'but you may be sure that she did not mean to harm you. You know how much she loved you all. I'm sure she – she – only appeared for your good. Will you take me to where you saw her?'

Clarissa swallowed, then nodded.

'I'll come too, Papa,' John said. 'I didn't see Mamma the first time. Perhaps she'll come to us again.'

Mr. Hale sighed. 'Don't count on it, my boy.' He called for a lamp and followed Clarissa and John as they retraced their tracks, finally arriving at the sliding door that led to the spiral staircase.

With the warm light from the lamp making their descent easier they soon reached the bottom of the steps. 'It was here that I saw Mamma,' Clarissa whispered.

There was no ghostly figure waiting for them this time, however. When Mr. Hale had lifted up the lamp and looked in the direction of Clarissa's pointing finger he gave a cry of horror. Only a metre from where they stood was a wide, open well, and, looking down, Mr. Hale could just see the black, oily water, waiting to receive and engulf anyone who might in the darkness have taken one step forward.

Mr. Hale hastily pulled the children back to safety. He shuddered when he realized how easily they might all have plunged to their deaths in that dark abyss. If it had not been for the spirit of their mother standing at the brink, warning them not to go forward, he would never have seen them again, and would never have known what had happened to them. They would have disappeared without trace. . . .

'Thank you, Isabel,' he murmured, and led the children away from horror into the simple ordinariness of everyday life.

Billy Bates's Story

My name is william joseph bates, though everyone calls me Billy Bates. I'm nearly thirteen – which is a better way of saying that I'm twelve and a half. I'm supposed to be good at writing stories, but that isn't why I'm writing *this* one. Something happened to me that I don't understand and I thought that writing it all down might explain things. Whether it will or not, I shan't know till I've come to the end.

This funny experience really began at school, which is a strange place for a ghost story to begin. You see, there was this special essay we had to write for a competition. One of the school governors had offered a two-pound book token for the best story called 'An Exciting Adventure', and I won it for my age-group. I was presented with the book token in front of the whole school, which I quite enjoyed, even though I did have to bash Phil Masters in the playground afterwards for squinting at me as I was going up to the platform and making me laugh right in the Head's face.

But now I wish I hadn't won that prize. If I hadn't I would have gone straight home to tea and afterwards met some of my pals in the park for a game of football, and then I shouldn't have been writing this. As it was, I went home on my own, the lads having decided to give me time to get over feeling big-headed at my success, though it really hadn't affected me at all.

I almost forgot to tell you that my prize essay was a so-called ghost story. On the main road near the flats where I

93

live there's an old derelict house. This was the house which had sparked off my story for the competition. I described it as a crooks' hideout and told how the gang and I had discovered this and then scared the crooks out of their wits by pretending to be ghosts. There wasn't much to it but it must have been more exciting than the other stories to win the prize.

As I walked home on my own I had to pass this house. The crumbling walls were covered with tattered creeper, and the garden was full of tin cans, dirty mattresses and broken boxes, partly hidden by a jungle of tall weeds. I looked round to make sure that no one was watching me, then gave a little bow. 'Thanks very much, house,' I said. ''Tis due to you that I was victorious.' I must have sounded like one of the Three Musketeers.

At that moment I caught sight of Phil Masters turning a corner into the road. I wondered if he'd seen me acting the fool, or if he wanted to return the bashing I'd given him, so I decided to play safe. I nipped smartly through the broken fence and entered the house through the broken-down door in the basement.

When I was inside I wasn't exactly scared, even though I didn't feel like laughing. It was pretty weird. The windows were boarded over and it was very dark. Most of the floorboards were rotten and it was a tricky job to avoid falling down one of the many holes. There was a smell like old cupboards, and a creaking noise that might have been caused by me treading on the broken boards – or by rats; a nasty thought when you hadn't got anything to throw at them.

I should have gone straight back to the safety of the outside world, but I was feeling pleased with the old house for helping me to win the book token, and I suddenly realized that I had never really explored it thoroughly. So, treading carefully, I made my way out of the basement and up the rickety stairs to the ground floor. I found myself in a big squarish hall but I couldn't make out many details because very little light came through the boarded-up windows. From the hall a door led into what was, I supposed, the front room. I pushed it open and went in. The door swung to behind me, closing with a little bang. The room was empty except for some rubbish in one corner, great pieces of wallpaper hanging from the walls and a huge fireplace which looked as though it might fall down at any moment.

Then, for no reason that I could think of, I went all hot and cold. My throat tightened and my heart started to pump away like mad. There's nothing to be afraid of, I told myself, hoping that I was telling myself the truth and, just to prove it, I began to whistle. The next moment I would have been out of that room like a scalded cat if the floor had been safe, for my whistling was interrupted by a voice. 'Hush, boy,' it said, 'I can't abide that tiresome noise.'

It wasn't an angry or threatening voice, but my hair was suddenly standing on end, and I must have looked pretty scared with my mouth open and my eyes popping out.

'There's no need to be frightened, child,' the voice went on.

Child! I may be only thirteen – nearly – but I'm tall for my age, and 'child' made me feel as though I were back in a sailor suit. 'I'm *not* frightened,' I lied, and my voice sounded like a transistor radio when the battery is running out. 'I just didn't see you, that's all.' I turned round and still didn't see anyone, and a cold shiver attacked me from stem to stern.

'No,' said the voice, almost in my ear, 'not many people do – but here I am.'

I tried to say 'Where?' but it was not easy to talk with my teeth chattering. In any case, there wasn't any need. She was there, right in front of me – a little old woman, not much taller than me, wearing a dark dress down to her ankles. There was just enough light for me to see her wispy white hair and pale wrinkled face, and I stopped trembling because it was a *kind* face, though anxious. I didn't know what to say next, but she kept the conversation going.

'I am so pleased that you have come,' she said, just as if she had been expecting me. 'It is not often I can get through and when I do manage it, there is never anyone here.'

'Get through where?' I asked, thinking that she meant on the telephone.

'Oh, just through – but never mind that. You wouldn't understand, child.'

Here we go again, I thought. 'I'm *not* a child,' I retorted, and then it was her turn to get flustered.

'Of course you're not – you're a big boy, I can see that now. So big and clever that I know you will do something for me.'

'I will if I can,' I said, 'but who are you and what are you doing here?'

'My name is Mrs. Cottrell,' she said after a pause, 'and this is my house.'

'But surely you don't live here,' I said, in a matter-of-fact voice.

She hesitated. 'For many years – I –' she began, then changed the subject. 'If you are going to help me, you must do so at once – there is no time to lose.'

'What is it?' I asked quickly, because it had just occurred to me that if this *was* her house she might think of asking me what *I* was doing there.

'I want you to take something to the authorities for me – the police, the vicar, the doctor – it does not matter which – so that Terence may be helped before it is too late.'

'O.K.' I said, then, in case she didn't like slang, I added, 'Very well. What do you want me to take?'

'My jewels, boy! They said that Terence had stolen them after he had frightened me to death, but he did no such thing! They also accused him of manslaughter, but fortunately he was acquitted.'

I gave a little laugh just to show that I had a sense of humour and knew that she couldn't have been man-slaughtered when she was standing there before my eyes. *She* didn't laugh, though, so I changed mine into a cough.

'Terence would never steal my jewels,' the old lady went on sternly, 'and they could find no proof that he had. But the stigma of thief was on him, and within a short time he went out of his mind.'

'You mean he went mad and was innocent all the time?' I asked, trying to sort out all this rigmarole in my mind.

'Exactly. For a long time I have tried to establish his innocence but nobody has stayed here long enough to give me the help that you have kindly offered.'

I puffed out my chest, feeling pretty smug. Then I had a worrying thought. 'But why haven't you gone to the police, Mrs. Cottrell?'

'I cannot go beyond these four walls,' she said abruptly. I waited to hear why, but she didn't seem inclined to tell me. 'Come, boy, I will show you where the jewels are hidden, then you can take the information to whomever you choose.'

She made for the door with a sort of skater's glide. I started to follow her, and then suddenly my whole world turned upside down. The door was closed – and she had passed right through it!

I'm not clear about the next few minutes. I know my head was spinning like a roulette wheel, and my heart was trying to force its way through my throat. I must have tugged the door open and stumbled down the stairs into the basement and then out into the garden. In the open air my legs gave way and I collapsed into a clump of rosebay willowherb in a dead faint.

I don't know how long I lay there and when I came to I wasn't clear about what had happened, but felt very frightened. I staggered through the gate, still groggy, and

The door was closed – and she had passed right through it!

straight into the arms of Mr. Meredith, who lives next door but one to me in the flats.

'Steady on, Billy,' he said. 'What's the matter with you? You're as white as a sheet – have you seen a ghost or something?'

Then it all came back to me. 'Yes, I have,' I blurted out and promptly fainted again, almost pulling Mr. Meredith to the ground with me.

The next thing I remembered was my mum coming into the bedroom with a bowl of soup. 'You did give us a fright, love,' she said as she plumped the pillow for me to sit up. 'Drink this and you'll soon feel better.'

I insisted that there was nothing wrong with me, but *she* insisted that I had caught a chill through some complaint she always called 'outgrowing your strength'. Mind you, the best way to pacify a worried mother is not to say, as I did, 'I haven't got a chill – I've seen a ghost.' All that did was to send her rushing downstairs for Dad. I tried to tell them everything, but it was no use. 'Take it easy, son, you'll feel better in the morning,' was Dad's reaction, and they went away, shaking their heads and clucking about sending for the doctor.

I had two big worries myself. The first was why I had been stupid enough to be frightened of little Mrs. Cottrell, ghost or no ghost, when it was obvious that she wouldn't have hurt a fly. The other was how to tell the police about the jewels if I didn't know where they were. I called myself all sorts of names for getting panicky at the wrong moment. After all, why *should* ghosts open doors if they don't need to? Then there was poor old Terence. How could I help him – whoever he was – without more information? And Mrs. Cottrell had said it was urgent. . . . I spent the next half hour making plans.

In the morning I hurried down to breakfast and flashed my biggest smile at Mum and Dad. I didn't give them a chance to tut-tut about my so-called chill. I left them in no doubt that I was fit enough to run the 1500 metres before eating a single cornflake. What convinced them that I was brimming over with good health was my offer to dry up before going to school. What's more, I did it! After I had put the last plate away I called goodbye to Mum and set off for school – or, to be more accurate, for the derelict house.

I felt more than a bit silly stumbling about the old house calling 'Mrs Cottrell – where are you?' But she must have decided that I was no use to her after all, for she didn't appear. I went to the back of the house and had a look round to see if I could locate any possible hiding-places for the jewels, but I might have saved my time. The rooms were in almost total darkness and there could have been a score of places. Reluctantly I decided I had better go to school.

The day was an awful drag, but I got through it somehow. After school I went back to the house. Still no sign of Mrs. Cottrell. So I went to the Police Station.

The police were all right but they treated the whole thing as a joke and told me to lay off cheese last thing at night and to remember that they were busy men. They also suggested that it would be better if I kept away from empty houses unless I wanted to get into trouble.

The vicar was more understanding and listened patiently without making any jokes. He said something about exercising the ghost, but I told him that Mrs. Cottrell was pretty old and didn't need much exercise. Then he explained that he'd said 'exorcizing', and that it was a kind of religious way of getting rid of ghosts. Anyway, we had a look at the parish registers for many years back and there wasn't a single Cottrell mentioned. That could mean, the vicar said, that she had probably been a Methodist or something. So I said goodbye to him and thank you, and went home none the wiser.

After tea I went to the library, and there I found somebody with some sense. It was Mr. Collins, the Reference Librarian, and if I'd been the Lord Mayor himself I couldn't have been better treated. I asked him how I could find out about a Mrs. Cottrell of 101, Netherton Road, and he went to work just as if a starting-gun had gone off in his ear. In a couple of minutes he produced the electoral registers of people entitled to vote going back to the Domesday Book by the look of them and left me to plough through them while he went off to attend to other people, though whenever he had a spare moment he would come back and give me a hand.

I began to get a bit fed-up after a time. It was a dreary job, not made any better by having to keep dead quiet because of all the people sitting around with their heads buried in books. It was rather like trying to do your homework in church.

Then suddenly the silence was broken by a loud, high-pitched cry, and everybody looked up and frowned – and Mr. Collins went as red as a tomato. It was he who had made the noise, you see. He coughed, straightened his tie, and whispered hoarsely, 'Diligence rewarded at last, old son.'

He pointed to a list of names on the sheet he was holding. There were dozens of names and numbers on it, but one of them almost jumped off the page and hit me. '101, Cottrell, Louisa Maude'.

'You see!' I said. 'There *was* a Mrs. Cottrell! But what does this mean?'

'It means,' said Mr. Collins, 'that your Mrs. Cottrell was living at 101, Netherton Road in 1935, but not –' He looked up another list and went on, 'not in 1936.'

'So she must have died in 1935,' I said, catching on quickly, 'or early in 1936.'

'Or else she moved out of the district.'

'No, she didn't move. I – I know that.' Mr. Collins didn't ask me why I was so sure, thank goodness, because I didn't feel like telling him the story in whispers. 'Is there any way of finding out whether she did die about this time?' I asked.

'Wait here,' Mr. Collins said, as though I'd got up to go, and hurried away himself. In a couple of minutes he had returned with two enormous bound books which he put on the table in front of me. 'Copies of the local paper for 1935 and 1936,' he murmured. 'I should try the later one if I were you.' Then he dashed away to answer the telephone.

I didn't much like the idea of going through all those newspapers. It would take hours and the library was due to close in forty-five minutes. But I opened the 1936 volume at random, somewhere near the beginning. Looking back, what happened seemed too good to be true and a bit mad, but at the time it didn't surprise me very much. I believe now that Mrs. Cottrell was helping me, because the very first item I saw was a headline: 'Adopted son cleared of manslaughter charge'. It was followed by: 'Terence Cottrell, adopted son of Mrs. Louisa Cottrell, a widow, of 101, Netherton Road, was acquitted yesterday. . . .'

But there's no need to give you the rest of it. To cut a long story short, this is what had happened. Mrs. Cottrell had lived alone in the house, apart from a woman who came in daily to do the cleaning. Terence, whom she and her husband had adopted when he was a baby, worked in an office at Barnet and didn't live at home. He gambled a lot and had got into debt. He daren't ask Mrs. Cottrell for money because she was opposed to gambling in any shape or form and wouldn't even buy raffle tickets at the Church Fête, and he had planned to sneak into the house when she was asleep and steal some of her jewellery. He actually broke into the house to make it look like an ordinary burglary, but Mrs. Cottrell heard a noise and waited for the intruder with a poker. According to Terence, when she saw who the 'burglar' was she must have had a heart attack, for she fell and hit her head on the marble fireplace. He panicked, left her lying there and ran out of the house – straight into the arms of a passing policeman. The doctor who was called confirmed that Mrs. Cottrell had had a heart attack. There was no proof that Terence had actually stolen anything, so he got off, and that was about all.

I thanked Mr. Collins and went home, trying to find the answers to all sorts of questions. Why had the house been empty all these years? If Terence had inherited it, why hadn't he sold it? Why hadn't he found the jewels afterwards if his story at the trial had been true? Had he really gone mad, as Mrs. Cottrell had said? Was he alive or dead? If alive, he must be about seventy now. Most important of all, where was he now?

It was hard work trying to be my usual cheerful self when I got home, but I had to try, otherwise it would have meant soup in bed again. Fortunately, Mum and Dad didn't suspect a thing.

I had been in bed about a couple of hours, tossing and turning all over the place, and at last faced up to the fact that I wasn't going to get to sleep. I knew that I had to go to the old house, and the sooner the better. *She* might be there, or if not, I might find a clue to some of the problems that were worrying me.

I slipped out of bed and dressed by the light of the moon. It must have been nearly midnight when I crept past my parents' room, tiptoed downstairs and let myself out of the front door. When I reached the old house and slipped through into the garden I felt a sudden stab of fear and wished like anything that I hadn't come. The front of the house looked like a hideous face, the two upper windows its sightless eyes, and the wooden slats of the lower ones were like misshapen teeth in a grinning mouth. I think I would have slunk away if there had not been a scuttering sound behind me. I ran for the basement door before I realized that it was only a cat, probably more scared of me than I was of it.

I took a deep breath and went in. I wondered what would happen if I disturbed a sleeping tramp, or fell and broke an ankle and had to spend the night with the mice and rats. . . . Then I remembered how Mrs. Cottrell had trusted me – how she had been sure that I would help her – and some of my courage came back. She would see that I didn't come to any harm – so I went straight to the front room. There was no tramp there – that was one problem out of the way.

'Mrs. Cottrell,' I called softly, 'are you here?' The only answer was my own voice bouncing back from the dead wood. I called again and again, but nothing happened. Then I said, 'I want to help Terence. I've found out what happened in 1936, but I don't know where he is. Won't you help me, Mrs. Cottrell?'

I was just about to give up and go when there was something that I can't describe – a change in the feel of the room. It was as though a breeze had blown through it very lightly without there having been an actual breeze. At the same time my scalp began to prickle. Then I heard a voice. It was very faint and seemed to be struggling against something. 'I can't come through,' it said.

'Where are you?' I turned round and round, hoping to see the old lady.

'It's no use,' the voice said, even more faintly.

I spoke loudly, as you do when you're trying to attract the attention of someone who is walking away. 'Where is Terence?'

From Mrs. Cottrell came two words. They sounded like 'Benfield Totting', but they were so muffled that I wasn't sure whether I had heard them properly.

'Please say that again,' I said, but this time there was no reply. For a minute or two I waited, straining my ears into the silence, but something told me that it was useless and there was nothing to do but give up and go home.

'Benfield Totting, Benfield Totting,' I kept on saying to myself on the way back, and I must have gone to sleep with the words on my lips.

The next night I went to the library again. I thought Mr. Collins would groan when he saw me but in fact he greeted me like his prodigal son. 'Ah,' he said, then gave his little cough. 'I'm glad you've come. I've found out something about your Mrs. Cottrell. There was a piece in another issue of the local paper about her will. She left everything – house and contents, and her jewels – to her adopted son. It seems, though, that after the trial Terence Cottrell had a breakdown and never actually lived in the house.'

'I wondered about that,' I said, trying to make my voice sound as grown-up as possible. 'I suppose it didn't say in the paper where he did go?'

'As a matter of fact, it did. He went to Burnfield's Clinic at Tottenham.'

You've read about people hitting the roof – I didn't exactly do that but it was a near thing. 'Benfield Totting!' I shouted. 'Benfield Totting – that's it – that's what she was trying to say!'

About a hundred and twenty people said 'Shush!' and Mr. Collins grabbed me and propelled me into the passage outside. 'My dear boy,' he said, breathing hard, 'you must *never* do that again.'

'I'm sorry,' I said, and I was, because I wouldn't have done anything to annoy Mr. Collins after what he had done for us – Mrs. Cottrell and me, that is. 'But what is this Burnfield's thing at Tottenham?'

'It's a hospital for the – er – mentally sick. I fear that if Terence Cottrell went there, he must have been very ill.'

'Would they let me see him?' I asked.

'I couldn't say – it would depend on how ill he is. Are you a relative?'

'No, it's just that I've promised his mother that I would try to help him.'

'His mother – you mean, Mrs. Cottrell?'

'That's right,' I answered, lost in thought.

'But – but she died in 1936. . . .'

'That's right,' I said again, smiled, thanked him, and hurried off, just in case he decided that *I* was due for a spell in Burnfield's Clinic.

I had enough information now to convince anyone that my story was worth looking into. But somehow I knew that no one would listen. Mum and Dad would put everything down to growing pains, the police would be too busy catching present-day criminals to bother about clearing someone wrongly accused over thirty years ago. If I went to the Clinic they'd be sure to turn me away. I thought I would try the vicar again. . . .

He was just as friendly as he had been before. He gave me a cup of tea and a biscuit and I told him every single thing that had happened. 'All I want to know, sir,' I said, 'is whether there is a Terence Cottrell at Burnfield's, and I've come to you because a vicar can usually get in anywhere.'

'I'm flattered,' he said, smiling. Then he began to puff at a foul old pipe. 'As it happens, I do go to Burnfield's occasionally, to visit one of my parishioners. I think I am well enough known there to be able to find out what you want to know. Wait here while I telephone.'

When he returned he said very thoughtfully, 'It is quite extraordinary.'

'Do you mean he *is* there?' I asked, jumping to my feet.

'*Was* there, Billy. I'm afraid that Terence Cottrell died about half past twelve this morning.'

I don't care who knows this but I sat down again and burst

into tears. Who was I crying for? I don't know – perhaps it was for myself because the whole story had suddenly collapsed about my ears; or for Mrs. Cottrell who would never get her wish for Terence to be cleared; or for Terence who had never known how she felt about him. Later on I realized why Mrs. Cottrell's voice had faded away. It must have been about half past twelve when I had said, 'Where is Terence?' – and at that moment she had met him again after more than thirty years. . . .

And that was the end of the story as I wrote it a year ago. I put it away, and the details had begun to grow a bit dim in my mind, though I never forgot I had seen the old lady's ghost. Then, a few days ago, a long stretch of Netherton Road was knocked down to make way for a new block of flats, and Number 101 was one of the first houses to go. For the first time since 1936 it hit the headlines again. 'Workman finds treasure in derelict house,' the local paper said.

I don't know what happened to the treasure and, since Terence is dead, I don't care. I daren't think what might have happened if Mrs. Cottrell had been able to show me where it was hidden, but I'm pretty sure that no one would have believed that I'd been guided by a ghost. So I've decided to add this postscript to my story. I've sent a copy to the police, and one to Mr. Collins at the library. Mum and Dad can read it too. After all this time they can hardly stop my pocket-money for sneaking out in the middle of the night. Perhaps they'll believe it – and perhaps they won't.

The Headless Horseman

'GOOD NIGHT, CHARLIE, and a safe journey to you!' The landlord of the *Harp of Erin* waved to his friend and retired to his warm bar, closing the door on a dark, unfriendly night.

Charlie Culnane turned his horse's head homewards and faced a long, lonely ride. 'Ay, 'tis all very well for you, Con Buckley,' he muttered. 'You haven't got nineteen kilometres to go before you see a fire. Nor did you have to go all the way to Fermoy to buy the things your wife wants for the Christmas dinner! Still, 'tis a fine stock you've got in that inn of yours, and I'm glad I was able to sample a drop of the hard stuff. . . .'

The road from Ballyhooley to Carrick followed very closely the course of the River Blackwater, though occasionally it diverged and passed through wild, rugged countryside. Charlie cantered on, heedless of the rain now falling heavily. The currants and raisins he had bought for his wife were carefully packed between the folds of a cloak strapped to the saddle in front of him. The cloak was part of the uniform of the Royal Mallow Light Horse Volunteers, of which he was a proud member – for wasn't he as bold a rider as any in Ireland?

Charlie began to be anxious about the effect the rain might have on his new snaffle reins, which he wanted to show off at the approaching St. Stephen's Day hunt. He became even more worried when he remembered how he had backed his old mare against Mr. Jepson's bay filly for a hundred pounds.

'I've not got a hundred pounds, nor anything near it,' he said to himself, and cursed for having been so rash as to make the bet. 'Me heart was too warm and me head not over cool. Oh, dear, what'll happen if I lose!'

At the bottom of Kilcummer Hill the mare reduced her canter to a trot. As they passed a ruined church Charlie's eyes fell on the tombstones in the graveyard, shining with wetness, and he shivered. 'Gee up, old mare,' he called, 'this is no place for lingering.'

He looked up at the sky to see if there was any break in the clouds foretelling an end to the rain and the saving of his new snaffle reins, but there was only the blackest blackness above him. No sooner had he lowered his eyes, however, than his attention was arrested by a sight so extraordinary that his first thought was that he had suddenly taken leave of his senses. Running just ahead of the mare was a large horse – no, Charlie realized with a gasp, the *head* of a large horse, with short cropped ears, large open nostrils, huge eyes – and no body. . . .

No body, no legs, no rider – but the head was travelling at a speed sufficient to enable it to keep up with the mare. Also startled by the unnatural sight, she snorted violently, and began to increase her pace as she struggled up the hill.

But the faster the mare went, so did the white head, and Charlie gazed at it with goggling eyes, his mouth hanging open as though the hinges of his jaws had ceased to work.

'Where – where's the body?' he thought numbly, and then gave another start when he saw the rest of the white horse was running alongside the mare. A head without a horse, and a horse without a head! 'Whatever's happening?' Charlie groaned. 'Maybe the world is coming to an end. . . .' And, just to make sure, he felt his own head to see if it was still attached to his body.

He glanced again at the horse running so smoothly by his

side, and then his heart lurched almost into his throat. 'Holy saints!' he gasped. 'Will this nightmare never end!' For now the headless body had a rider – a man who looked to be over two metres tall and who was dressed in a scarlet hunting coat of a very old-fashioned cut. It reached to the saddle and there were two huge shining buttons on the tails.

Charlie's dazed eyes took in the coat and then travelled upwards to see the mysterious huntsman's face. He peered through the darkness intently, but it was a full minute before the horrid fact was plain that there was nothing to see above the figure's collar – not only was the horse headless, so was its rider!

Charlie almost fell off his mare – something he had never done before in all his years of riding. 'May the saints preserve me! A horse without a head – a head without a horse – and now a man without a head – ach, it's too much for me poor mind to take in, that it is!'

But more was to come to befuddle Charlie's wits, for the headless rider suddenly spoke! 'Look again, Charlie Culnane,' it said hoarsely, 'and you'll see you've made a mistake.'

Charlie looked in the direction from which the voice had come and saw, under the figure's right arm, the head which should have been on its shoulders. . . .

The face was ashy pale, the skin stretched over it like the parchment of a drum. Two fiery eyes were gazing at him, and a mouth that reached almost from ear to ear was parted in a horrid grin. The head was topped by matted hair hanging in greasy locks.

Although Charlie had the reputation of being one of the bravest men in County Cork, it took all his courage to prevent him from yelling at the top of his voice for help which he knew would not be forthcoming. The horseman, without the aid of whip or spur, and disdaining the use of stirrups,

There was nothing to see above the figure's collar — not only
was the horse headless, so was its rider!

which dangled from the saddle, rode steadily by his side. Sometimes the head was hidden in the folds of the coat, sometimes it appeared in all its horror as the horse's movements caused the arm to move to and fro. The silence of the night was broken only by the clattering of hooves and the sound of distant thunder rumbling over the hill as both horses trotted purposefully forward.

After a time, as the headless rider seemed to have no evil intentions towards him, Charlie, being naturally of a talkative disposition, and having become a little more reconciled to the strange situation, plucked up his courage to address him. 'Your honour rides mighty well without the stirrups,' he observed. What he wanted to ask was why he carried his head in such an unusual position, but he thought he would lead up to the subject gradually so as not to anger or annoy the apparition beside him.

'Humph,' growled the head from under the horseman's right arm.

It was not an encouraging beginning, but Charlie decided to ignore the brusque answer, so he cleared his throat and tried again. 'Ahem – that's a mighty fine coat your honour is wearing, though it's a little too long in the waist for present taste.'

'Humph,' said the head again.

Charlie wondered what on earth he could talk about that the horseman would find more to his liking. ''Tis a sensible head, at any rate,' he thought, 'for 'tis plain enough that it doesn't care for flattery.' He racked his brains for another topic of conversation, and thought he would make a comment on the headless horse, jogging alongside his old mare; and as he was considered to be very knowledgeable about horses he felt more hopeful. 'To be sure, that's a brave horse your honour rides,' he observed.

'You may say that with your own ugly mouth,' the head

growled.

Charlie was not very pleased at the reference to his looks, but at least he had got a proper answer, so he felt emboldened to continue. 'Maybe your honour wouldn't be thinking of riding him across the country?'

'Try me, Charlie Culnane, just try me,' said the head, and a look of ghastly pleasure spread over the face.

'Faith, I'd do that willingly,' replied Charlie, 'but I'm afraid of laming my old mare, the night being so dark. What's more, I've got a hundred pounds on her for the St. Stephen's Day hunt, and I want her to be in good shape.'

'Will you take my word,' the head went on, 'that if we have a race your mare will come to no harm?'

The voice sounded so confident that Charlie's doubts disappeared. 'Done!' he cried, and dug his heels into the mare's flanks.

So away they went, old grey mare and headless white horse – flying like birds over every obstacle, ditch and wall, hedge and bush. Never had the old mare galloped so fast, even in daylight. It was as if she had swallowed some magic potion that had lent wings to her hooves. Soon she had passed the white horse and was drawing steadily farther ahead, though the bodiless head was still in front of her and seemed likely to remain so.

Suddenly the voice called out, 'Charlie Culnane, stop! Stop, man, I tell you!'

Charlie pulled up hard, and the headless horse reached his side. The mare was panting and snorting, but the white horse made never a sound. 'You will always beat me by a head,' Charlie said in disgust, 'because your horse's head isn't attached to its body, but if we were racing neck-and-neck, just as my old mare will be with the bay filly, then I'd beat you hollow.'

The head became quite talkative when he heard this, and

said in a friendly tone of voice, 'Charlie, you have a stout heart, and that you're a good rider you've proved beyond any doubt. You're the sort of man for my money. Now you shall hear my story. . . .'

'Ah,' said Charlie, pricking up his ears, 'I felt sure you would have one, your honour.'

'A hundred years ago,' said the head, 'my horse and I broke our necks at the bottom of Kilcummer Hill, and ever since then I've been trying to find someone who would dare to ride with me as you have done, but I've never succeeded until tonight. If you will always ride so bravely, never baulking at a ditch, nor turning away from a stone wall, then the headless horseman will never desert you, and your mare will never let you down.'

'Thank you kindly –' Charlie began, looking at the head to see if it had been in earnest, but he stopped with a gasp – the head was not under the arm, but snugly lodged in the huge pocket of the horseman's scarlet hunting coat. When he had torn his astonished gaze away from the bulging pocket his senses were rocked by another sight. The horse's head was no longer moving steadily in front of the mare, but was rising perpendicularly into the sky, and the rest of the horse was climbing after it! Soon the white horse and its scarlet-coated rider were but faint blotches high up in the sky, and after a few moments had disappeared altogether.

Charlie remained open-mouthed for several minutes, lost in a mixture of perplexity and wonder. The driving rain, the ingredients for his wife's pudding, the new snaffle – all were forgotten. For the rest of the journey he rehearsed the story he would tell his friends and neighbours as soon as he arrived home.

He did tell his story, first to his wife, but she was more concerned about her currants and raisins, then to all the neighbours, then to his friends in the village inn, and then at the St. Stephen's Day hunt to anybody who would listen. He was furious when, after all the pains he had taken to describe the head, the horse and the man in great detail and with strict accuracy, everybody laughed and said, 'Charlie, you had taken a drop too much of Con Buckley's hard stuff! A headless horse and a man with his head under his arm – why, 'tis not in the nature of things.' And the more Charlie protested that his story was true, the more they laughed at him.

All the same, Charlie's old grey mare beat Mr. Jepson's bay filly by three lengths, and Charlie pocketed the hundred pounds. Feeling the golden coins jingling pleasantly as he rode home Charlie said to himself with a chuckle, 'They may not believe me, but if I didn't win that race with the help of the headless horseman, then I don't know *how* I did it!'

Fisher's Ghost

PENRITH WAS A SMALL SETTLEMENT about sixty kilometres from Sydney, in New South Wales, and about the middle of the 19th century a middle-aged farmer named Abel Fisher lived alone in a tumbledown wooden farmhouse surrounded by rich cornland and fields in which hundreds of fat sheep grazed contentedly. Although Fisher's appearance was shabby, and he shuffled about like a tramp, he was actually a rich man, and his lands and stock were the envy of his less fortunate neighbours.

Most of the farmers of Penrith travelled into Sydney every Thursday, the market day. They bought and sold their produce and drank great quantities of beer when their business was done. They did not return home until the late evening, and usually in a befuddled state.

Abel Fisher went to market with the others, but he did not join them in their drinking. He told them that he did not like the taste of beer, but the other farmers declared that he was too mean to spend his money and preferred to put every penny he could into the bank.

One Thursday Fisher did not appear in the market. Several people noticed his absence but thought nothing of it. When, the following week, he was again absent, more voices commented on the odd fact. 'Surely he has not given up farming and gone to live on his fortune!' one burly farmer said with a laugh.

'Not Abel!' said another. 'He'll never stop scrimping and

saving till he dies. He must be ill or he'd be here all right.'

'He's not ill, and he's not given up,' a new voice put in. 'I know what's happened to Abel Fisher.'

The two farmers turned round and saw a tall man, dark and lean. His face was deeply lined, and his eyes were sunk far back in his narrow skull. He stood with folded arms, regarding the weather-beaten faces of the Penrith men with a confident smile on his lips. 'You won't see Abel Fisher for two or three years,' he went on.

Ben Weir, short and fat, looked up at the stranger suspiciously. 'Who are you, and how is it you know so much about Abel Fisher?' he demanded.

The tall man unfolded his arms and thrust his hands in his pockets. 'My name's Smith – Harry Smith,' he said. 'I've just arrived from England and brought some news for Fisher about his brother Reuben. The poor man is dangerously ill – likely to die within a few months, and Fisher decided on the spur of the moment that he would go back to the old country to see his brother. His plan is to stay with him till the end, then look round for a wife, and come back overland, seeing as much of the world as he can on the way.'

His listeners gasped. 'Abel Fisher's doing that!' Ben Weir cried. 'Who'd have thought it of the old skinflint!'

'Meanwhile,' the man called Harry Smith said, 'he has appointed me as his agent.' He took a legal-looking paper from an inside pocket. 'Here is a document authorizing me to act for him in any way I think best during his absence.'

'Then the farm belongs to you, as near as makes no odds?' enquired one of the farmers.

Smith nodded, the smile on his lips once more. 'You could put it that way – until Fisher comes back.'

Ben Weir shrugged his plump shoulders. 'Funny that Fisher didn't tell any of us that he was going,' he said. 'You'd think he'd have said goodbye to his nearest neighbour.'

'I don't know,' his friend said. 'I reckon that's just how he would go. Ah well, we shan't miss him much. Let's forget him. How about a drink, Ben? Will you accompany us, Mr Smith?'

'No, thank you.' The dark stranger was already moving away. 'I still have things to see to. In any case, I prefer to be alone.'

The snubbed farmers gazed after him. 'I think we'll be able to get along without him for a cobber. . . .' Ben Weir spluttered indignantly.

During the next six months little was seen of Harry Smith, and nothing at all was heard of Abel Fisher. The farmers' gossip died down as more interesting things attracted their attention. Then, one Thursday night, Ben Weir, who had a small farm near Penrith, was returning home from market when he saw something that made his hands jerk on the reins and caused his horse to rear up alarmingly. On the fence that ran alongside the dusty white road gleaming in the moonlight a man was sitting, a bent, shabby figure that turned its head as Ben's cart drew near.

'Abel Fisher!' the farmer cried out in surprise. He pulled tighter on the reins and the old mare came to a stop. 'Is that you, Fisher?' he shouted.

There was no answer from the man on the rail. Ben Weir dismounted hurriedly and groped his way across the rutted road to the grass verge. 'Fisher –' he began, stretching out a hand to greet the stranger. Then 'Fisher!' he shrieked, and threw up his hands in horror.

The figure had turned a face to the frightened farmer, a face of a ghastly greenish-white colour, its eyes glowing dully, the mouth open slackly showing broken, blackened teeth. For a moment the two men stared at each other. Ben Weir closed his eyes to shut out the sight, and when he opened them again the figure had vanished. There was the moonlight silvering

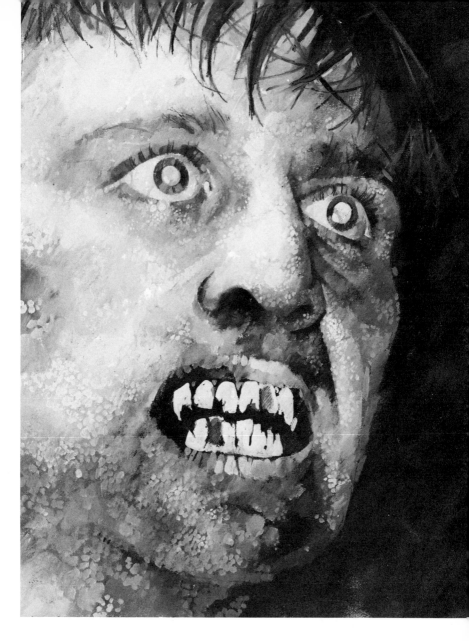

The figure had turned a face to the frightened farmer, a face of a ghastly greenish-white colour.

the road with its grass verge, the wooden rail, and that was all.

The farmer staggered over to the rail and put his hand on it as though to reassure himself that the fence, at least, was real. 'It was here he sat,' he muttered to himself. 'I'd better mark the spot. . . .' And he broke some branches of a sapling which grew nearby. Returning to his cart he looked back once and saw the evidence of his grotesque experience marked by the stiff, twisted branches.

As soon as he got home he told his story to his wife, and her reaction was not unexpected. 'Rubbish!' she sniffed. 'You were drunk. People don't sit on fences and disappear!'

Ben Weir stubbornly resisted her suggestion. 'I was not drunk,' he said. 'I *did* see Abel Fisher.'

'But Fisher's in England, isn't he?' Mrs. Weir cried. 'How could he be in two places at once? Someone was playing a trick on you.'

'It was no trick – Fisher was sitting on that rail,' her husband insisted quietly. 'There's something very odd about the whole thing, and I'm going to get to the bottom of it.'

The next morning the farmer went to see Mr. Grafton, a justice of the peace, who lived near him, and repeated his story. 'I know it sounds impossible,' he finished, 'but it's *true!*'

The magistrate was at first inclined to treat the account lightly, but he was impressed by the sober earnestness of Ben Weir's manner, and after consideration he called one of his workmen, an aboriginal native, and talked to him in his own tongue. Weir listened, not understanding a word, wondering what it was all about.

Mr. Grafton dismissed the native and got up from his chair. 'I have arranged to meet my servant at this place you speak of at sunrise tomorrow,' he told the farmer. 'Will you be there too, to help us in our investigations?'

'I will be there,' the farmer promised.

The early morning was cold, the sky tinged with a smoky pink, and a chill breeze rustled through the trees as Ben Weir waited for the magistrate and his servant at the fence by the tree with the broken branches. They came at last through the half-dark, turning from black shapes to recognizable human beings as they drew near.

'This is the place,' the farmer whispered, pointing to the rail, 'and there's where he sat.'

Mr. Grafton said nothing, and the alert aborigine began to move about, almost on all fours, looking intently at the ground. Suddenly he stopped. He beckoned his master nearer. 'Body here,' he grunted.

The two white men crouched over the place the native had indicated. They could see nothing out of the ordinary. To them the ground there looked just as hard and undisturbed as it was all round them. The magistrate questioned the man sharply. He nodded his head several times and repeated the words, 'Body – body here. . . .'

Not a single shower of rain had fallen for several months, not even to lay the dust of the road. What grass there was was short, the ground itself hard-baked. Yet the aborigine, turning away from the spot, walked unerringly in the direction of a pond which Ben Weir knew to be about four hundred metres away. 'Man go this way,' the aborigine said, his keen eyes on the ground ahead as he walked. 'I see marks. Man pull body.'

The two men followed, the magistrate grim-faced and preoccupied, the farmer shaking a disbelieving head. When they reached the pond the native walked round and round it, examining the sedges and weeds springing up round the edges. At first he seemed baffled. There was no clue anywhere to show that anything had been sunk in the pond. He scratched his wiry black hair and thought hard. Then he stretched himself flat and looked with narrowed eyes along the surface of the smooth, stagnant water. The white men held their breaths. Suddenly the native sprang up, uttering a peculiar cry. He clapped his hands and pointed to the middle of the pond, which had, in one spot, a slimy coating streaked with prismatic colours. 'There!' he cried. 'White man – down there!'

The magistrate looked at the farmer. 'If he says so, then it is so,' he said soberly. 'We will go back to the farm and get men and implements to drag the pond. Fortunately the level of the water is much lower than it usually is, owing to the lack of rain.'

It was not until early afternoon that the gruesome task was completed. Below the spot in the water the native had indicated, a body was discovered, and attached to it by rags was a large stone. . . .

The men looked at it, their faces white. Ben Weir peered down and touched the sodden clothing gingerly. 'It's Abel Fisher,' he gasped. 'That's his coat – I'd know those buttons anywhere.'

When the body had been taken to the mortuary in Sydney and the coroner informed, an inquest was held, and the remains formally identified as those of Fisher. Rumours spread round the neighbourhood as thick and black as locusts, and the finger of suspicion pointed unhesitatingly at the man Smith. For some days Smith stalked about on his business, gaunt and grey, speaking to nobody, apparently indifferent to the gossip, but when eventually he was arrested for the murder of Abel Fisher, he broke down and confessed.

The story came out at the trial. He had killed Fisher on the very rail on which Weir swore that he had seen Fisher's ghost, and had dragged the body to the pond and sunk it with a heavy stone. Then he had concocted the story of Fisher's journey to England and carried out his plan to possess himself of the dead man's property and wealth.

Smith was hanged and buried, unmourned. The talk then centred round Mr. Grafton's servant, and admiration of his tracking skill was expressed. 'Not one of us could have seen what he saw – even in the full light of day,' was the general opinion. 'Those natives are real clever. . . .'

Ben Weir's part in the capture of the murderer was somehow overlooked, and when he insisted 'But I saw Fisher's ghost – don't forget that!' his drinking companions laughed and reminded him that it was possible to see all sorts of things when returning from market.

In time Weir began to wonder whether his friends were right and that he had imagined the whole episode. But the stubborn part of him refused to accept the obvious answer, and when, driving home from Sydney, he saw the tree with the dead branches near the rail, he would mutter to himself, 'I *did* see Abel Fisher – sitting on that very rail – come to ask me to find his murderer. . . .'

The Black Ribbon

In 1665 a son was born to Lord Tyrone, a wealthy Irish landowner. The child's title was Lord Decies. A year later a girl called Nicola Sophie Hamilton was born, also of rich parents. The two children had the same tutor, and grew up to be close friends. When the time came for their ways to part they were broken-hearted, and thinking that they might never see each other again, they made a vow. The first to die would return to the other. As it happened, they were able to see each other fairly frequently during the years that followed, and though the promise was never forgotten neither of them mentioned it nor thought much about it.

Nicola Hamilton married Sir Tristram Beresford in 1687. Lord Decies' father died in 1690 and he became Lord Tyrone. Three years later in the October Sir Tristram and his wife went on a visit to Nicola's sister, Lady Macgill, at Gill Hall in County Down. One morning Lady Beresford came down to breakfast looking very pale and drawn. She seemed to have something on her mind, something that had frightened and confused her.

'Are you well?' her husband asked her. 'You look as though you slept badly.'

Lady Beresford brushed aside his question. 'I am all right,' she said indifferently.

Then her husband noticed that she had a wide black ribbon round her wrist. 'What is the matter with your wrist? Have you sprained it, my dear?'

Lady Beresford moved her hand so that the ribbon could not be seen, remarking, 'My wrist is not sprained. You are mistaken, there is nothing the matter with it.'

'Then why –' her husband began, but she interrupted him: 'Tristram, I want you to promise me that you will never ask me again about this black ribbon. I shall wear it all the time and you will never see me without it. But, please, never ask me why I am wearing it.'

Her husband was a good-natured man. He shrugged his shoulders and smiled tolerantly. 'Very well, my dear, you shall have your wish. Now we will change the subject.'

Breakfast continued but Lady Beresford still showed signs of agitation, glancing repeatedly at the window and at the door.

Finally, her husband put down his cup. 'My dear, there *is* something the matter,' he said. 'I have never seen you behaving like this before.'

'I am expecting a letter to tell me that my old friend Lord Tyrone is dead – that he died last Tuesday at four o'clock.'

Sir Tristram stared at her. 'You must have had a bad dream,' he declared. 'I beg you to forget all this nonsense. Come now, be your usual cheerful self.'

Lady Beresford smiled sadly. 'I wish I could be,' she murmured, staring out of the window at the lawns and flower beds which surrounded the lovely old country house. 'I shall be able to tell you something else soon, something that will please you very much.'

At that moment the butler entered, carrying a tray on which were some letters. Sir Tristram picked them up and turned them over. One letter was sealed with black wax.

'He *is* dead!' Lady Beresford exclaimed. 'I told you – Lord Tyrone *is* dead!'

She seemed to be scarcely listening as her husband read the letter. It was from Lord Tyrone's steward. His master had

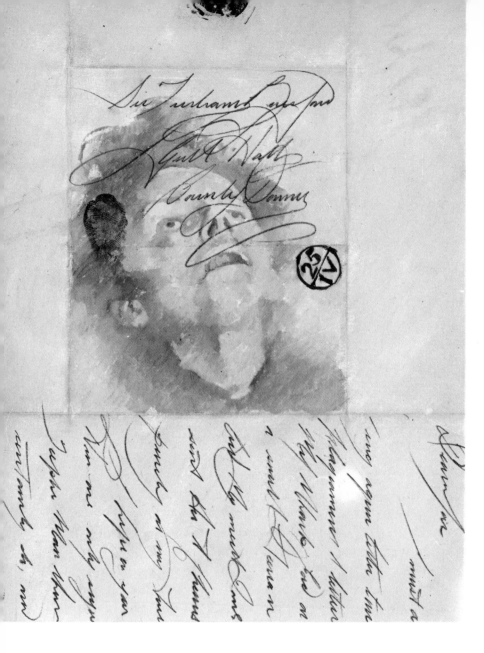

One letter was sealed with black wax. 'He is dead!' Lady
Beresford exclaimed.

died the previous Tuesday, at four o'clock. . . .

Sir Tristram put the letter on one side as his wife stood up. 'I will go to my room,' she said. 'But I will give you my other news first, and this will make you happy. I am going to have a child, and that child is going to be a son.'

'How do you know?' Sir Tristram asked, but there was only the gentle closing of the door for answer. He looked down at the letter again, shook his head in a puzzled way, and muttered, 'Lord Tyrone's death has something to do with the news of the child – but what? And how did she know that her old friend was dead? Why is she wearing a black ribbon?'

Sir Tristram never found the answers to his questions. His son was born some months afterwards, and when the boy was six years old Sir Tristram died.

For the next few years Lady Beresford lived the life of a recluse. She avoided all her former friends, kept to her house in the county of Derry, and seemed to prefer solitude to all human contact. The only family she would visit occasionally was that of Mr. and Mrs. Jackson of Coleraine. Mr. Jackson had a brother-in-law named Colonel Gorges. He was much younger than Lady Beresford, and everybody was surprised when, in 1704, after having been a widow for some years, she married this young soldier. Her friends and neighbours prophesied an unhappy marriage, and they were right. Colonel Gorges turned out to be selfish, cruel, and a spendthrift. The former Lady Beresford had a son, two daughters, and later a second son.

The day after the birth of the second son was Nicola's forty-seventh birthday. She asked her eldest son, Sir Marcus Beresford, twenty years old; her married daughter, Lady Riverston; the Archbishop of Dublin; and an old clergyman friend who had christened her, to make up a small party to celebrate. She greeted her family and friends with pleasure, and they sat in her bedroom chatting and admiring the new baby.

'You look very young for forty-seven,' said the old clergyman, looking fondly at his hostess.

'Nay, but I am forty-eight today,' protested Lady Beresford, 'and I feel very well. Well and happy,' she added with such gaiety in her voice that the others looked at her in surprise. It was many years since she had been so cheerful.

'You are mistaken,' said the clergyman, 'you are forty-seven. I looked up the date of your baptism just before I came here, as I was not sure of your age. You should be glad, dear lady, that you are a year younger than you thought you were. Most women would rejoice at such a discovery!'

But Lady Beresford had turned white and was trembling. 'Surely not,' she protested. 'Am I really only forty-seven?'

'There is no doubt about it,' the clergyman assured her.

'Then you have signed my death warrant,' she told him. 'I know now that I shall die very soon. I thought the danger point had been passed, but I was wrong. I must make all the necessary preparations. Please leave me, all of you, except my son and daughter. . . .'

When they were alone her children plied her with questions. What did she mean? Why was she going to die? Why did she want to be forty-eight rather than forty-seven?

Lady Beresford silenced them with her raised hand. Lying in the large fourposter bed from which thick curtains of crimson velvet hung, she looked very small and lost in the expanse of white sheets and huge pillows. The new baby slept peacefully in a cot near the bed.

'I have told you that soon I shall die,' she began, 'and now I will tell you why. You know that Lord Tyrone and I were very close friends, and when we were separated at an early age we made a solemn promise that whichever of us died first would appear to the other. One night, just over twenty years ago, when your father and I were staying at Gill Hall, I awoke to find Lord Tyrone sitting on the edge of my bed. I screamed and shook your father, but could not wake him. I asked Lord Tyrone why he had come in the middle of the night without warning. He asked me if I had forgotten our vow. "I died last Tuesday," he said, "at four o'clock, and I have come to tell you things you ought to know."

'I struggled up and pulled a cloak round my shoulders. "What things?" I asked.

'Although he was so near to me I felt as though there was a great distance between us. He gazed at me solemnly. "You are going to have a son," he said, "and in the fulness of time that son will marry my daughter. In a few years your husband will die. You will grieve for a long time but you will marry again, and your second husband will ill-treat you and make you unhappy. You will have more children, and you will die in your forty-eighth year."

'I could hardly take in what he was saying. His mournful tones and dark eyes seemed to cast a spell on me. "Give me a sign," I cried, "a proof that your appearance is real, so that when morning comes I shall know this was not a dream."

'"What can I do?" he asked. "I cannot touch you for that would injure you."

'"I don't mind a small blemish."

'"You are a brave woman," he said, and laid his marble-cold hand on my wrist. As he touched me the sinews shrank up and the nerves withered. "Now," he went on, "while you live, let no mortal eye ever see your wrist." I looked down at my hand, and when I looked up again he had vanished.

'I felt chilled with horror, and a cold sweat came over me. I fell asleep in a flood of tears. The next morning I bound up my wrist with black ribbon before going downstairs, and I have never taken it off. After his first enquiry your father did not mention it again.

'You, my son, were born the following July, and your father died six years later. I then made up my mind that I would give up the pleasures of society so that I would not meet anyone who might persuade me to make a second marriage; but, alas, in the one family I remained friendly with I met the man who was destined by Fate to prove my undoing. Children were born to me, and all Lord Tyrone's prophecies had come true, with the exception of *your* marriage, Marcus, and the forecast of *my* death. Today, I thought, was my forty-eighth birthday. I thought I had passed my forty-eighth year and that the worst would not now happen. I was happy – I was going to live! Now I have been told by the man who christened me that I was mistaken about my age, and that the dreaded time has not passed. The prophecy can still come true, and will!

'When I am gone I want you to take the black ribbon from my wrist, and before I am buried you alone will see where Lord Tyrone touched me. Now, please leave me.'

Sir Marcus Beresford and his sister left the bedroom, their hearts heavy with sorrow, their minds buzzing with the questions they had been unable to ask. For an hour all was quiet. Then a bell in the bedroom rang violently. They hurried back, but before they could reach the bedroom door they heard a servant call out, 'She is dead – my mistress is dead!'

Sir Marcus told the servant to leave the room. He and his sister knelt by the side of the bed, unbound the black ribbon and found their mother's wrist just as she had described it, with every sinew shrunk and every nerve withered.

Lady Beresford was buried in the Cathedral of St. Patrick in Dublin. Later Sir Marcus Beresford married the daughter of Lord Tyrone. The black ribbon was kept among the family possessions and handed down from father to son, a constant reminder of the ghost whose prophecies came true.

The Obstinate Ghost

OLD MRS. PRINGLE and her middle-aged daughter Cissie lived together in a small semi-detached house in a suburb of Macclesfield in Cheshire in the 1930s. At the age of eighty Mrs. Pringle was thin, upright and sprightly, with a firm jaw and flashing eyes. Her hair was still only grey, and she wore it pulled back into a tight little bun into which she jabbed hairpins as if it were the wax image of an enemy. She was an 'I-stand-no-nonsense' person who, after her husband's death, had run his hardware shop much more successfully than he had. Her sharp tongue had quelled all who dared to argue with her, and in retirement she was still feared by the milkman and baker, the grocer's boy and the laundryman.

Cissie was nearly everything that her mother was not. Plump, sloppily dressed, hair never in place, slow-moving and inefficient, she ran the household with amiable confusion. In her spare time, mainly to get away from her mother, she attended meetings of the local Women's Institute and the Gardening Club.

People who did not know Mrs. Pringle or Cissie very well often said that it was a mystery how such a pair could be mother and daughter, but closer acquaintances would point to the one thing that the two women had in common – their quite extraordinary obstinacy.

The old lady's determination to get her own way was direct and open, but Cissie's was of a more subtle nature. Cissie's mother argued, ordered and nagged; Cissie would smile, agree, and go her own way. She was adept at pretending she had misunderstood her mother's orders, and she goaded the old lady into fury several times a day by her seemingly innocent sabotage of the arrangements her mother made for her own comfort.

This state of affairs, far from making the two women unhappy, gave them extreme pleasure, and both delighted in thinking up new ways to annoy the other. Only in one respect had Cissie given up the struggle to get the better of her mother. This concerned her mother's armchair, a hideous piece of furniture of Victorian design, too large for their sitting-room, its grey covers faded, its bottom sagging and its arms splayed. Her mother declared that it was the only chair in which she could be comfortable, and insisted on having it in the one corner of the room that was free from draughts, and in a position that got most of the fire's heat and the light from a standard lamp. Furthermore, it was protected by a tall screen that stood behind it, covered with pictures cut from long-dead magazines, and in this cosy corner the old lady spent every evening, her feet on a stool, a shawl over her shoulders and a rug over her knees.

One evening Cissie, crouched in her chair on the opposite side of the fire, was struggling with her crossword. One side of her froze while the other roasted. Her mind was churning with resentment as she held her paper to catch the light. 'Yes, you may sit there with your face as smug as a cat that's got the cream,' she muttered to herself, jabbing her pencil into the paper, 'but one day things will be different. There'll come a time when I shall do what *I* want – all the time –'

'The potatoes were lumpy at lunch,' her mother announced.

'Eight letters, beginning with D,' Cissie said dreamily. 'It should be DEVILISH, but it doesn't fit in with 3 Down.'

'Did you hear what I said? The potatoes –'

'Yes, dear. Mine were all right – I expect it's your indigestion. You know the doctor said you shouldn't eat potatoes.'

Her mother sat bolt upright. 'There's nothing wrong with my digestion! The potatoes *were* lumpy.'

'I'll speak to the greengrocer about it,' Cissie said soothingly, noting with glee her mother's growing irritation.

'The greengrocer didn't cook those potatoes – you did!' The old lady sank back in order to gather strength for the next onslaught, and Cissie thought up various remarks that would add fuel to the flames.

This enjoyable bickering was not to last much longer, however. In spite of screen, shawl and rug Cissie's mother caught a chill that turned to pneumonia. She weakened rapidly. Almost the last words she spoke to Cissie were, 'You left the window open and I was sitting in a draught. You wanted me to die!'

'Now, Mother, you mustn't say such things.' Cissie started to smooth the pillows but the old lady moved irritably.

'Don't think that when I'm gone I shall let you alone. I want everything to remain just as it is, especially my chair. Don't you dare move my chair. And don't you dare sit in it. It's a symbol that I shall still be mistress here. If you touch it I'll – I'll haunt you!' She glared at her daughter, tried to sit up, gave an exasperated 'Oh, drat!' and died.

After the funeral Cissie entered the silent house with a feeling of mounting excitement. She stood in the doorway of the sitting-room, drawing off her black gloves and unbuttoning her too-tight coat, gazing round, making plans. 'A bright new wallpaper,' she decided, 'some gay cushions and a three-piece suite. That old screen must go for firewood, and as for the armchair –' She crossed over to it and pushed it out of its usual position. 'I like mother's nerve. Don't move it, indeed, and don't sit in it – why, it's ridiculous.' She pulled it towards her and slumped into it so heavily that it gave a protesting wheeze. 'I'll sit where I like in my own house –'

Suddenly she was on her feet again, her hand to her back. 'Ouch!' she exclaimed. She looked at where her back had rested. 'There must be something sharp sticking out – a pin or a piece of wire. It's strange that mother never felt it.' She passed her hand over the faded material but could find nothing that could have caused the sharp pain.

She decided that it had been a twinge of rheumatism, and sat down again gingerly.

Once more she was on her feet, her face contorted with pain. That had been no rheumatic twinge but a definite, bad-tempered nudge!

Then puzzlement succeeded pain. 'It can't be . . .' she cried, 'but she did say – oh, but it's impossible!'

She examined the chair from every angle, even getting on her knees and peering underneath. Then she got up, her lips pressed together. She addressed the air angrily. 'If it's you, Mother, who is playing this trick, I must say that dying hasn't changed your bad temper. You seem to be as fratchetty as when you were alive! But I'll not be beaten, so there!' And determinedly she sat down again in the chair, leaning against the back and clutching its arms defiantly.

For three minutes only could she bear it, then the constant poking, like a bony finger digging into her back, forced her out.

She stumped about the room in an agitated way, talking half to herself and half to the chair. 'It can't be you, Mother – you're dead – and I don't believe in ghosts – I know you said you'd haunt me if I sat in your chair – but – but – it's impossible! And yet – there's nothing else that could be responsible – and I didn't imagine it – something hurt me beyond endurance – but what was it –?'

At last, breathless, she had to stop and lean against the

table. 'I'll try again tomorrow. Everything will be all right tomorrow. . . .'

The next morning Cissie carefully ignored the sitting-room until she had finished the shopping and the housework. She was too nervous to eat any lunch, and hesitated for a long time outside the sitting-room door. Finally she pushed it open bit by bit, as though there might be something behind it waiting to pounce on her.

But of course there was nothing, and she went in more confidently and looked at her mother's armchair standing four-square and empty, and as harmless and ugly as it had ever been. 'Nothing is going to happen, nothing is going to happen.' She repeated the words as though they would form a spell that would wrap her in safety. Then she sat down. 'Mother, stop!' she cried, on her feet in a flash, pressing her hand to the spot which felt as if it had been gored by a twisting finger-nail. 'You think you've won, don't you? You think I'm going to leave this monstrosity here and spoil my plans. But I can be as obstinate as you – just you wait. . . .'

She pushed, pulled and tugged the armchair to the door, upended it to get it through, then, heaving and straining, manoeuvred it up two flights of stairs and finally, with a last heave that left her red-faced and panting, got it into the dark, dusty attic. She hurried out, locking the door. 'There!' she gasped, shaking her fist at what was behind the door. 'You can do all the prodding and poking you like! But you won't prod me again!'

The sitting-room looked strangely empty without her mother's chair. Cissie felt a momentary unease when she crossed the space where the chair had stood in order to draw back the curtains and let the sunlight in, but triumph soon overrode all other feelings, and she hummed happily as she continued to plan the room's new look. 'When this room is finished I'll start on my bedroom,' she decided, 'then the kitchen. Oh, what a relief to have that ghastly chair out of the way.'

Cissie's plans reached fruition in a remarkably short time. New curtains went up and a new carpet went down. The furniture arrived soon after and she spent an enjoyable hour getting it exactly where she wanted it. When it was all done she stood in the doorway surveying the room proudly. 'Victory!' she cried, snapping her fingers towards the ceiling in the general direction of the attic.

But Cissie's triumph only lasted three days. In the mornings she cleaned, swept and polished the already pristine sitting-room; in the afternoons she sat by the window with her knitting, frequently turning a loving eye on her new possessions; and at night she sat by the fire, luxuriating in draught-free comfort, nibbling at soft-centred chocolates and making half-hearted attempts to finish the day's crossword puzzle. Never had she felt so relaxed and happy.

On the fourth day the first inexplicable event occurred, when she was sitting at a small table near the window, playing a game of Patience. It was a long time since she had been able to indulge in such a pastime, for her mother had flatly refused to allow a pack of cards in the house. She was feeling very content because the game showed every sign of 'coming out'. She had to leave the room to answer the postman's knock, and when she returned all the cards were scattered over the floor and the table was lying on its side.

'Oh, dear, how could that have happened?' she exclaimed. 'I don't think I knocked the table over as I got up.' She stooped to retrieve the cards. 'The game was going so well too – now I'll have to start all over again.'

That evening, while boiling milk in the kitchen for her evening drink, she turned from the cooker to get a cup, but when she turned back the milk was already sizzling and frothing over the edge of the saucepan. She stared at it in amazement, quite forgetting to turn the gas off. 'I've never known milk to boil so quickly before,' she said to herself. 'I'm sure the gas wasn't as high as that. What a mess. . . .'

Those two incidents were only the beginning, however. The next day brought one minor accident after another. Sewing on a button that had mysteriously detached itself from her cardigan, the needle stuck itself sharply into her thumb. Cissie yelped with pain and put her thumb into her mouth. While she was trying to stem the trickle of blood her eyes fell on the wallpaper by the fireplace. Horrified, she hurried over to it and saw a black stain disfiguring the dainty pattern. It was just as if somebody had thrown a bottle of ink against the wall. 'But I've never used ink in here for days,' she wailed. 'How *could* it have happened?'

Later in the evening her bath water overflowed and soaked through the floor to make a wet patch on the ceiling below. Cissie could not think how that could have happened, because the water had been running for only a couple of minutes and it took five minutes at least to fill the bath three-quarters full. When at last she sank into bed, exhausted and miserable, she found that her hot-water bottle had burst and the sheets were soaking wet.

The following morning, wondering what the day would bring forth, she went to the front door to get the morning paper and found it smeared, of all things, with strawberry jam. Before she realized what had happened her sticky fingers had transferred the jam on to the door, her dress, and her hair when she tried to brush away a wasp that had been attracted by the sweetness. Retreating to the kitchen in extreme distress she found that the teapot had apparently poured its contents on to the table cloth of its own accord.

Cissie sat down and burst into tears of mixed rage and grief. 'What's happening?' She beat her fists upon the table. 'Why are all these things happening to me?' Her agitated

She beat her fists upon the table. Her agitated tattoo upset the milk jug.

tattoo upset the milk jug, and when she jumped up to get a cloth she knocked her elbow against a pile of dishes that fell to the floor with a crash. 'Oh – oh – my best set –' Cissie's tears poured down her plump cheeks. She blundered into the sitting-room and collapsed into one of her new chairs.

'All right, I give in,' she sobbed. 'I know it's you, Mother. Just because I took your chair away. You said you'd haunt me, didn't you? Well, I can't stand it any more, do you hear? I give in – you've won!'

She dragged herself to her feet and wearily climbed the stairs to the attic. Getting the chair down to the sitting-room was more difficult than she had anticipated, but she managed it. She had to move the furniture around so that the chair could be restored to its former position, and when she had finished she stood in the now overcrowded room, looking around her with dissatisfaction. 'Ugh!' she exclaimed. 'How I hate this room now.'

That evening she sat in her usual draughty seat, her crossword on her knee. On the other side of the fire the empty armchair took up far too much space and received all the warmth. 'Ugly old chair,' Cissie said bitterly.

There was a creak from the chair as though something had settled itself comfortably in the sagging seat.

'As for you, Mother,' Cissie went on, 'I hope you're pleased with yourself now that you've ruined my happiness. Why couldn't you rest in peace like other people's mothers?'

She was answered by a contented chuckle that seemed to say, 'I *am* at peace now,' and the chair creaked again.

'You were obstinate when you were alive,' Cissie sniffed, 'and now you're an obstinate ghost. . . .'

First Performance

WHEN ABRAHAM BENZ, the great German composer, died a few years ago, music-lovers all over the world were sad, though no one was very surprised, for he was ninety-seven when the event occurred.

Benz had been famous for his eccentric behaviour as well as for his music. He had quarrelled with other composers, with conductors, singers and orchestras. He had walked out of concerts of his own music, and once he had interrupted the performance of one of his operas with a demand for the leading soprano to 'keep to the tune I wrote'. Everybody had a story to tell of his outrageous actions, yet at the same time he was loved by a great number of once-struggling singers and musicians to whom he had given either advice, encouragement or money.

His music was admired without reservation. He had written symphonies, concertos, songs, operas – even the occasional pop song (under an assumed name) when he needed money quickly to help one of his deserving causes. So when, a few months after his death, his stepson, the conductor Franz Freiden, announced that he had found a new symphony among Benz's papers, the musical world hummed with excitement. It was likely to be one of Benz's major works, Freiden said, and was certainly the longest. The excitement grew when it became known that the first performance would be given in London and that it would be conducted by Freiden himself.

It was common knowledge that Benz had always disliked Freiden, and that Freiden had considered his stepfather to be a silly old man, but this did not worry anybody. The concert would be a musical occasion of the first importance, and everybody who *was* anybody was determined to be present, as well as several thousand members of the general public.

London's largest concert hall was sold out two hours after the booking opened, and a great success was predicted for Benz's Fifteenth Symphony. Such was the enthusiasm that the entire audience had taken their seats several minutes before the concert began. There were no late-comers, no stragglers who had lingered over their coffees in the foyer. The members of the orchestra lost no time in getting to their places: they tuned their instruments immediately, then waited silently for Franz Freiden to arrive.

As soon as he appeared, a tall, spruce figure with a shock of grey hair, the applause broke the silence like a sudden thunder-clap. Freiden walked briskly to the rostrum, acknowledged the applause with a grave nod, then, with baton raised, faced the players. The last cough was stifled, the last programme rustled. With a neat gesture Franz Freiden brought the symphony to life.

The gently rhythmic tune, played by the violins, violas and cellos, cast an immediate spell. The double-basses joined in and gave it greater depth, then the woodwind instruments had their say and after them a single French horn gave it a mellow glow. Freiden, with eyes closed, swayed to the rhythm, carried away by the beauty he was creating. Never had he imagined that any orchestra could play so superbly. It was going to be a performance of supreme perfection. . . .

Freiden knew the music by heart and prepared himself for the coming violent intrusion of the brass and percussion that would change the mood completely. Soon all the instruments except the violins had trembled into silence, and Freiden turned to the violin section, bringing the sound down to a thin, sweet thread. The last few notes were played in unison. It was time for the thread to snap – when suddenly the air was jarred by the sourest, most discordant note that any violin had ever played.

The harsh, unexpected sound brought the violinists to a faltering stop. Freiden screwed up his face in agony. He almost cried out in anger, but controlled himself just in time, and contented himself with a furious glare at the violinists. He tried to identify the culprit. Surely it must have been the one on the back row, the player with the strange mocking grin on his face. He peered closer at the man, then gave a start and almost dropped his baton. Wasn't that – but it couldn't be – it was too ridiculous – and yet – oh, I must be going mad, Freiden thought. He blinked rapidly and shook his head as if to dispel an unpleasant vision, and remembered just in time that the music had to go on.

He turned towards the brass section, opened his arms wide, and gave them the beat for the entry of their martial tune. When it came the hall reverberated with the tremendously exciting noise. It was as if the Day of Judgement had been announced. Magnificent! thought Freiden. Now we can forget that terrible moment. . . .

The tune reached its climax; then it was repeated, first by the trumpets to a background of plucked strings, then by the French horns. The tubas added their version, and a drum roll announced the trombones.

The trombones started beautifully – deep, but with the right touch of hoarseness. But the smoothness of their last sliding notes was interrupted by a crude sound that could only be described as a raspberry. . . .

Again the audience was shaken out of its rapt mood, and a loud murmuring broke out. This time Freiden did drop his baton. In a mixture of rage and despair he shook his fists above his head and uttered a savage exclamation. He cast a withering look at the startled trombonists, then stepped back as though trying to avert an unexpected danger. 'No, no – I *must* be going mad,' he muttered. 'It can't be. . . .' He looked again at the trombonists. There had been four. But now there were only three – where had the fourth one gone? He could have sworn there were four when he mounted the rostrum.

He leaped off his rostrum and pushed his way to the back of the orchestra. 'Vhere, vhere, vhere? You, you and you – vhere is he?'

The leader of the orchestra hurried up to him. 'Mr. Freiden, please calm down.' He started to pat the conductor on the shoulder, making ineffectual noises.

But Freiden was not to be soothed. 'He's hiding some-where, ze old – how you say – cheat!' he gasped. He approached the first trombone with such a menacing look in his eyes that the player stretched out the slide of his instrument to the full to keep him at bay. 'Vhere you hide him, eh?'

'I'm not hiding nobody,' the first trombone twittered, forgetting his grammar in the heat of the moment.

'Ach,' said Freiden and pushed past more players until he reached the tympanist. 'Let me look behind your tymp, eh? Perhaps you hide him.'

'Who, m-me?' the tympanist asked, with a sickly grin.

Freiden wriggled his way between the three kettledrums and addressed the other percussion players. 'Vhere he hide? Beneath your drum – under ze glockenspiel? I must find him. . . .'

While all this was going on the people in the hall, shattered first by the music and then by its bizarre sequel, were pushing and struggling to get a better view of the fantastic proceed-ings. The members of the orchestra were adding to the confusion by arguing excitedly among themselves about what had happened.

Freiden blundered about the platform like a maddened bull, knocking over chairs and upsetting music stands in his attempt to locate the mysterious fourth trombonist. Vainly the leader appealed to the players to sit down and be calm, and in the auditorium the stewards were doing their best to restore order. The manager of the hall and the orchestra manager, together with their assistants, had appeared on the platform and were chasing after the frantic conductor like huntsmen in full cry after a fox; and a flustered nurse, clutching a bottle of sal volatile, brought up the rear.

At last Freiden was surrounded by his pursuers and he disappeared in the scrum. When he emerged, dusty and tousled, all the fight had gone out of him. He was dusted down and consoled. He was promised that a searching inquiry would be held and that the practical joker who had been responsible for the disturbance would be severely dealt with. After a great deal of muttering and head-shaking he agreed to continue with the concert. He made his way back to the rostrum to a burst of applause from the audience, a rather hysterical sound made up of relief that the concert was going to be resumed and gratitude for the unexpected entertainment they had witnessed.

Freiden decided to start again from the entry of the brass. This time the notorious trombone passage went off without a hitch and in a short time the music had woven its spell round all the eager listeners.

With a great sweeping movement the conductor launched the players into the last great tune of the movement. It swirled thrillingly through the hall like a waterfall cascading down a mountainside. Then he alerted the orchestra for the two pauses that punctuated the end of the movement. The flood of sound was halted for a count of three. There was another climax, another pause before the last breathtaking chord. The first pause was perfection; the silence could almost be felt. The re-entry of the orchestra was like a mighty shout of triumph. Freiden brought his baton down for the second pause. One – two – and on the third beat the silence was broken by a clear, piping 'Cuckoo!'

In the pandemonium that followed all hope of further music that evening dwindled and disappeared. Freiden hurled his baton from him and, roaring at the top of his voice, stamped off the platform and made his way blindly to the conductor's room. There he locked the door and burst into tears.

Eventually the doors of the concert hall were closed against the last reluctant newspaper reporter. Backstage, the musicians had been questioned about the events of the evening, but no explanation of the interpolations that had ruined Benz's symphony was forthcoming. All the violinists vigorously denied having caused the sour note; the three trombonists were positive that the raspberry had not come from them, and everybody was insistent that the cuckoo sound had not come from any of their instruments. Yet the sounds had been made – but by whom?

The manager allowed the musicians to leave. 'I suppose it could be a conspiracy,' he said to his assistant, 'but why should anyone deliberately try to ruin such an important occasion?' With a baffled groan he went to the conductor's room and knocked on the door. 'Please let me come in, Herr Freiden,' he pleaded.

'Go avay,' came a muffled shout from the conductor. 'I vill not come out from here – ever! I am disgraced – ruined – nobody vill ever vant me to conduct again!'

It was long after midnight when they gave up hope of persuading him to change his mind. 'We'll just have to let him stay until he comes to his senses,' the manager said. 'Perhaps when he's really hungry he'll decide he's had enough solitary confinement. Anyway, I'm going home. Goodness knows what my wife will say. . . .' He turned to the chief steward. 'Mr. Bulstrode, I'm going to leave you in charge. You'd better stay here till something happens – if anything does.'

'That's all right, sir,' said Mr. Bulstrode cheerfully. 'Poor chap, I can understand how he feels. I locked myself in the kitchen once when I thought I'd won the pools and then found I'd forgotten to post the coupon. Terrible, it was. I've got over it now, but –'

'Yes, yes,' said the manager hastily. 'Quite. Well, I must be off. . . .'

So everyone went home and the chief steward was left alone with the heartbroken conductor. He tapped at the door and called out, 'Would you like a nice cup of tea, sir, and maybe a biscuit? The kettle's on – I'll have it made in a couple of shakes.'

He waited, head on one side, but there was no reply. 'Well, I could do with a cuppa meself, seeing as how it's going to be an all night sitting,' he muttered, and ambled off to his room in the basement.

When all was still the door of the conductor's room opened slowly and a white-faced Freiden peeped out. He made his way carefully along a dimly lit corridor and entered the pitch-dark auditorium. When he had found his rostrum he stepped up on to it and gazed into the blackness around him, first towards where the audience had been, and then he turned round as if the orchestra were waiting for his baton to summon them to their task.

Fresh tears came to his eyes. 'Vhy, oh, vhy did this have to happen to me?' he cried, then gave a little jump as the echo of his words rumbled round the hall. And as the poor man stood wiping his eyes with a handkerchief, the echo died away and there came from somewhere in the gloom around him a

When Frieden had found his rostrum he stepped up on to it and gazed into the blackness around him.

loud, musical 'Cuckoo!'

Freiden felt the hairs at the back of his neck rise, and he shivered with fear. 'Who – who – is there?' he said in a quavering voice, in his native German.

'Franz, you know very well who is here,' came the answer.

He did know – there was no mistaking that querulous tone, even though it did seem to be echoing in a cavern. His fear disappeared, and he faced where he thought the voice had come from. 'Abraham Benz! Then it was you, stepfather!'

The answer was a chuckle.

'So it was *you*,' Freiden went on bitterly, 'sitting among the violins, grinning like a fiend. *You* were the fourth trombonist. And it was *you* who cried "Cuckoo". . . .'

'Yes, it was I,' said the voice. 'I did it all rather well, don't you think?'

'But – but you are dead –' Freiden spluttered. 'Then – then it's your ghost who has played these tricks!'

'You may use that term if you like,' the voice said impatiently. 'But I will show you that Abraham Benz is as much alive dead as he was alive!'

And a formless glowing cloud emerged from the back of the hall and slowly moved towards Freiden until it was only a metre from him. Freiden shrank back, covering his face with his hands. Gradually the glow subsided, the edges of the cloud hardened and took on the shape of an old man. Abraham Benz stood before the terrified conductor, apparently as real and solid as he had been in life.

'Look at me,' he commanded.

Freiden let his hands drop. He stared at the ghost of his stepfather.

'Do I look like a ghost?' demanded the old man.

Freiden shook his head, 'But you are. . . . Tell me, why did you ruin everything tonight? The music was sublime, the orchestra was playing brilliantly, the occasion would have added still more lustre to your name. Yet the evening ended as a fiasco. I dread to think what the papers will say tomorrow. Why did you do it?'

Abraham Benz's ghost growled. 'Stop playing the fool, man. Use your wits and tell *me* why I stopped the symphony. Why pretend that you don't know?'

Freiden stepped down from the rostrum, groped for a chair and half collapsed on to it. 'I thought nobody would ever find out,' he groaned. 'I know that what I did was wrong – but I *had* to do it. How could I know that you would interfere?'

'Foolish man,' said the ghost. 'Do you understand now that what I did was for your own good?'

'Yes, yes, I see that now. I was mad to think that I could get away with it,' Freiden said humbly.

'If I had not interfered as I did,' the ghost went on, 'the evening would have been a resounding success, as we know. The world would have again acclaimed Abraham Benz. What a genius! they would have said. It is not many composers whose last work is their greatest. That is what they *would* have said. Now the world is going to know the truth.'

Freiden rose to protest, crying, 'No, no!' But the ghost moved too and towered above him.

'The world will know that Benz did not write that symphony – that Benz's Fifteenth Symphony is really Franz Freiden's First!'

Freiden spread out his hands in despair. 'How can I explain that *I* wrote the music? Would anyone believe me?'

'That is your problem,' said the ghost. 'But – I warn you – if you ever conduct Benz's so-called Fifteenth again I shall assist you just as I did tonight! But if it is Freiden's First, then I shall be an invisible power at your side, helping you to create the performance of a lifetime. Choose. . . .'

'You make it very difficult,' Freiden complained. 'I would never have deceived the public and tried to pass off my work as yours if I had thought its true worth would have been recognized. But who would have come to a concert to hear music by *me*? A handful of my friends, perhaps, and one or two critics convinced in advance that nothing I wrote could be any good. I knew my symphony was good. When I was going through your papers the idea came to me. . . . I copied your writing and your musical notation until your style was mine. Then I wrote my own score just as you would have done it. The result – a new symphony by Abraham Benz!'

There was a more sympathetic tone in the ghost's voice. 'You were wrong, though I understand why you acted as you did. A true artist cares nothing for what the critics say. If your music had not been so fine I would not have bothered to interfere. Where I am now fame is not important. But at last *you* have justified yourself by composing music I would have been proud to call my own. After tonight, because of what has happened, your name will be on everyone's lips. You will be besieged by reporters tomorrow, and you will tell them the truth! Then you will give a repeat performance of Freiden's First, and I shall be there – listening. . . .'

'I will do that!' Freiden straightened himself up, his eyes lit up with hope. 'Thank you, dear stepfather –'

But his stepfather was no longer there, and though he strained his eyes through the gloom he could see nothing. 'Where are you?' he called.

The only answer was a faint 'Cuckoo!' that seemed to be coming from the depths of a distant wood.

Mr. Bulstrode, the chief steward, nearly dropped his cup of tea when he heard a tap at the door of his basement room and Franz Freiden, tired-looking but happy, stepped over the threshold.

'Ah, my friend,' the conductor said, rubbing his hands together expectantly, 'so I have found you! I think, perhaps, I will accept that cup of tea, if there is still one in the pot, huh?'

Ghost at Sea

ON A COLD stormy November evening Captain Johnson sat in
the company of a few friends in the bar-parlour of an inn in
the sea-port where he lived. The glow from the fire made the
pewter tankards glint and shadows dance on the walls,
creating a cosy atmosphere that was in sharp contrast to the
savage wind and hammering rain outside.

The little group of men had been friends for many years,
and knew each other so well that there were seldom any new
things to talk about. They had grown accustomed to the
comfortable silences between bursts of conversation, and
puffed contentedly at their pipes or took long draughts of ale
from their tankards.

The silence was broken at last by old Jed Puller, a craggy-
faced farmer with a deep voice that reverberated in the low
rafters like a small thunder-clap. ''Tis on a night like this,' he
said, looking challengingly round him, 'that ghosts
walk. . . .' He put his pipe back in his mouth and clamped his
teeth round the stem.

It was just as if he had lit the blue paper on a firework, for
the others suddenly crackled with laughter. Captain Johnson, however, could only manage a faint smile.

'Jed's off again!' said Amos Cottam. 'Hark at him now!'

'Him and his old ghosts,' Len Wilson sniffed. 'Clanking
chains that turn out to be old tin cans. . . . You're full of
superstitions, Jed!'

'What if I am?' Jed asked in his rumbling voice. 'There's

nothing wrong with that if they happen to be true.' He fixed the captain with a glare. 'What do you say, Jack? There's nothing wrong with superstitions, eh?'

The captain gave another uneasy smile. 'I suppose not, Jed. We sailors have enough of them, anyhow. In the old days they used to nail a horseshoe to the mast to keep witches away, and they'd whistle up the wind in calm weather, although some said that to do that would call up the devil. It was believed that a voyage begun on a Friday was bound to be unlucky, and as for seeing a stormy petrel – well, there's not a sailor alive who doesn't know that it means foul weather. Mother Carey's chickens, we call the nasty creatures, and I'd as soon not see any, I can tell you. Aye, superstitions are catching, right enough, and it would be a bold man who denied having any.'

Jed nodded wisely, determined to press home this advantage. 'Ghosts, now,' he said. 'What about them, Jack? Do you believe in ghosts, too?'

Captain Johnson froze for a moment, holding his pipe in mid-journey to his mouth. His expression became worried, and his eyes seemed to be tinged with fear. Then he said hesitantly, 'It would be a bold man, too, who denied that there were such things as ghosts. Anyone who's seen one, as I have, wouldn't dare.'

Jed gave a sigh of satisfaction. 'You've seen one? That's more than I have. Heard the clanking, I have, but nothing more.' He leaned towards the captain, and said in a stage whisper, 'This lot think we're daft, Jack, but we *know*, don't we? Tell us about the ghost you saw!'

'It's not a nice story,' the captain said, 'and I don't think –' But before he could say any more his friends were clamouring to hear the story, and reluctantly he agreed.

Jack took a pull from his tankard, then twisted round in his seat so that he was looking into the heart of the fire. His eyes narrowed, and it seemed to his listeners that he could see in the red-hot cavern the events he was about to describe.

'It happened about thirty years ago, yet I can remember it as if it were yesterday,' the captain began soberly. 'I was second officer on board the *Morning Star*, and as she sailed through the Channel the weather was much as it is tonight, with driving rain, a bitter wind and a sky full of low, scudding clouds. Our destination was Hong Kong, and Port Said was the first port of call. We had a mixed crew – English, Scottish and French, with Chinese firemen and greasers.

'Everybody seemed edgy, and some were downright bad-tempered. Apart from sailing on a Friday, it was New Year's Eve, and the Scotsmen in particular were disgruntled at having to give up their Hogmanay celebrations. The storm, however, kept everybody alert and busy, and there wasn't much opportunity for real trouble to break out. When we reached the Bay of Biscay and there was no improvement in the weather, we all felt so sorry for ourselves that, strangely enough, the atmosphere improved. As we entered the Atlantic and sailed down the coast of Portugal things gradually became normal, and when some bright winter sunshine took the place of wind and rain we grew quite cheerful.

'We were through the Straits of Gibraltar, heading for Port Said, when the first mysterious incident happened. I had the middle watch – twelve noon till four p.m. and twelve midnight till four a.m. – and I fully expected it to pass uneventfully. I was on the navigation bridge, and I re-member marvelling at the placidness of the Mediterranean after the turbulence we had been through a few days before. Two bells had been rung about ten minutes before. . . . Suddenly there was a terrible sound. It was halfway between a groan and a scream, but more animal-like than human.

'"What on earth –!" I shouted, and then I saw the look-out on the fo'c's'le collapse in what seemed to be a fit or a faint. "It's Miller," I said to Grimes, the quartermaster. "He must have been taken ill. Look after him, will you? Get him below and put somebody in his place."

'Grimes quickly summoned help, and I saw two men carry Miller's inert form away. The quartermaster reported back to me shortly afterwards. Miller had come to, he said, but was still in no condition to account for his collapse. "The doctor's with him now, sir," Grimes added. "I daresay he'll pull himself together soon."

'For the rest of my watch Miller's cry rang in my ears. I had heard the cries of frightened men before, but I had never heard a noise which contained so much sheer terror, and I could not shake off its ghastly echoes. For my own peace of mind – and perhaps for Miller's too – I knew that I must see him and discover what had scared him so badly.

'He lay in his bunk, blank-eyed and shrivelled-looking. The doctor had given him something to make him sleep, but so far it had not taken effect. I asked him if he remembered what had happened. He shuddered and looked at me as if pleading with me not to press him. Nevertheless, he tried to explain.

'"It wasn't much at first," he said. "I was on the look-out over starboard when I thought I saw something over on the port side. Under the rail, it was, sort of black and round, like – like a head. . . . I went over to port, but when I got there it had gone. I couldn't make it out – it's not like me to see things that aren't there. A few minutes later I saw it again, and it seemed to be nodding at me from the other side of the boat. When I moved towards it there was nothing there. . . . This time I thought someone was playing tricks – one of those Frenchies, perhaps – and I didn't like that at all. A joke's a joke, I said to myself, but this one has gone too far. Then – *it* happened. . . ." He fell silent.

'"Carry on," I said quietly. "Tell me what happened."

'"It grew – this black thing. It grew to the size of a man. It rose up and came through the rails as though they weren't there. It came towards me with its arms outstretched – all smooth and wet and silent. Closer and closer it came, and I couldn't move. Not for a fortune could I have moved one step. I saw its dark, grinning face and glaring eyes, but more than that – I saw its neck – there was an ugly red mark round it, as if – as if – fingers had been pressing hard. . . . I tried to speak, to tell it to go away, but no words would come. Then it was almost upon me and – and that's all I remember. . . ."

'I didn't know what to say. In the end I managed to whisper, "Try to sleep now and you'll feel better tomorrow," and I left him alone.

'A couple of days later Miller returned to duty. His nerves had settled down, and the horror of his experience seemed to have faded. I wondered how he would feel doing his duties during the night watch, but the first night passed without incident, and when it was over Miller was almost unnaturally lively – probably from a sense of relief.

'The next night the weather was perfect. It was the sort of night when one thanks the stars one is a sailor. The half-moon gave enough light to soften the hard outlines of the ship and deepen the dark blue of the sea. The wind was fresh and scented. The rumbling throb of the ship's engines seemed hushed, as if they were trying not to waken the shades of those Phoenician sailors who had sailed these very seas more than two thousand years ago.

'The shriek, when it came, split the air with jagged sound. This time I saw the figure too, but did not realize at first what it was. I saw Miller moving towards the starboard, then I became aware of someone appearing behind him. The figure reached him, put its arm around his neck, and swung him

I saw its dark, grinning face and glaring eyes.

round so that they faced each other. It was then that Miller screamed.

'This time, leaving the quartermaster on the bridge, I hurried to Miller myself. He lay writhing on the deck, shouting unintelligibly. The commotion had brought out several of the crew, and between them they got him below and roused the doctor. The thing that had attacked Miller had disappeared, but this time *I* had seen it, and I knew that he was not suffering from hallucinations. My watch seemed interminable, and I finished it in a terrible state of nerves.

'The next day I visited Miller. The doctor had warned me that I was in for a shock, but I was not prepared for what I saw. The previous day Miller had had a fine head of brown curls, and a lean face deeply tanned by sea-winds and tropical suns. The man lying in the bunk had white hair, an ashen complexion, and a drawn, lined face. He had aged thirty years overnight. But what gave me the biggest shock was the angry-looking red mark round his neck.

'His vacant eyes looked into mine. I thought at first he couldn't see me, then came a flicker of recognition. "Are you feeling better?" I said stupidly, at a loss to know how to begin.

'He made no reply, but continued to fix me with his eyes. A sudden flash of understanding made me blurt out, 'You *know* why this has happened, don't you?"

'After a long pause he answered, feebly yet with some determination, "Yes, I know. I can't escape now – ever."

'"Are you going to tell me?" I asked gently.

'"Aye, I'll tell you. I'm dying, you know. . . ."

'I shook my head, about to reassure him, but he cut me short. 'I *am* dying, and I must confess. Confession is good for the soul – and my soul needs a bit of goodness. It was Parry, that – that thing – the figure. David Parry. I murdered him in Melbourne three years ago. I hated him, you see. There was a girl there I was going to marry – Greta, her name was. It was all fixed – until Dave Parry stole her from me. He was a strong, fine-looking chap with a winning way, and he turned her against me with the smoothness of his lies. When he told me *he* was going to marry Greta it was the last straw. That night I made an excuse to get him away from our usual haunts. We drove out of Melbourne and when I saw my chance I strangled him. And as I squeezed the life out of his body he told me what he'd do. He would haunt me, he said, until the time came when he could murder me – and that's what he's doing. He's haunting me – and soon he will kill me.'

'Miller sank back and almost immediately fell asleep. I wondered whether he would have forgotten the story when he woke up in the morning for I was more than half convinced that what he had said had been the ramblings of a sick man. And yet – I had seen – what? Dave Parry?

'I was unable to sleep that night. I tossed and turned for an hour or two until in despair I dressed myself and went on deck. I had been gazing over the side for a minute or two when the silence was shattered by the now familiar cry of anguish. I looked round but could see nothing. I dashed down to Miller's cabin. His bunk was empty. I leaped up the companionway and back on deck. There I saw a small group of men on the fo'c's'le, strangely still. I joined them and looked where they were looking. Crumpled on the deck, peaceful in death, lay Miller, and it was only necessary to look once to see that he had been strangled.

'I shivered. Dave Parry had indeed been a strong man and he had carried out his dying threat with ghastly success. . . .'

There was a long silence after the captain had finished. Then Jed Puller gave a nervous laugh. His hands were shaking as he applied a match to his pipe. 'Aye, there – there you are then,' he stammered. 'That's ghosts for you – Amos, would you be walking my way home tonight?'

Requiem for a Ghost

ON THE HEIGHTS BEHIND PALERMO, a coast town in Sicily, stands the great cathedral of Monreale, the walls of which are covered with ancient mosaics.

One evening, many years ago, as the setting sun was bathing the stones with a mellow, honey-dark gold, a Knight of Malta approached the church, panting slightly as he climbed the rugged incline from the town.

He was a tall, powerful-looking man with dark, close-cropped hair and the weather-beaten face of a traveller. Originally the Knights of Malta were called Knights of St. John of Jerusalem, an order founded to help Christian pilgrims who were on their way to the Holy Land. Each member of the order was a soldier as well as a priest, as used to fighting as to praying.

The knight opened the huge main door on the western side of the cathedral and slipped quietly into the dim, scented interior. Its shade was very welcome to him after the heat of the day and his stiff climb, and he stood for a moment to enjoy the feeling of peace. The sunset streamed through the long windows and the mosaics glowed with rich colours. One lovely arch melted into another, and the knight felt as though he were in the middle of a poem.

He gasped at the beauty all around him. 'I must transfer all this to paper,' he murmured to himself, 'so that I can live this moment again when I am far away.' He took out a sketchbook and a piece of charcoal from his haversack, sat down on a wooden seat and began to draw.

After a time he realized that he could scarcely see the paper in front of him. The light of the sun had waned and its radiance had faded into a grey blur. The corners of the great church were black with shadows, and the vaulted roof had disappeared into a dark mist.

The knight had not noticed the approach of darkness. He put down his charcoal and paper and suddenly shivered. It had grown cold and the dampness from the stone floor seemed to rise and invade his body. 'I can do no more here,' he said. 'I will go back to the inn at Palermo where there is warmth and comfort.'

He picked up his things and made his way to the western door, stumbling in the deepening gloom. He turned the heavy handle and pushed. The door would not open. He pushed again, harder, and pressed his whole weight against the wood. The door remained immovable.

'Locked in!' the knight exclaimed in annoyance. 'I must have been so engrossed in my sketching that I did not notice the church being locked up for the night. No doubt I shall find another door open.'

He went to the side doors. They too stood firm against him. So did the door to the sacristy, the room containing the cathedral's vestments and holy vessels.

The knight was not so much frightened as irritated. 'I'll make a noise,' he thought. 'Someone at the nearby monastery will be sure to hear me and come to my rescue.'

He shouted until his voice grew hoarse, and hammered at the main door until his hands were sore, but nobody heard and nobody came. The knight was alone in the dark, gloomy church and would have to stay there until the morning.

His annoyance left him when he realized there was nothing to do but make the best of the situation. Sighing at the thought of the meal and the comfortable bed he would miss at the inn, he sat down with his back against a pillar, wrapped his cloak around him, and prepared to spend the night.

While he sat there, his eyes drooping at last into sleep, the moon rose, and through the windows the silvery light cast a shimmering halo over everything around him. The effect was as lovely, in a different way, as when the sunset had stained the walls with ruby and gold. Each avenue of arches was like a fairy-tale palace. Pools of moonlight splashed on the floor, and the statues and ornaments looked as though they had been dipped in quicksilver.

'I could never capture this loveliness with any material aids,' he thought. 'It would be useless to try. I must drink it all in with my eyes so that I can remember it for ever.'

Suddenly from above came a booming sound – the clock outside was striking the first note of midnight. Just before it quivered into silence the second stroke broke in, then another and another. The knight counted twelve. The cathedral grew deathly cold, as though it had turned into a huge empty grave. He drew in his breath sharply, glancing rapidly round the church.

His eyes came to rest on a figure that had appeared from the west door and seemed to be floating rather than walking up the nave. It wore a monk's robe and the cowl was drawn right over its head, hiding the face completely. Its hands were folded in the sleeves and its sandalled feet made no sound as it slowly glided along.

After his first shock the knight sighed with relief.

'I've been missed,' he thought. 'The landlord of the inn has informed the monastery, and one of the monks has come to find me.'

He got up and started to move towards the figure, now only a few paces from him. Its head was bent low, its shoulders were hunched and the face was still in shadow.

The knight broke the silence. 'I am glad you have come –' he began.

But the figure took no notice. It passed the knight, looking neither to left nor to right, and as it did so the knight heard a soft sighing sound coming from beneath the hood, and a few whispered words, so faint that he was not sure whether the figure had uttered them or whether he had imagined them. 'Is there no good Christian who will say a mass for my poor soul?'

The figure moved on swiftly, reached the high altar, slipped behind it and disappeared.

The knight stood as if turned to stone, his eyes straining through the darkness, as if the intensity of his gaze would bring the strange figure back again. The moonlight picked out the altar and the vessels on it. The chancel was as empty as ever it had been.

The knight clasped his hands to stop them trembling. With a great effort he pulled himself together. 'I do not know what I saw,' he said to himself, 'but – I do not like it – I wonder where the monk came from. . . .'

He fumbled his way to the west door, expecting that it would open as easily as it must have done to let the strange monk enter. His arms ached with his efforts, but they were in vain. Baffled and defeated, the knight returned to his former resting place and sank down, this time not to sleep, but to watch. He kept his eyes on the altar, determined to see where the mysterious figure appeared from, if it appeared again.

An hour passed, and the knight's eyes were swimming with tiredness and the strain of watching. The cathedral clock suddenly jerked him to wakefulness with a single tremendous clanging sound. One o'clock. . . .

Nothing happened at the altar, but the knight felt the hairs at the back of his neck begin to bristle. Slowly he turned round. There was the monkish figure, again coming from the

The figure wore a monk's robe.

door, floating up the nave, the dark robe flowing, the head bowed. As it passed him he again heard the whispered words, a mere sad wisp of sound. 'Is there no good Christian who will say a mass for my poor soul. . . .?' The figure moved steadily on towards the altar.

The knight stirred into action. 'I'll find out this time where he goes,' he muttered. He followed the monk down the nave and into the chancel. At the altar he stopped. There was no one there. The monk had passed round behind and vanished.

The knight gazed at the spot where the monk had been. All he could see were the flagstones of the floor and the walls behind. There was neither door nor window through which a man could have gone.

'A trick of the light!' the knight panted. 'I have seen nothing – it was a mixture of moonlight and shadow – an illusion brought on by tiredness –' He stopped. He *had* heard the softly spoken words – that he could swear to. *They* could not be accounted for by the moon! Feeling the first pricklings of fear, he returned to the pillar and prepared again to keep vigil.

During the next hour nothing happened and the knight, needing all his will-power to keep himself awake, began to think he had dreamed all that had happened. He longed for the light of day, and for the arrival of someone from the monastery to open the door and let light and sanity flood into the cathedral. When the clock struck two and the intense cold penetrated his bones once more he rose slowly and turned to the door. He knew what he would see. . . .

For the third time the monk travelled slowly through the church. For the third time he reached the knight and uttered his sorrowful plea. 'Is there no good Christian who will say a mass for my poor soul?'

'Yes!' the knight found himself saying, his voice harsh and

loud. 'I am priest as well as soldier. I will say a mass for you!'

The monk stopped and turned his face towards the knight. But it was still in shadow, and the knight could not see the features. He felt a pair of eyes burning into him, and he shuddered.

Side by side they approached the altar. When they had reached the steps of the chancel the knight said, 'You must serve the mass. There can be no mass without a server. What do you say?'

The monk bowed his head as if in agreement. The knight took the last few steps and stood before the altar. He felt the presence of the monk at his side, and saw that he had thrown back his cowl. Instead of a face a skull grinned at him.

The bones were yellow, the teeth brown and crooked, the empty eye-sockets held only blackness. The knight lurched forward, almost falling on the altar. With an effort he steadied himself, but he was trembling so much that his arm knocked against a holy vessel, which would have fallen if the monk had not stretched out a fleshless hand, taken it from him and carefully put it back in its place on the altar.

The knight put his hands up to his head as if to try to steady the whirling thoughts in his mind. What had happened? Had he gone mad? Was there really this – this *thing* standing next to him? He stole a look sideways. Yes, it really was there, a skeleton in a monk's robe, the skull bowed as though in prayer, the bones of its hands clasped together, prepared to take its part in the service.

I shall wake up soon, the knight told himself fiercely. This cannot be happening. Did the ghostly figure intend some evil? he wondered. Had it appeared to warn him of danger? Or was it simply a poor unhappy ghost who would not find peace until a mass *had* been said for its soul?

Forcing himself to concentrate on the prayers, the knight began the introduction. . . . 'Eternal rest give to them, O

Lord; and let perpetual light shine upon them. . . .' The Introit over, his voice strengthened a little as he went into the Kyrie. 'Kyrie eleison . . . Lord have mercy. . . .'

'Christe eleison . . . Christ, have mercy. . . .' came a whisper from his side.

'Day of wrath, that day shall dissolve the world in ashes. . . .' mumbled the knight-priest, and the mass continued.

The moonlight shone on the altar and illuminated the two figures before it. The unearthly silence was broken only by the low voice of the priest and the responses of his shadowy companion.

Then it was over. 'Requiem aeternam dona eis Domine; et lux perpetua luceat eis,' the priest whispered.

'Amen.' The ghost's head dropped to its chest. There was a long silence. Then, with a moan, the knight-priest collapsed and fell unconscious in front of the altar.

In the morning, when the monks came into the church, the knight was found, still unconscious. He was taken to the monastery and put to bed in the infirmary. After some hours, during which an anxious monk watched by the bedside, his eyes flickered open. He looked around him, blankly at first, then heaved a deep sigh. 'Thank God he has gone,' he murmured.

'Who has gone?' asked the monk, putting a glass of water to the knight's lips.

The knight began to tell his story. When he had finished the monk, his eyes wide with amazement, went to fetch other monks, and they listened in silence as the knight repeated the account of the ghost who had served the mass. When their guest was well enough to get out of bed he was taken to the abbot, and in the bare polished room he retold his experience for the third time. 'Who was he?' he asked, aware of the abbot's tight-lipped mouth and hooded eyes.

'I do not know,' the abbot said slowly. 'There is nothing in our archives about a monk who needed a mass to save his soul. No other monk has ever reported seeing him. Are you sure you were not dreaming?'

'I was awake and as close to him as I am to you,' the knight cried. 'You must believe me!' He stretched out his arms in appeal, his face expressing his anxiety.

The abbot pursed his lips together and shook his head. 'I fear –' he began, then stopped. 'Brother Anselm!' he said. 'He is the one who would know. He is the oldest monk in the monastery, nearly a hundred years old. He spends most of his time sitting and dreaming in the cloisters. He knows every story and legend about Monreale for hundreds of years back. Come, we will go to him. . . .'

They found the aged brother sunning himself on a stone seat in the cloisters. He was very thin and frail, with watery eyes and hands twisted with rheumatism. But his smile was sweet, and he bowed his head gravely as the abbot and the knight approached. 'Peace be with you,' he quavered.

He listened with a hand cupped to his ear as the knight again went over the happenings of the night, and his old head nodded several times during the telling. Then he seemed to withdraw into himself and was silent for a long time, his eyes looking past the two men into the distance.

'I haven't heard about that monk for – for at least fifty years,' he said at last, 'and the story goes back much, much further. Nobody knows when it really happened. I am old and my mind is not clear, but I remember hearing about a monk named Gregory. . . .'

'Yes?' the knight said impatiently.

'It is indeed a beautiful morning,' Brother Anselm murmured dreamily. 'On mornings like this I realize more than ever that God is good –'

'Brother Gregory!' the knight interrupted. 'What about him?'

'Ah, yes.' The old monk's voice grew softer. 'He committed a grave crime, so the story goes. In those days the abbot was a stern, unforgiving man, and he ordered that Brother Gregory should be buried alive under a flagstone behind the altar. Before it was done the poor man pleaded that a mass should be said for him so that his soul might find peace, but even that was denied him. They forced him, protesting and screaming, into the hole dug beneath the stone, and pressed the heavy cover over him. It was done secretly, at dead of night, with only the moonlight to guide the monks in their unholy work. . . .'

Mungo

THE DEFEAT of the last Bourbon king in the French Revolution of 1830 inspired the people of Belgium to a revolt of their own.

For some years the Netherlands and Belgium had been united under King William Frederick, but it was an unsatisfactory state of affairs because, although the Belgians were not oppressed, they were very different from the Dutch, both in language and religion, and hated being tied to them politically. Catching the spirit of revolution that was rife in Europe, the people of Brussels decided to rebel.

When the revolution began, at the end of August a large force of Dutch troops, loyal to the king, advanced towards Brussels. It was while the regiment, the 20th Foot, was encamped outside the Belgian capital that Lieutenant-Colonel de Witt first heard of Mungo.

He was in his tent when he overheard a conversation between two privates who were digging a drain outside at the back. It was a sultry day and the men were hot and tired. The colonel smiled sympathetically as he listened to the complaining voices of Forster and Berg.

'Join the army and dig!' Berg grumbled. 'Learn to be a grave-digger in civilian life.'

'This is a mighty big grave,' said Forster, 'big enough for both of us. Would you like a pleasant sleep in the grave, my friend? I've just enough strength left to shovel the soil over you.'

Private Berg snorted. 'Someone would be sure to dig me up in time to go on guard duty!'

'That's all right,' said Private Forster. 'You could continue your sleep while you were on duty, like you know who!'

The colonel heard Berg chuckle. 'You mean Jokel Falck,' he said. 'He'd sleep anywhere. When the last trumpet sounds Falck won't hear it!'

'Nor will we, for his snoring,' laughed Forster.

The colonel frowned. He had already heard rumours about the sleepy Private Jokel Falck. It was said that the man slept every single moment when he was not on duty, as well as some of the time when he was. On his rounds as Field Officer he had never actually caught Falck sleeping, though occasionally he had been suspicious of the faraway look in the man's eyes. Perhaps Berg and Forster would give away a few secrets. . . .

'He's been lucky, has Jokel,' Forster said, after a short pause. 'Only last night he missed being caught by the skin of his teeth. Leaning against a corner of the wall, dead to the world, he was. The officer of the guard was making a spot check and was within a few metres of Jokel when – know what happened?'

'Of course I do,' said Berg. 'Don't we all?'

I don't, thought the colonel, his curiosity aroused.

'Aye,' said Forster, 'if it hadn't been for Mungo, Jokel Falck would be feeling very sorry for himself today.'

'I don't know how many times Mungo has saved him,' Berg said in an awed voice.

'Mungo is a very valuable friend,' Forster said. 'He's saved many a man from punishment besides Falck.'

The colonel, puzzled by what he had heard, considered making his presence known in order to find out more about the mysterious Mungo, but a captain entered the tent with a message that the general wanted to see him. The privates' conversation slipped from his mind and he forgot to make any further investigations.

On a clear, moonlit night, a few weeks later, Lieutenant-Colonel de Witt was taking his turn as Field Officer for the day. As he and the mounted orderly were approaching one of the outposts of the camp he saw the sentry stretched out on the ground, fast asleep.

At that moment a movement attracted his attention, and he was surprised to see a large Newfoundland dog trotting purposefully towards the prostrate man. As the colonel and the orderly drew nearer, the dog lowered his head over the sentry's ear. The sentry jumped to his feet and brushed himself down hurriedly. He stood, swaying slightly, trying to look alert as the colonel reached him.

'You were asleep at your post!' the colonel shouted. 'Don't answer back, I saw you with my own eyes,' he added as the man began to stutter an excuse. The colonel turned to the orderly. 'Fetch a file of the guard and put him under arrest, and send another sentry to replace him.'

The orderly galloped off and the unfortunate sentry, his face a picture of misery, tried to persuade the colonel not to take such an extreme step. 'No, sir – please, sir – I haven't – wasn't –' He knew only too well that his words were slurred, and silently regretted the extra wine he had drunk earlier that evening. When he saw that nothing would shake the colonel's resolve he changed his tune. 'So be it,' he murmured. 'It's all the fault of that wretched Mungo – missed me – missed me.'

After the sentry had been taken away the colonel continued his tour of duty, reflecting on what the man had said. 'Mungo,' he said to himself. 'Where have I heard that name before?' But he could not remember, and decided that it was merely a soldiers' new slang name for drink.

He was surprised to see a large Newfoundland dog trotting
purposefully towards the prostrate man.

Two evenings later the colonel was returning from a visit to his brother, whose regiment was stationed nearby, when he again saw the same large Newfoundland dog. It was just ahead of him, and he watched with interest to see where it was going. Leaning against a wall, legs crossed and arms folded, was a sentry. The dog appeared to trot up to the man who at once pulled himself together and began marching smartly back and forth with true military bearing.

When the colonel reached the man he saw that it was Private Jokel Falck, and remembering his reputation for sleeping, felt sure that he had almost caught him out. But not quite. Falck had avoided discovery by a hairsbreadth, for the colonel knew he would not be justified in taking action on mere suspicion. He decided, however, to warn the sentry.

'Take care, Private Falck,' he said. 'I've half a mind to put you in the guard-room.'

'Sir!' Falck answered promptly and saluted.

'I believe I should have caught you sleeping,' the colonel went on, 'if that dog hadn't roused you. Then you would have been in real trouble!'

As the colonel turned away he noticed the ghost of a smile on Falck's face. 'That's odd,' he thought, 'that's unlike Falck. On other occasions when I've reprimanded him he has looked very downcast.'

He turned to his batman. 'Whose dog is that?'

'I don't know, sir!'

The colonel let the matter drop. He was rather angry, but knew that it would not do to vent his feelings on either the sentry or his batman.

That evening in the mess Colonel de Witt overheard the end of a conversation between two of his junior officers. 'It's quite true, I believe,' the subaltern was saying, 'and they call him Mungo. . . .'

The colonel was interested to hear the word again. The

incident with Jokel Falck had reminded him of his previous encounter with the sleeping sentry, and he edged nearer the two officers. 'Did I hear you say Mungo?' he asked. 'Is that a new name the men have got for Schnapps or beer?'

The young subaltern laughed. 'No, sir, it's the name of a dog.'

The colonel drew in his breath sharply. 'Is it a black Newfoundland with a large white streak on its flank?'

'So I am given to believe, sir.'

'I have seen a dog like that a couple of times – I saw it earlier this evening, as a matter of fact. Whose dog is it?'

The subaltern glanced at his companion, a confused expression on his face. 'I – er – I'm afraid – well, sir, that's a difficult question –'

'Come, man,' the colonel said impatiently, 'who is the owner of the dog?'

By now some of the other officers at the table had begun to take an interest in the conversation. 'Do you mean to say that you have actually *seen* Mungo?' one of them called to the colonel.

'If Mungo is the dog I have just described then I have certainly seen it, and tonight. But what is all the mystery? Will someone please tell me the name of the dog's owner?'

There was an uneasy silence at the mess table, broken at last by the rasping, tetchy voice of Major Rugen, a quick-tempered man who rarely spoke without giving the impression of sneering. 'Captain Tetjen is supposed to know more about Mungo than anyone else here,' he said. 'Perhaps he can answer your question, Colonel de Witt.'

Captain Tetjen was the oldest officer present. He was also the one who had been longest in the regiment, having joined as a private and reached his present rank through hard work. Although he spoke little he was an expert on the regiment's history, and could remember names and events stretching far back over the years.

Colonel de Witt turned to Captain Tetjen. 'Does the dog belong to Jokel Falck, captain?' he asked.

'No, sir,' the captain answered quietly. 'The dog doesn't belong to anybody – now. Once he belonged to an officer called Joseph Arveld.'

'An officer of the regiment?'

'Yes, sir.'

'He is dead, I presume?'

'Yes, sir,' said Captain Tetjen. 'He is dead.'

'And the dog has attached himself to the regiment?'

'Yes, sir.'

Major Rugen leaned across to the colonel. 'That is not all,' he said. 'According to Captain Tetjen, Mungo is not a real dog at all, but the ghost of a dog.'

There was a ripple of laughter from the men round the table, in which even the colonel joined. A preposterous story, he thought. Then he noticed that the captain had remained unsmiling. 'Really, Captain Tetjen – a ghost!' he spluttered. 'Surely you don't really believe that?'

'I believe it, sir, because I know it to be true,' the captain answered.

The colonel's immediate reaction was to pour scorn on the idea of a ghost dog, but he hesitated to ridicule the captain, who was held in great respect; he turned away impatiently, changing the subject, and once again Mungo was forgotten.

The following weeks were hectic ones. The army advanced into Brussels and there was much confused fighting. Later, the regiment withdrew to Antwerp, and while they were there the city was besieged by the French, and the Dutch were penned inside the city walls.

Time passed heavily and discipline grew lax. One night Colonel de Witt saw Mungo again, in circumstances similar to the previous occasion. A dozing sentry was awakened and an arrest was averted just in time.

This time the colonel sought out Captain Tetjen at once, taking care that their meeting should be in private. 'I saw your friend Mungo last night,' he declared bluntly.

Captain Tetjen frowned. 'Did you, sir? I suppose the sentry was asleep?'

'Er – yes, he was,' said the colonel, surprised. He had not even mentioned the presence of a sentry. 'Do you seriously believe that this dog is a – well, a hallucination, and not a flesh and blood creature?'

'I do, sir,' said the captain, 'and now I will tell you all I know about Mungo, and you will be able to judge for yourself. You know that I have been in the regiment all my life. In fact, I was born in it – my father was a sergeant in No. 3 Company. I have seen Mungo myself at least twenty times, and I know of others who have seen him many more times than that.'

'Surely,' the colonel persisted, 'it could still be a living dog that has attached itself to the regiment?'

'No, sir.' The captain shook his head. 'It's the *time*, you see. I've seen Mungo during the last fifty years, and my father saw him frequently long before I was born.'

'Fifty years. . . .' The colonel's bewilderment grew. 'But are you sure it's the *same* dog that's been seen over such a span of time?'

'I'm sure, sir. There couldn't be another dog with that large white streak on his flank, nor would you find one with the remarkable habit of keeping sentries awake, sober sentries, that is. For some reason Mungo doesn't like heavy drinkers. Apart from that, Mungo has saved many a man from punishment. To tell you the truth, sir, he came to my own rescue once. It was many years ago. My sister was married to one of the regiment, and naturally there were festivities. You know how these affairs go, sir. I drank more than was good for me that night, and when I mounted guard my head was a bit fuzzy and I dropped off into a light doze. I would have been caught if it hadn't been for Mungo. He must have known that it was a special occasion and that I did not drink very often.'

'How did he wake you?' the colonel asked with suspicion.

'He gave a short, sharp bark right against my ear. I jumped up, startled, just in time to see him vanish.'

'Tell me, captain, does Mungo only protect the men of our regiment?'

'Yes, sir, only the 20th. The story is that after the Battle of Fontenoy in 1745 a large black dog was found lying beside a dead officer. Although it had a terrible sabre wound in its side and was exhausted from loss of blood it would not leave its master's body. It even refused to leave the graveside when the officer was buried. The men were so moved by such faithfulness that they dressed the dog's wound and fed and tended it until it recovered.

'Then the men taught the dog to make a round of all the guards and sentries to make sure they were awake. When, after many years, the dog died it was buried with great ceremony – with full military honours, you might say. Since then the dog has repaid the kindness of the soldiers in the way you have seen for yourself.'

'The white streak on its flank is the sabre mark, I suppose,' said the colonel, almost convinced by the captain's obvious sincerity. But he would require much more proof before he was fully satisfied. 'I wonder someone has not fired at him!'

Captain Tetjen looked appalled. 'God forbid that I, or anyone, should do such a thing. The tale goes that a man did so once, and never had a moment's luck afterwards.'

The colonel was not convinced. 'But if it is really a ghost, a bullet could do it no harm.'

'Perhaps not, sir, but I'd rather not put it to the test. In any case, what would be the point? I believe in Mungo, so I have nothing to prove.'

'Yes, I see that,' the colonel answered thoughtfully. 'Perhaps one day I might believe in him too. . . . Thank you for your story, captain.'

Inside the besieged city during the days that followed, Colonel de Witt thought a lot about Captain Tetjen's story, but decided that he simply could not believe in ghosts, whether of dogs or humans. Tetjen is different, he told himself. He comes from peasant stock and accepts such things as ghosts as part of everyday life.

In order to settle the question one way or the other, however, the colonel carried a pistol, ready primed, whenever he went to inspect the sentries. If Captain Tetjen was right, then a bullet would pass through the animal and do no harm. If, as the colonel suspected, Mungo was a real dog who had been trained by the men to give them warning of an officer's approach, then the bullet would quickly put an end to its tricks. 'And a good thing too,' the colonel said to himself.

He was frankly disappointed not to see Mungo during his tours of duty. The men were less inclined to doze off while on guard, for the general himself had threatened severe disciplinary action against any sentry committing such an offence.

Colonel de Witt made no secret of his plan to put an end to the mysterious dog if he got the chance, and told his fellow officers in the mess.

'I'd like to take a pot-shot at Mungo myself,' grunted Major Rugen. 'If I thought I'd a chance of seeing him, I would try it. But I've never set eyes on the beast!'

'Your best chance is when Jokel Falck is on duty,' said one of the subalterns with a laugh. 'He'll soon forget the penalties threatened by the general. If it hadn't been for Mungo, Falck would have spent most of his soldiering days in the guard-room!'

'If I could catch him I'd put an ounce of lead into this mungo-jungo, or whatever his stupid name is,' the major muttered, returning to his drink.

Captain Tetjen stood up and looked at the major gravely. 'Better not, sir,' he said, and left the room, followed by some good-natured laughter.

A week later Colonel de Witt was passing the guard-room on his way to his quarters when a mounted orderly rode up, called out a file of the guard and gave them instructions to take a prisoner.

'What's the matter?' the colonel called.

'A sentry has been discovered asleep at his post, sir,' the orderly replied.

'Jokel Falck, eh?' exclaimed the colonel. 'Caught out at last. Well, I'm not surprised, though it looks as if Mungo has neglected his duty!'

'No, sir.' The orderly's voice was almost defiant. 'Mungo was there all right and would have roused the sentry, had not Major Rugen shot at the dog.'

'What, did he kill him?'

The orderly did not reply, but saluted and rode away. Colonel de Witt smiled to himself, and decided to ask the major himself what had happened.

But the colonel saw Major Rugen much sooner than he expected. It was barely daylight when he was awakened by his batman with the news that Major Rugen was outside and was very anxious to speak to him. 'I'm eager to speak to him myself,' the colonel yawned, 'but not as early as this. However, show him in at once.'

The colonel knew that something was wrong the moment the major entered. The familiar sneer was absent. He looked worried and ill.

'My dear fellow,' said the colonel kindly, 'whatever is the matter?'

The major tried to answer, but no words would come. He pulled out a handkerchief, collapsed into a chair and began to weep as freely as a child.

'Has something happened to your wife?' asked the colonel.

The major shook his head. 'No, no,' he moaned, 'it's my son, my poor Fritz!'

Colonel de Witt decided that Fritz must have been injured in a skirmish with the French. The boy was a private in the regiment, trying to earn his commission, and he knew the major's heart would break if anything happened to his son.

The major began to pull himself together. He took the handkerchief away from his eyes. 'If only I'd listened to Captain Tetjen!'

'What has happened to Fritz?' the colonel demanded again. 'And why is the captain involved?'

The major began his story in a slow, halting way, entirely foreign to his usual brusque manner.

'I was Field Officer yesterday. When I was going my rounds last night I asked my orderly which of the men were on guard. One of the names he mentioned was Jokel Falck, and that reminded me of our conversation about Mungo a few nights ago. I didn't expect to see the dog, as I had never done so before, but I loaded a pistol and put it in my pocket so that if anything happened I should be ready for it.

'I met the general as I was riding through the Place de Meyer. He rode with me and we talked about military matters. I had forgotten all about the dog, so you can imagine my surprise when we reached the rampart above the Bastion du Matte and I saw it trotting along below us! Even in the darkness I could see clearly the white streak on its flank. I knew that there was a sentry immediately below the rampart even though we could not see him. The dog was obviously on its way to warn the man of our approach. I grabbed my gun and fired, then I jumped off my horse to look over the bastion and catch a glimpse of the sentry. The general was completely taken by surprise, but he dismounted too and joined me. We caught the sentry all right. He had been awakened by the shot and was just crawling to his hands and knees.'

'What about the body of the dog?' the colonel asked.

'There was no body,' the major answered. 'There was neither sight nor sound of any dog. I hit him – I must have done. I could hardly have missed from where I was. The general said that there was no dog, that I must have been seeing things. He saw nothing, but I did – I did – and so did the orderly. . . .'

The major fell silent, lost in horrified memories of the night's activities. The colonel began to wonder if the major was quite sane. What had all this to do with his son?

'But where does Fritz come into all this?' he asked impatiently.

The major lifted up his tear-stained face. 'Don't you see? The sentry was Fritz – my son. If I had caught him I would have punished him, of course, but I was not alone. The general is determined to make an example of him. There is to be a court-martial this morning, and Fritz will be shot unless the general grants him a pardon. I beg you, as a friend as well as a superior officer, to intercede on my boy's behalf. . . .'

Colonel de Witt promised to do all in his power to save Fritz, but his efforts were in vain. The general listened politely but firmly rejected his plea. Being the son of an officer was a disadvantage for the unfortunate Fritz. Not only would it appear to be favouritism to spare him, but he was expected to be an example to all the other soldiers.

Fritz was found guilty and shot. His mother died soon after, heart-broken at the fate of her son. The major left the service after his wife's death, his own life in ruins.

The colonel never saw Mungo again, nor did he try to catch the dog on its errand of mercy. The subject was a barred topic in the mess. The only reference to Mungo was made in private by Captain Tetjen.

'Are you convinced?' he asked the colonel. He did not mention the dog's name, but the colonel knew what he was referring to.

'I was convinced *then*, I admit,' he answered, 'but now – well, I don't know what to think. *Can* one believe in ghosts?'

'Perhaps – perhaps not,' said the captain, shrugging his shoulders. 'But if you'll take my advice, sir, you'll leave *your* pistol in its holster in future!'

The Haunting Skull

SIR HENRY GRIFFITH was the owner of a large estate between Bridlington and Driffield in the East Riding of Yorkshire in the early 17th century. When he died he left all his property between his three daughters, who decided that the former house was too big and that they would have a new and smaller one built.

This was finished in 1628, a lovely mansion known as Burton Agnes Hall. The famous architect Inigo Jones had designed part of it, and the ceilings were encrusted with exquisite carvings, and paintings by Rubens hung on the walls.

The youngest of Sir Henry's daughters was Anne, and she was particularly interested in watching the new building grow and in planning what she and her sisters would do when they moved in. She loved the house right from the beginning, and was overjoyed when the builders and decorators had finished and they could say, 'It is ours. Our new home is ready at last.' Anne was sure that her future would be peaceful and happy at Burton Agnes Hall.

Soon after the sisters were installed, Anne received an invitation to visit some friends who lived not far away at Harpham Hall. At first she was reluctant to go because there was so much to do in the new house, but eventually she decided to accept the invitation. This would be a splendid chance to tell her friends all about the plans she had for making Burton Agnes Hall the loveliest house in Yorkshire.

She set off one afternoon with her sisters' warnings fresh in her mind. 'You must be very careful,' said one, 'the roads are very unsafe.'

'You know there are many beggars roaming the countryside,' said the other. 'I have heard of lonely travellers being robbed.'

'Have no fear,' replied Anne gaily. 'I have Patch with me and he would scare any stranger. He's the fiercest-looking dog in the district.'

'And the gentlest,' said the first sister in worried tones. 'I really don't like you going alone, Anne. Why not take one of the servants?'

'They are too busy getting the furniture straight and putting the pictures up,' Anne cried impatiently. 'I shall be all right, I tell you. Besides, it's such a short way. I shall be there in a quarter of an hour.' So, with her fawn-coloured dress billowing out behind her, she strode off, her dog at her heels.

She had travelled over half the distance and was enjoying the fresh breeze and the spring sunshine when two men stepped from behind a tree and stood in front of her, blocking the narrow lane.

'Excuse me, Miss,' said one of them. His tone was civil but there was an evil glint in his eye.

'What do you want?'

'I suppose you wouldn't care to help a couple of poor travellers on their way?'

'You are right, I would not,' Anne replied spiritedly. 'Besides, I have no money with me. Move aside and let me pass.'

The other man spoke. 'You have a very pretty ring on your finger. I daresay that would fetch a good price.'

Anne's eyes flashed with anger. 'That ring belonged to my mother. I will not give it to you. Get out of my way!'

'Mother or no mother,' the ruffian said gruffly, 'we mean to have it.'

The two men moved closer to her. She could see their dirty, unshaven faces and smell their ragged clothes. Only at that moment did she begin to feel afraid. 'I'll set my dog on you,' she cried. 'Patch, seize them! Bite them, Patch!'

Patch bounded up to one of the men and laid a stick at his feet. Then he sat back, tongue hanging out, tail wagging, ready to play his favourite game. The man gave a hoarse laugh, picked up the stick and flung it contemptuously over the hedge and into a field. Patch barked happily and scrambled through a hole after it.

'So much for your savage dog!' sneered the beggar. 'Come on, Miss, your ring.'

'No!' Anne cried desperately.

Suddenly they closed in on her. One of them grasped her wrist. She struggled furiously, managed to break away and started running down the lane. The men set off after her. She could sense them almost upon her, and half turning, she saw one of them raise a heavy club. A blinding pain shot through her head, then all went black.

Anne Griffith was not found until her friends from Harpham Hall sent out a search party, several hours after she should have arrived. She lay just as she had fallen, and her hair was matted with blood and dirt. Sitting near her was Patch, watching his mistress wonderingly.

Anne was conscious, but only just. The searchers carried her carefully to Harpham Hall and a doctor was called. When he had examined her he shook his head gravely. 'The injury is very serious. I fear she has not long to live.'

'I must go back home,' Anne managed to get out through dry lips. 'Please – please take me home – if I am to die I must die in the house I love.'

The doctor shrugged. 'It will make no difference where she

is,' he told Anne's friends. 'If she will die happier at home she might as well be there.'

So Anne was taken back to Burton Agnes Hall and lingered on for five more days. Most of the time she was unconscious, growing weaker every hour. Just before she died she spoke again. Her sisters leaned over her bed, straining to catch every whispered word.

'You must promise me,' Anne said, 'that when I die, though my body is put in the ground, my head will stay in this house. I should not rest if part of me were not here. I love this house more than anything else in the world. I must stay here! Promise me – do what you will with my body, but let my head remain. . . .' She lifted a weak hand. 'If you don't I shall haunt you for ever – I will make this house unfit to live in. . . .'

Her two sisters looked at one another. The same thought was in their minds. She does not know what she is saying – she is delirious – we had better humour her so that she can die happy.

'We promise,' they said.

Anne gave a tired smile. Her eyelids fluttered and she died.

The sisters did not refer again to Anne's last words, nor to the promise they had made, and she was buried in the family vault next to her parents.

A few days after the funeral the elder Miss Griffith was sitting at her desk writing letters when she heard a loud crash from her bedroom above, as though a large piece of furniture had been knocked over. 'Whatever are the servants doing!' she exclaimed, and laying down her pen she hurried upstairs to see what had happened.

There was nothing to see. No one was in the bedroom and every piece of furniture was in its accustomed place. She went from room to room on that floor and found nothing unusual. The servants were all downstairs, and as far as she could see no human agency had caused the crash. Puzzled, she went downstairs, sought out her sister and told her about the strange happening.

The next night the whole household was aroused by a series of violent noises – doors slamming, bells ringing, bumps, knocks, thuds and loud, unearthly groans. They seemed to come from every part of the house at once. The frightened sisters woke up all the servants. They searched the house in twos but could find nothing to account for the terrifying sounds. All was silent in the room they happened to be in, but as soon as they had left it the banging and groaning started again. As the first light of day broke greyly over Burton Agnes Hall the noises stopped. The two sisters and the servants, huddled together in groups in one of the downstairs rooms, gradually relaxed and began to breathe more freely. With many a backward glance they returned to their own rooms, and what was left of the night passed without incident.

At breakfast the two sisters sat facing each other. They were both grey-faced and drawn from lack of sleep and tortured minds. 'You know why we were plagued by those dreadful sounds?' one said, and the other replied:

'Yes, it was Anne's ghost come to haunt us.'

'She said she would make this house unfit to live in if her head were not kept here –'

'We broke our promise –'

'And Anne is keeping hers –'

The elder sister got up from the table. 'We must see the vicar,' she declared. 'He will advise us.'

The vicar heard the story and his advice was simple and direct. 'You must have Anne's grave opened,' he said, 'and her head must be brought back here. Only then will the noises cease.'

When the gravediggers opened the family vault and forced open the lid of Anne's coffin they found her body quite perfect. But her head, which had somehow become separated from the body, was already a skull, though she had only been buried a few days.

The skull was borne back to the house and reverently placed in a velvet-lined box on a table in Anne's bedroom. The door was locked and nobody was allowed to go near the room. Inside, as time passed, the dust gathered and the spiders spun their webs over the furniture and curtains. After the sisters' grief at Anne's tragic death had lessened, life in the house went on peacefully.

Years passed. One day, a new servant girl who knew nothing about the story of Anne Griffith, intrigued by the room with the locked door, found a key that fitted the lock. She poked an inquisitive head round the door, wrinkled her nose at the sour and musty smell, and tut-tutted at the sight of the dust that lay thick on everything. 'What this room needs is a good cleaning,' she muttered.

She advanced to the window and drew back the dingy faded curtain. She saw the wooden box on the table and peeped in. 'Oh, the nasty thing,' exclaimed the unimaginative girl, 'whatever is that doing here? I'll throw it away.'

She opened the window, picked up the skull and hurled it out, thinking it would fall on the soft earth below. But she flung it further than she had intended and it landed in a cart that was passing under the window on its way to the stables.

The girl's hand flew up to her mouth to check the scream she suddenly let out. At the moment the skull landed on the load of hay the cart stopped, the horse and driver froze into the stillness of death. They might all have been carved out of marble. One of the driver's hands rested loosely on a rein, the other was arrested in mid-air. The horse remained with one front leg raised in the act of stepping forward. The eyeless sockets of the skull gazed on the outside world and a groan issued from between the yellow grinning teeth.

The servant girl could not believe her eyes. 'They're bewitched!' she gasped. 'Something terrible and awful has happened.' She flew downstairs and met the housekeeper in the hall. 'Oh, Madam, come quickly, please come quickly!' She began to stammer. 'I – I was in the locked room – the skull – it's bewitched Sam Caunt and the horse – oh, what have I done – the skull. . . .'

'What on earth is the matter, you silly girl?' exclaimed the housekeeper. 'What are you trying to tell me?'

For answer the girl dragged her through the front door and round the corner of the house. 'Look!' She pointed with a shaking hand.

The housekeeper's face went white. 'Dear God,' she whispered, 'what will become of us now. . . .'

From behind them in the house came the sound of great bangings, as though a mighty wind were hurling itself against every door and smashing it open. Above that rose a wail so frightful that it seemed to freeze the blood in the two women's veins. For a moment they stood with trembling limbs and ashen faces. Then the housekeeper, breaking out of the trance of horror with a great effort, ran up to the low cart and plunged her hands over the side. With eyes shut and face averted she felt around till her hands closed on the marble-like coldness of Anne Griffith's skull.

The wailing in the house grew louder. The crashes were like thunderbolts falling. The scared faces of servants appeared at the windows. The housekeeper lifted the skull from the hay and held it in front of her as though its touch would contaminate her. Slowly, fearfully, like a sleepwalker, she carried it back into the house, up the stairs and into the room where it had lain for so many years. Carefully she placed it in its velvet-lined coffin. She backed out of the room, closed the door and collapsed on the landing outside.

The moment the skull found itself in its familiar home the

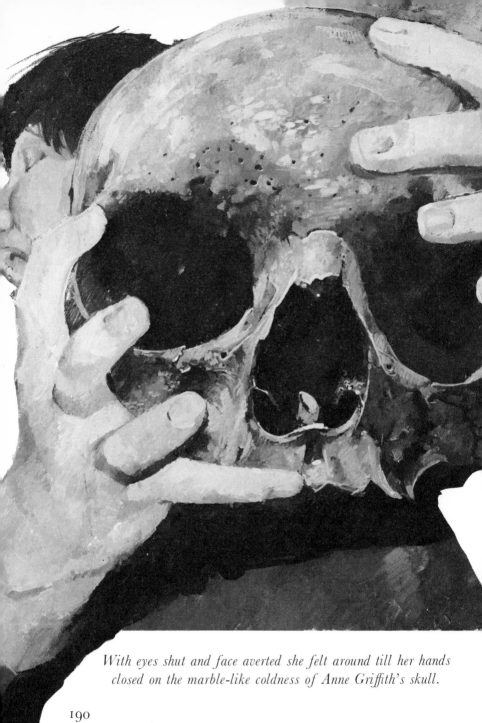

With eyes shut and face averted she felt around till her hands closed on the marble-like coldness of Anne Griffith's skull.

noises stopped. The horse outside put down its foreleg, the driver's hand fell to his side. Old Sam Caunt looked round him vacantly, shook his head in a puzzled way and drove on to the stables. The silence that succeeded the wild wailing was almost as eerie as the noise had been.

Life returned to normal at Burton Agnes Hall. Eventually the skull was bricked up in one of the walls of the house. Nobody knows exactly where it is now, so there is little fear that it will ever again be disturbed.

The ghost of Anne Griffith is quiet but still haunts her old home. She has been seen on many occasions as the girl who set out on a bright spring day to visit her friends. A small thin figure in a fawn dress has been seen coming through the garden, going up the steps and disappearing through the front door. Whenever she has been approached she has vanished.

Anne Griffith loved her new home when she was alive, and for over three hundred years she has continued to love it. Many families have lived in the house, have died or left, and are forgotten. But Anne Griffith lingers on, and her story will never be forgotten as long as Burton Agnes Hall still stands.

The Golden Guinea

Fish hill street is near London Bridge, and there, in 1780, lived a merchant with his wife and children. They had one maid, a woman from the country named Rebecca Griffiths who was very hardworking, meek in her manners, and very plain. But she seemed to get along all right without good looks, and was happy working for a family which liked her and treated her well.

One day a young man came to stay at the house in Fish Hill Street, a distant relation of the merchant, from the East Indies.

Carl Dupree was handsome, rich and gay, and poor, plain Rebecca Griffiths fell in love with him the moment he arrived; she tried to serve him in every way, expecting nothing in return but a smile and a few kind words. These the good-natured young man gave her willingly, for he liked everybody and wanted everybody to like him. No wonder Rebecca's feelings for him grew stronger with every day that passed. She forgot her plainness, and gradually she became convinced that he felt the same towards her. She worked harder than ever and sang round the house like a lark.

The day came when Carl Dupree's visit came to an end. Rebecca fully expected that he would make arrangements to see her again, and when he came to the kitchen to say goodbye she waited for him to say the words.

But all he said was, 'Thank you for all you have done for me, Rebecca,' and pressed a golden guinea in her hand.

Rebecca, speechless, could only gaze at the coin and then up at him.

'Now I must hurry – my chaise is waiting at the front door. Goodbye, Rebecca, God bless you.' And he left the room without a backward glance. Rebecca stood there motionless, all her hopes and dreams slipping away from her as the sound of horses' hooves died in the distance.

Then suddenly the shock and disappointment changed Rebecca into a mad woman. She started to scream and wave her arms about. Her eyes grew wild, and her already plain face was ugly and distorted with anguish. She tore off her apron and rushed through the house, out of the front door and into the street.

The chaise had almost disappeared – but Rebecca began to run after it calling loudly, her long hair streaming behind her, her arms stretched out in appeal. 'Come back! Oh, come back!'

By this time the other members of the household had been roused by the noise, and the merchant and his wife ran out after Rebecca, seized her arms and prevented her from pursuing the chaise. Rebecca fought the restraining hands fiercely, but eventually she was overpowered.

A doctor was called and she was pronounced insane. She was taken to the Hospital of the Star of Bethlehem, commonly called Bedlam, an asylum in Moorfields which stood on the site of what is now Liverpool Street Station.

Rebecca never recovered. She was an old lady when she died, still an inmate of Bedlam. In all the long years she was there she never once let the golden guinea out of her possession. Night and day she clutched it in one of her work-roughened hands. The coin grew dirty and tarnished, but Rebecca held on to it determinedly, and never more so than in her dying moments. 'Bury it with me,' were her last words.

When she was dead a dishonest and heartless keeper prised

open her cold stiff fingers and stole her richest treasure, her only wealth, the only reminder she had had of the young man who had driven away, not knowing that she loved him.

Rebecca Griffiths was buried in the asylum graveyard with not a soul to mourn her, and the authorities did not spare her memory a further thought – until Rebecca began to be seen again at nights, moving silently along the corridors, opening cell doors and peering in at the inmates. Her grey and ghostly figure could be seen disappearing round corners, dissolving into nothingness when a scared keeper put out a hand to ward her off. She spoke only a few words in a voice of deep sadness, 'Give me back my golden guinea . . . give me back my token. . . .'

Her appeal went unanswered. The thieving keeper had long since spent it. Besides, how could you return money to a ghost? Still Rebecca haunted the asylum and became a familiar figure in its dim and melancholy interior. Her pleading words continued to float hollowly in the air, and her ghost was as little regarded as she had been in life.

In 1812 a new Bedlam began to rise on St. George's Fields, near the junction of Lambeth Road and Kennington Road, and after three years the old building was pulled down. All the inhabitants were transferred – except one. The ghost of Rebecca Griffiths was never seen again. No more did her pitiful cry, 'Give me back my golden guinea . . . give me back my token. . . .' echo round the stone walls.

Somehow the ghost of the servant girl who went mad for love had found peace at last.

Ghostly Treasure

MISS BESWICK WAS AN OLD LADY who lived at Birchen Bower, near Hollinwood in Lancashire, in the 18th century. The house, quaint and gabled, was built in the form of a cross, and was set in beautiful surroundings. When Miss Beswick realized that she could not live for many more years a great fear possessed her mind and caused her much distress.

'I have a horror of being buried alive,' she told her doctor, 'and I am determined to prevent such a thing happening.'

'But, my dear lady,' Doctor White began, 'such a thing is hardly possible –'

'It happened to one of my brothers,' Miss Beswick told him obstinately, 'and I don't want it to happen to me. You see, he fell into a trance that lasted so long everybody thought he was dead. He was put in his coffin and the lid was being closed when one of the undertaker's men noticed the faint flicker of an eyelid. You can imagine the consternation! He was lifted out immediately and put back to bed where he remained in a trance for several days. Then he revived and lived for some years after. It was a terrible experience, and he never fully got over it.'

'Then we must see that such a thing does not happen to you,' the doctor said soothingly, as if speaking to a child, for he wanted to humour the old lady in her unlikely fancies.

But she would not be soothed so easily. 'How will you make sure?' she asked sharply, and the doctor, who was not prepared for such a question, puffed his cheeks out and pretended to consider. 'Well –' he began.

'You need not go on, doctor. I can see that you do not think I am serious. But I am, and I have thought of a plan. I want you to arrange that my body will never be put underground! You may put it in a coffin, but the lid must never be screwed down, and the coffin must never be buried. In that way,' finished Miss Beswick triumphantly, 'if I am not really dead I shall be able to rise from my coffin and walk again.'

'Good heavens!' cried the startled doctor, rising up from his chair, 'I've never heard of such a suggestion!'

'Then you've heard it now! Sit down, doctor, and I'll tell you the rest of my plan. I want you to arrange that my body, wherever it finds itself, is returned to Birchen Bower every twenty-one years, and is to remain there for a week.'

The doctor struggled for words. 'Such – such nonsense –'

'Perhaps you won't think what I'm going to say now is such nonsense. If you will do all this for me I will leave you all my property. There now, is that nonsense?'

The doctor made no further protest. He thought of all the land the old lady owned, the fields, woods and farms. Giving in to an eccentric whim would be a small price to pay to gain possession of such wealth. Besides, he told himself, she would never know if it were not possible to do what she wanted.

Miss Beswick seemed to be reading his thoughts for she gave a small cackling laugh. 'And if you don't fulfil all the conditions of my will I'll come back and haunt you!'

The doctor shivered. There was something witch-like about his old patient. Perhaps she *could* haunt him. He decided to put all thoughts of disobeying her right out of his mind.

Miss Beswick lived for many years after making her pact with the doctor, and when she did die, Doctor White had her body embalmed with tar, covered with bandages, put in an open coffin with the face exposed, and for many years kept it

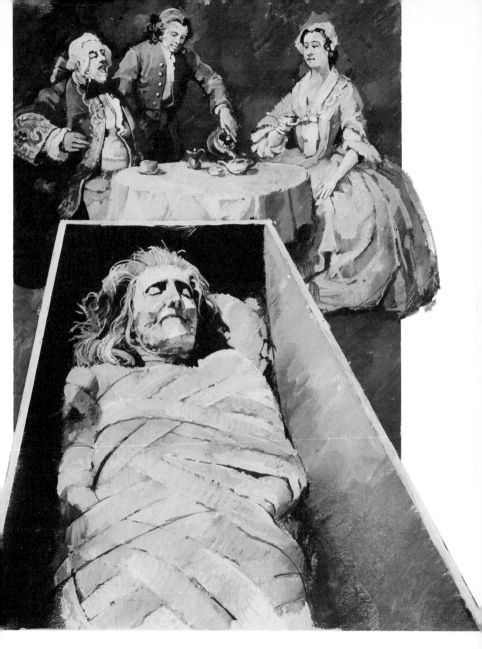

Doctor White had her body put in an open coffin and for many years kept it at his home.

at his home.

After his own death, the body in the coffin somehow landed up in the rooms of the Manchester Natural History Society in Peter Street, and stayed there on view until 22 July, 1868, a hundred years after her death, where it became an object of great popular interest. In 1868 the Society's exhibits were being rearranged, and it was decided that the poor wizened remains of the long forgotten old lady should be properly buried at last. Now they rest in Harpurhey Cemetery, in Manchester.

But before that happened, Miss Beswick's ghost had been active for many years. It had not haunted Doctor White because he had obeyed her instructions, but it had been a source of trouble to certain of her relations who had refused her dying request, and it happened like this.

In 1745, Scottish rebels under Prince Charlie had reached Lancashire on their way south. Miss Beswick was afraid that the intruders would seize all her money so she got together all the cash she could collect quickly and buried it in various places about the premises – where, nobody ever knew. The invading Scotsmen did not in fact reach Birchen Bower, but Miss Beswick could never be persuaded to tell her relatives where the hidden treasure was.

When she was very old and could no longer manage her affairs she retired to a little stone cottage which stood on the edge of a stream that flowed through the gardens of Birchen Bower, and was looked after by some of her family. Then the time came when she knew the end was very near. 'Carry me back to Birchen Bower,' she pleaded. 'I must die in my old house. Then I'll tell you where I hid the money.'

'Yes, we will,' they promised, 'tomorrow.'

The next day she asked again. 'Please take me home.'

'Tomorrow,' they said again.

But Miss Beswick's 'tomorrow' never came. She became

suddenly worse and died. Her secret died with her and her relations were never able to lay hands on the hidden hoard.

Although her mummified body lay in Doctor White's home, her ghost haunted Birchen Bower. Her coffin was taken to her old home every twenty-one years and put in a granary over one of the barns according to her instructions to the faithful doctor. And there it stayed for a week. When it was time for it to be taken back it was found that the horses and cows were loose, and sometimes a cow would be found in the hay loft, a place where it was impossible for an animal to get of its own accord.

By this time the house had been divided into several flats. One family grew so familiar with the little ghost in the black silk gown that they were never frightened when it made its occasional appearances. They heard a rustle of silk at the door, saw it glide through the room and go straight into the parlour. It would always disappear at one particular flag-stone in the floor. 'Here she is again,' one person would remark to another, 'and there she goes!'

In another part of the house a tenant had a treadle-lathe for wood-turning. Sometimes he would go into his workroom and see the lathe busily turning, being worked by an invisible presence.

In the 19th century most of Birchen Bower was pulled down. Only the southern wing was left standing, and the rooms there were taken over by handloom weavers and their families, victims of a depression caused by the high price of flour and a scarcity of bread. They too became used to the ghost of Miss Beswick, and were not upset by her appearance or disappearance in the parlour by the flagstone in the floor.

One day a weaver nicknamed 'Joe at Tamer's' decided to put up a loom in the parlour for one of his children to learn to weave. He prised up a stone in order to dig the treadle-hole and was surprised when his iron bar hit against something that was not the dry earth he expected. He groped about the space and pulled out a tin vessel. The lid was rusty and difficult to get off, and when at last he succeeded he was staggered to find it full of gold pieces.

'The old lady's treasure!' he gasped, and decided to say nothing to anybody else in the house. He hurried off to Manchester as soon as he could to a goldsmith named Oliphant in St. Anne's Square. There he sold each piece for three pounds ten shillings. Joe and his family were able to live in comfort for many a day, stinted for neither food nor clothing, which made everybody marvel at their prosperity when the rest of the weavers were so poor.

Years passed before the source of Joe's wealth was discovered, and the tin vessel is said to be still kept by his descendants.

But did the weaver discover the whole of the treasure? Miss Beswick continued to haunt Birchen Bower even after the money was found. She forsook the house and the parlour, however, and was seen in the open near the old well by the brookside, in the large barn which had the initials of the Beswick family carved on the front, or near a pool from which her horses used to drink.

Sometimes, on a dark winter's night, there would be strange unearthly noises in the barn, as if the devil were holding a party there, and a red glare of glowing heat would show through the cracks and crevices, as though the interior were on fire. Neighbours would knock up the farmer and tell him his barn was on fire, and they would all rush to see what was happening. But as soon as the door was opened and before the premises could be searched the noises and the lights disappeared. Everything was in order, and the puzzled men would retire to talk over yet another of the old lady's tricks.

The last time Miss Beswick was seen was about eighty years

ago. A farm worker was going to the well to get a pail of water but when he got there he stopped short. In front of him was a tall lady, wearing a black silk dress and a white frilled cap. It was dusk and her outline was dim and uncertain. But the man could see that her attitude was threatening by the streams of angry blue light that flashed from her eyes. Slowly she moved towards him, one arm raised menacingly. The farmhand dropped his bucket and fled. . . .

Does the rest of Miss Beswick's treasure still lie somewhere around Birchen Bower? Is it hidden under the floor of the barn, down the well or beneath the water of the horse pool? Was she trying to guard these places from inquisitive strangers when she was seen there, or was she trying to tell people where it could be found? If the ghost of the old lady ever appears again perhaps it will lead whoever sees it to an even richer store than the poor weaver found.

Corpse-candle

MANY YEARS AGO, in a village in North Wales, lived two cousins, Tom Llewellyn and Evan Pugh. They had grown up together on neighbouring farms, but when Tom was eighteen and Evan sixteen, the Pughs moved to another village eleven kilometres away, and so the cousins were separated.

The two lads missed each other very much. Together they had fished from dawn till dusk, and together they had made boats and sledges. Now Tom no longer found it fun to go off on fishing expeditions in the winding mountain streams, and Evan lost interest in making things from wood.

'It's no good you moping, see,' Tom's mother would say to him, 'that won't bring Evan back. You must make the best of it.'

And Evan's mother would say, 'Why don't you make new friends here? There are plenty of young people in the village.'

But it wasn't the same thing at all, and after a time it was arranged that each weekend the boys would visit each other in turn. It was a good arrangement, not only because it brought the friends together but also because each visit seemed like a holiday at the end of a week's hard work on the farm.

One autumn weekend it had been Evan's turn to visit Tom. They had had two grand days together with the lovely countryside bathed in cold, crystal sunshine, but now it was time for Evan to begin his eleven-kilometre walk home. As it was the custom in Wales for a host to walk part of the way with his departing guest, Tom wrapped a thick scarf round his neck and called to tell his mother that they were leaving.

'Goodbye, Evan bach,' Mrs. Llewellyn called back, 'safe home with you now.'

'Goodbye, Auntie Gweno,' said Evan, 'see you again in two weeks. And thank you for a nice time.'

The boys turned left on the road to Evan's village. They chatted as they walked and made plans for the next weekend when Tom would visit Evan. Slowly the sun sank in the sky as they walked along, and the thick, jagged clouds faded into a dark blue-black until it was difficult to see ahead.

'You'd better go back now, Tom,' Evan said at last, 'you must have come three kilometres.'

'I'll come as far as the chapel at the cross-roads,' said Tom.

As they approached the chapel and passed the sinister-looking graveyard edged with groping trees, both boys fell silent, and Evan shuddered.

'Take my scarf if you're cold,' Tom suggested. 'You have further to go than me.'

'I'm not cold,' Evan replied, 'but I feel strange – eerie-like. It must be the graveyard, though I've passed it before and never felt anything.'

Tom chuckled. 'Those trees look like great ghosts stretching out their long arms specially to frighten you,' he said, and waved his arms over Evan's head, moaning weirdly. His cousin laughed, making a lunge at Tom, who dodged and ran through the low hedge surrounding the graveyard.

Evan could only just make out Tom's form as he dashed away into the darkness but he followed the direction of his running feet. No sooner had he set foot on the grass beyond the hedge, however, than he was brought to a halt by Tom's hand urgently gripping his arm and Tom's voice whispering. 'Stay still, for heaven's sake, stay still! Look!'

Evan froze to the spot. 'What is it, Tom?'

On the far side of the graveyard, still and menacing, was a strange ghostly light, bluish in colour. As the two boys watched, it seemed very, very slowly to flicker into life. Evan sucked in his breath sharply and repeated his question. 'What is it, Tom?'

Tom answered, his voice slow and quavering, 'The *canwyll corph* – the corpse-candle. It comes when someone is going to die – to warn them.'

Evan felt a thrill of horror. 'But who is holding the candle?'

'No one,' Tom said, 'that is – no one real. But it has the face of the one who is going to die.'

The light slowly moved among the graves. Evan, panic rising in him, muttered, 'Come on, Tom, let's go – quickly. It's coming this way . . . please, Tom.'

Tom's grip on his cousin's arm tightened. 'No, stay,' he said, 'it can't hurt us. It isn't coming here. It's taking the route the dead body will take to the grave.' He fell silent for a moment, then added, 'I wonder who it is. Shall we try to find out?'

Evan was shivering violently with terror. He wanted to run all the way home and find himself in a warm, lighted room with friendly people around him. 'No – no – let's go –'

Tom did not seem in the least frightened. 'Don't be afraid! Look, it's not coming this way. It's the first one I've seen, though Gareth Price has often talked about them. If you can get to the door of the church before the light goes inside, you can see who the corpse will be. Will you come with me?'

Evan could only produce a strangled croak. 'No – no, Tom! I don't want to see it and I don't want to know who's going to die.'

Tom gave a laugh. 'All right, if you're too frightened I'll go alone.'

'Don't, please, Tom, don't. Let's go. I *am* frightened. Come on, let's get out of here.'

'No fear!' his friend exclaimed. 'I'm not letting a chance like this go. I never really believed old Gareth, but this will prove it. For the last time, are you coming?'

'No,' said Evan. 'It's evil, I know it is.'

'Then wait for me on the road. I'll go alone.' Tom released Evan's arm and took a step towards the church. Evan darted back, leaped over the hedge and fell panting with relief on the grass verge of the road.

Tom, following the progress of the ghostly light, crept stealthily towards the door of the church. He felt no fear, only intense curiosity. His reason told him that a faint bluish light could not hurt him. He was superstitious but he was no coward. If the legend about corpse-candles were true he might see something horrifying but harmless. After all, he told himself, Saint David had brought about the candles as a friendly warning so that a person might not be taken unawares by the approach of death.

At last he reached the church porch and was surprised to find the big doors wide open. He wondered whether to go inside the porch but decided against it. Dangerous or not, it would be safer to be in a position to run away as soon as the candle had passed by. Then he saw that the flame was almost upon him. Slowly it moved around the last gravestone and then along the path towards the church door. Tom held his breath. Suddenly he felt cold, numb to the ends of his fingers. It was coming. . . . He stared as though hypnotized as the light came nearer and nearer. It was at the porch. It turned to enter the church. At one moment it was just a flickering blue flame – then it became a horribly leering face, a face that Tom felt he knew and yet could not put a name to. He gave a shriek that echoed round the empty, night-shrouded graveyard and began to run blindly between the gravestones, tripping and stumbling in his anxiety to get away from the grinning horror.

At one moment it was just a flickering blue flame – then it became a horribly leering face.

Somehow he managed to blunder over the hedge and on to the road where Evan was waiting.

'What is it? What happened?' Evan asked.

Now it was Tom who could not talk from fear. 'N – nothing,' he stammered. 'Don't ask me – it was nothing. All wrong – Gareth is a fool – it was nothing –'

'Then why did you yell?'

'I didn't – that is, I don't know. Go home, Evan, go home now.'

'Yes, I'd better. All this has made me late. Are you all right, Tom?'

'Yes,' said Tom, 'I'm all right. Go on – good night.'

'Good night,' said Evan. 'See you next week.'

There was a pause as Tom stood still on the road. Then he answered, with an odd urgency in his tone, 'Yes, next week. . . .'

The two boys parted, Evan running quickly towards the comfort of his home, Tom walking slowly and thoughtfully towards his.

For the next few days life went on as usual for Tom. He had recovered from his shock, though the memory of what he had seen was with him all the time. Sometimes he would stop working and gaze blankly in front of him until his father spoke to him sharply. On the Friday morning he began to feel ill. Usually, he left for Evan's village immediately after work on the Friday, but by the afternoon he had fainted three times, and after the last attack he found that he could not walk.

'It's a fever you've got,' his mother told him. 'The treacherous weather has given you a chill. To bed with you, my boy. There'll be no visit to Evan Pugh this week.'

Tom felt too weak to protest and submitted readily to being helped to bed. He had no wish to eat or do anything but lie still, his eyes wide open, staring at the whitewashed wall of his bedroom. In a weak voice he begged his mother, 'Please send a message and ask Evan to come.'

'No, Tom. You are not well enough. Just you rest there, and you'll be up and about in a few days.'

'Please,' he insisted anxiously. 'I *must* see him.'

'But you saw him last week. He'll understand. You are ill and it won't help for you to be worried by visitors. We'll get word to him and explain,' his mother said, in a final way.

Tears welled into Tom's eyes. He was far too tired and weak to argue any more. All he could do was to say again, in a pleading whisper, 'Please. . . .'

Mrs. Llewellyn looked at her son's white face and enormous dark eyes and relented. Perhaps it would help Tom to get better if Evan could see him. 'All right,' she said. 'He'll come, just try to sleep now.'

Tom's father was only too eager to drive over to the Pughs in his pony-cart, so it was only a matter of an hour or two before an anxious Evan ran into the farmhouse to question Mrs. Llewellyn about what had been happening. Then he tiptoed into Tom's room. Looking down at the figure in the bed he was shocked. His cousin seemed to have shrunk to half his former size. The old husky, energetic Tom had disappeared; this frail, ashen-faced invalid was almost a stranger.

Then Tom opened his eyes, and gradually they focussed on Evan and a bitter half-smile appeared on his lips. He began to speak but the words were so faint that Evan had to sink to his knees by the bedside and put his ear close to Tom's mouth.

He managed to catch the merest wisp of sound disturbing the heavy silence of the room. 'Evan – tell no one this – last week – the light in the graveyard – you asked me what I had seen –'

Tom's head fell back on the pillow.

'Yes?' Evan asked urgently.

After a long time Tom spoke again. 'I saw – that the light –

had a face – horrible – like a corpse – I didn't realize at the time – but it was my own face. . . .'

The voice faded away. Evan rose to his feet and looked down with horror at the dead features of the boy who had seen his own corpse-candle.

Ghost at Halloween

The preston family, after six years in India, arrived back in England at the beginning of an autumn of rain and gales, of brown leaves falling and pools of water gleaming on roads and pavements.

Their first task was to find somewhere to live that was convenient for Mr. Preston's work – he was an engineer whose firm's headquarters were at Alton in Hampshire. Mrs. Preston insisted that it must be in the country; she wanted the soft glowing greens of the countryside after the hot vivid colours of India, and they finally decided on a dilapidated old farmhouse. It was far enough from the nearest village to satisfy Mr. Preston too, who wanted nothing that would remind him of the bazaars of Bombay.

The first month was spent in furnishing and decorating the farmhouse, and making it warm enough to withstand the cold blasts of winter winds. Then the three Preston children, who had been staying with their grandmother in London, arrived, and the family was complete.

Laura was the eldest child. She was nearly fourteen, a quiet, gentle, rather plain girl whose chief love was reading, and who usually preferred being on her own. But she was no hermit. She could sparkle and laugh like any girl of her age when she wanted to. She had developed a successful method of dealing with her rowdy young brothers, George, aged nine, and Thomas, three years younger, by playing football better than they did, beating them at Monopoly, and making model aeroplanes that would really fly.

One day during the last week in October the family were having breakfast when Mrs. Preston looked up from her morning paper and announced brightly, 'Do you know what Saturday is?'

'Yes,' said Thomas, 'the day before Sunday. Can I have some more toast?'

'*Please*,' his mother added automatically. 'No, the date, I mean. It's 1st November – Laura's birthday. She'll be fourteen!' She turned to her daughter. 'I'm afraid we've been so busy there's been no time to think of anything. We can't even give a party because we don't know anybody in the village yet.'

'I don't mind,' Laura said, smiling good-naturedly. 'When you get to my age parties aren't all that important. We can have a special tea for ourselves.'

'I'm sorry to put a damper on the idea,' Mr. Preston said, folding his paper and getting up from the table, 'but I have to go into Alton on Saturday morning and probably won't be back until very late. I flatly refuse to let you have a party without me!'

'Oh, dear,' Mrs. Preston murmured vaguely.

'Look out, Daddy,' Laura said, 'I think Mother's going to have one of her ideas.'

Mrs. Preston sat up briskly. 'Of course! Why didn't I think of it before? We'll celebrate Laura's birthday the night before. Do you know what Friday is?'

Mr. Preston chuckled. 'Here we go again!'

'The day *before* Saturday,' Thomas said wearily.

But Laura's dark eyes were gleaming. 'I know – it's Halloween!'

'That's right, dear, and we'll have a Halloween party. Now that we're living in the country we must keep up the old customs.'

'What's Halloween?' George asked. 'Will there be lots to eat?'

Laura leaned forward eagerly. 'It's the night that's all mixed up with ghosts and witches and bonfires. In the old days witches used to hold one of their sabbaths at Halloween, and people were frightened and lit fires to keep them away. And they'd make a lantern out of a hollowed-out turnip and put a candle inside and stick it on a post –'

'I say, that sounds super,' George said. 'Can I make one?'

Laura was remembering all she had read about Hallow-tide. 'We'll play Duck-apple and Snap-apple, and we'll put hazelnuts on the bars of the grate.'

'What for?' Thomas wanted to know, but Laura did not reply.

'We'll tell ghost stories round the fire,' she went on, 'and stick apple pips on our cheeks and toss the peel over our shoulders, and we'll put a thimbleful of salt on a plate to see who's going to die during the year –'

'We will *not!*' Mrs. Preston said firmly.

'And we'll put a sprig of rosemary and a new coin under our pillows to see who we're going to marry –'

'I'm going,' Mr. Preston said, 'before things get really complicated. . . .'

During the next few days preparations for Halloween went on apace, with Laura and her mother full of enthusiasm. Mr. Preston regarded the proceedings with amused tolerance, and the boys, in spite of themselves, were gradually drawn into helping. They were mollified by the unusual amount of cooking their mother was doing, and grew excited when big tins were filled with sausage rolls, ginger cake, and a strange kind of biscuit made of oatmeal, butter and treacle. Laura said it was called parkin and was always eaten at that time of the year.

When Halloween arrived the excitement had reached its

peak. Laura, in a sweet party dress, looked almost pretty. The boys had brushed their hair for the occasion. Mr. Preston had come back early from Alton, bringing bags of apples and nuts, and Mrs. Preston, humming happily, was setting the supper table in the sitting-room.

They decided to start the party with Duck-apple and Snap-apple, and to play them in the kitchen because of the mess that was likely to be made. Mr. Preston had filled a large tin bath with water and had put in several apples, which floated lazily on the surface, occasionally bobbing up and down as if impatient for the game to begin. Then Laura and the boys knelt before the bath, their hands behind their backs, and at a signal from their father they tried to grab an apple in their teeth and take a bite out of it. . . .

Thomas won that game, apparently because he was not frightened to push his face right under the water and pursue the apple as though he were a submarine.

After the spilt water had been mopped up they played Snap-apple. For this game Mr. Preston had fixed an apple and a candle on either end of a stick which was suspended from a beam by a string. He lit the candle and swung the stick gently in a clockwise direction, then the children took turns to try to grab the apple in their teeth as it swung towards them, avoiding both the candle flame and the grease which spattered out. George got his eyebrows singed and Thomas received blobs of grease on his nose. Laura managed to steer clear of both hazards and sank her teeth in the sweet flesh. 'I've won!' she gasped, and skipped round the kitchen triumphantly.

Mrs. Preston looked at the clock. 'Supper,' she announced. 'Time's getting on and we mustn't miss the rest of the rituals.' She ushered the family into the sitting-room, where the boys made an immediate dive towards the table.

Laura was the last to leave the kitchen. She looked round

the untidy room, smiling reminiscently at the fun they had had, and was just about to turn towards the door when she stopped suddenly. The stick to which the apple and candle were attached, which had slowed to a standstill after the game, was now swinging again, quickly but jerkily, as though someone had clumsily set it in motion.

Laura felt her heart beat quicker, and she backed to the door, still staring at the jerking stick. She closed her eyes and shook her head. When she looked again the stick was still. She decided that a sudden gust of wind had been the cause, and then forgot all about it.

Supper was a noisy and hilarious meal. Mrs. Preston prophesied upset stomachs the next day, but smiled indulgently as the plates were rapidly emptied. When even George refused the last piece of parkin they drew up their chairs round the roaring fire. Mr. Preston switched out all the lights except for a small one on the chimney-piece, and they sat in a cosy circle of light, secure from the shadows licking at its edges and the wind rattling at the windows.

Laura gave a quiet sigh of happiness. This is how I would like to be always, she thought – all of us together, with nothing to frighten us. . . . The heat began to make her drowsy, and once or twice her eyelids dropped.

Mr. Preston had put five hazelnuts on one of the bars of the old-fashioned grate, and the others fixed their eyes on them. 'Watch to see which of them pops first,' Mrs. Preston said softly, 'and we'll see who is going to get married first. . . .'

George stirred restlessly. 'Who's going to tell us a ghost story?' he demanded.

'Not me!' said Mr. Preston. 'I don't know any!'

'Nor me,' said Mrs. Preston. 'I always get the plot mixed up. It'll have to be Laura – she's always reading.'

Thomas edged nearer to his father. 'Don't make it too

scary, will you, Laura?'

Suddenly Laura's mind was a blank. It wasn't that she didn't know any ghost stories, it was as if something had taken all power of thought away from her. There was a lightness in her head. She felt as though she were outside herself, unable to think or speak for herself. In spite of the heat she shivered.

Her mother was looking at her curiously. 'Are you all right, dear?'

Laura did not appear to hear her. Words were forming in her mind, but they were being put there, they were not her own. Slowly, dreamily, she began to speak.

'What I'm going to tell you about happened here, in this house, fifty years ago, and it happened at Halloween. . . . There was a girl called Meg, who lived here with her father and mother. They were a very happy family. Meg was nearly fourteen –'

'Just like you,' George interrupted.

'Sh!' said his mother, still gazing at Laura in a puzzled way.

'Early in the evening,' Laura went on, 'she was waiting for her father to return from the market – he had promised to take her to a neighbouring farm for a Halloween party. She kept running to the window to see if she could see him coming up the drive. She was wearing her best party dress covered with flowers, and her hair had been specially put into ringlets for the occasion. . . .'

'Just like you again,' Thomas interrupted. 'I hope you're not going to be the ghost, Laura.'

'Meg was specially excited because the following day was her birthday, and she knew that she was going to receive most of her presents at the party,' Laura went on. 'When seven o'clock came and her father had not returned, Meg grew impatient. She kept asking what could have detained him.

but her mother, busy in the kitchen, could give no reason. All she could do was advise her daughter to be patient. Then it was eight o'clock, then half past. Meg was on the verge of tears. The party would have started without her – she was going to miss all the fun. At nine o'clock there was a knock at the front door. Meg flew to answer it. A stranger was standing there, stammering out some dreadful news. Her father's horse had stumbled just as he had left the market town; he had been thrown off and killed. . . .'

'Laura,' her mother said, 'do you think you ought –?'

Laura did not turn her gaze from the fire, whose dancing flames seemed to have a hypnotic effect on her. 'The night was endless,' she continued in the same dreamy voice. 'Inside Meg felt frozen, and she could not cry. But something told her that more sorrow was to come. Her mother took the news badly and moaned and sobbed all night long. Nothing that Meg could do or say would comfort her. Nor did she improve in the days that followed, for the shock had turned her brain and it was as though she had drowned in grief. In the end she had to be taken away and Meg was sent to stay with an aunt and uncle in London. Although they were kind and meant well, they could not give her the deep affection that her father and mother had always given her. Then too, she hated the town and longed to be back in the country. Before many months had passed she became very ill. She died the next Halloween – the day before her birthday. . . .'

Laura's voice died away. She sat in her chair, her hands folded in her lap, as still as though she, too, had no life left in her.

'But where's the ghost?' George said indignantly. 'I don't call that much of a story!'

Laura stirred slightly. 'Meg has been seen occasionally, but only at Halloween, and only when there have been children in the house. She comes to share their happiness and only wants to be treated as a friend. But everyone who sees her is frightened, and their fear shuts her out. Sadly she disappears until she hears children's voices again.'

Laura's face was paper-white. Mrs. Preston got up and hurried over to her. 'Whatever is the matter, my dear?'

For a moment Laura looked at her mother as though she were a stranger, then the deadness went out of her eyes and she gave a wan smile. 'I'm sorry, Mother, have I been asleep?'

Mrs. Preston and her husband exchanged anxious looks. 'Asleep? No – you've been telling us a story –' Mrs. Preston began. 'About a girl called Meg –'

Laura put her hand to her brow. 'Oh, yes, of course.' She gave an embarrassed laugh. 'Stupid of me to have forgotten.' Then she yawned heavily. 'Oh, dear, I'm so tired all of a sudden.'

Her mother spoke firmly. 'Then bed for you at once, and if your colour hasn't come back in the morning I shall call the doctor!'

'Not on my birthday, *please!*' Laura stood up and began to move towards the door. 'Good night, all.' She yawned again. 'Sorry to leave the party, but I can't keep my eyes open.'

But George for one was paying no attention to his sister. He was looking hard at the grate and frowning in a puzzled way. 'Dad, how many nuts did you put on the bar?'

'Five, of course,' Mr. Preston replied. 'One for each of us.'

George pointed to the grate. 'Well, there are six now. Where did the other one come from?'

Laura slipped out of the room while they were deciding that their father had miscounted, and slowly climbed the stairs to her little bedroom. Moonlight was struggling through the leaden window-panes; it fell in pale lozenges over the flowered counterpane on the bed, the faded carpet and the polished oak furniture. For some reason Laura did not switch on the light. She went to the dressing-table and looked at her reflection in the mirror. A pale, thoughtful face, framed by dark hair, stared back at her. Automatically she picked up her silver-backed hairbrush, and with long strokes began to brush her hair.

Glancing down she saw an apple on the dressing-table. She smiled, deciding it must be a present from one of her brothers. She picked it up with her free hand and began to nibble the apple as she continued brushing. The old superstition about seeing the face of one's future husband at Halloween stirred in her mind as she continued to stare into the mirror.

Suddenly she gave a little gasp. A mist had crept over the mirror and she could no longer see herself. But there was no mist outside. The moon was still bright, and all the objects on the dressing-table stood out clearly. As she stared, the mist slowly faded and the mirror was as clear as before. But now she could see, not only her own face, but another just behind her shoulder. . . .

She blinked several times, but the face would not go away, and Laura was surprised to find that she was not at all frightened. She felt, in fact, as though she were on the verge of recognizing someone she had once known well. It was not long before recognition came. 'Meg. . . .' she whispered.

A smile appeared on the face at her shoulder. 'Yes, I'm Meg – and you are Laura.'

Laura made as though to turn round but Meg, with a quick indrawing of breath, said, 'Don't, Laura – don't turn round – or I shall have to go. Keep looking in the mirror. . . .'

'Somehow – I thought you would come tonight,' Laura said. 'You used me to tell your story, didn't you? I didn't know what was happening at the time, but now I think I understand.'

Meg nodded. 'I can only appear when there are children in the house, and only at Halloween. I tried to join in your

*She blinked several times, but the face would not
go away.*

games – it's such a long time since I was able to play. And I put the apple here so that the old Halloween ritual would help you to see me.'

'Can you stay?' Laura asked hopefully. And her eyes were shining.

Meg looked back at her out of the mirror, and the smile deepened.

'Tell me you can stay,' Laura begged.

'Not for long. But even a little time is wonderful. To talk to someone like you – to know that I have made a friend – such happiness will last me a long long time. Everyone else who has seen me in the past has screamed and rushed away. I'm so glad you didn't decide to do that, Laura.'

A sudden thought struck Laura. 'It's your birthday tomorrow!'

'Yours too,' said Meg. 'Oh, I know so much about you – I've been here ever since you came to live in the house.'

'And you'll be here even though I can't see you!' Laura exclaimed. 'I shall be friends with a ghost! You don't mind me calling you that, I hope?'

A chuckle came from behind her. 'Why should I? That's what I am! And don't forget, I shall see you again at Halloween next year – and every year while you are still here. Oh, Laura, I don't think I shall ever be lonely again. . . .'

'Nor me,' said Laura. 'Meg, there's so much I want to talk about –' She forgot Meg's warning and span round, eager with questions – but her ghostly friend had disappeared. A faint 'Laura . . .' sighed in the air, then there was silence.

Laura turned back to the mirror and stared into it as though she might conjure up Meg's ghost again, but all she saw was her own distressed face. . . .

Laura awoke the next morning with an aching head. She went over to the dressing-table and listlessly she took up her hairbrush. Then something unfamiliar caught her eye, and a little cry broke from her. She picked up the object. It was a gold locket on a thin gold chain, and it gleamed dully in the morning light. She pressed the tiny catch and the front of the locket sprang open. Inside was a photograph browned by age. She looked at it closely. It was Meg, her hair falling about her round face in ringlets. She was smiling, her eyes glinting with excitement. She must have looked like that as she prepared for that Halloween party all those years ago, Laura thought.

Suddenly Laura's sadness fell away. 'A happy birthday, Meg!' she whispered. 'Thank you for your present. I'll keep it always. It shall be my greatest treasure.' Then, as she slipped the slender gold chain round her neck, she murmured, half-smiling, 'See you again *next* year!'

The Ghost in the Barrel

SOMEWHERE ON DARTMOOR stands a large house which was once the vicarage belonging to a near-by church. Even though it is now deserted and in a state of disrepair passers-by are often curious about its odd shape. Parts of the house are obviously later additions, others are as primitive as the cottages in the village, and the styles fail to match harmoniously.

People who venture into it find one feature more than any other that makes them wonder at the quirky ways of some past occupant, for in the main room, which originally was large, high and elegant, each of the four corners has been filled in with a mixture of stones and mortar. This makes the shape crudely octagonal rather than rectangular, and from above the effect is like a snapshot mounted in an album.

These cut-off corners serve no useful purpose, and anyone who wished to renovate the house could have them removed with ease – if he could find a builder who would do the job. To find such a man, however, he would have to travel far afield, for no man who lives in the village would lift a finger to help and would be reluctant to explain why. But a persistent questioner might, in time, elicit the details of a strange story. . . .

About a hundred years ago a new parson named Graves came to the village. Having a wife and three children he soon decided that the vicarage, which at that time was little bigger than the cottages near by, needed to be enlarged. He wanted a study for himself, bedrooms for the children and the servants, and a larger sitting-room to replace the poky one where there was hardly room to swing a cat. The alterations were started within a week of his arrival, and stone-masons and carpenters worked hard to get them done. Mr. and Mrs. Graves were impressed at the speed the new wings went up, and the villagers regarded their go-ahead vicar with approval.

On the evening of the day that the last workman had taken his tools and gone, leaving the vicar and his family in proud possession, things began to happen. . . .

Mr. Graves sat by the fire in his handsome sitting-room with its grey walls and red velvet curtains, making notes for his next sermon. Opposite him Mrs. Graves was busy knitting. The children, tired by the day's excitements, were in bed. Suddenly the companionable silence was broken by a swishing sound, as though someone wearing a floor-length garment had walked across the room, and a cloth that covered a small table in one corner whisked into the air, sailed across to the vicar and fell squarely over his head. At the same time his wife's workbasket toppled to the floor, its contents spilling over the hearthrug, and the wool jerked itself from her knitting-needles.

Mr. Graves, enveloped in the cloth, thought his wife must have suddenly taken leave of her senses, and began to protest. 'My dear, this is no time for pranks! You know I must get my sermon finished tonight —'

Mrs. Graves, believing that her husband's satisfaction with his new home had made him playful, cried, 'William, whatever are you doing?'

Mr. Graves removed the tablecloth and saw his wife angrily picking up reels of thread. She glanced up and noticed his dishevelled hair and the cloth in his hand.

'I didn't do it!' they said together, then they both span

round as a rusty cackling came from the doorway.

'Was – was that the wind?' Mrs. Graves quavered, for there was no human being in sight who could have made the sound.

'Perhaps it was a bird,' Mr. Graves suggested, but with little conviction in his voice, gazing round as though expecting to see the fluttering wings.

They were both far from easy as they put out the lamps and went to bed, but they would have been horrified if they had known what was to happen during the next few weeks. Locked doors were found open; open doors closed of their own accord with loud bangs. Clothes neatly hung up in wardrobes were found in crumpled heaps on the floor. Flower vases overturned and water dripped on carpets, scratches appeared on polished furniture, and pictures and ornaments detached themselves from walls and shelves. And all the time, everywhere, there were footsteps – sometimes loud, as if stamping in anger, sometimes soft, creeping in search of fresh mischief; and the footsteps were accompanied by a swishing noise like a heavy garment sweeping the floor.

The vicar and his wife grew more and more worried, but pretended to each other that all the incidents had a natural explanation. But the three children were terrified and at night called for their parents when their nightlights were blown out, their bedclothes pulled off, and their sleep interrupted by sinister cackles and chuckles.

The room that was most affected was the sitting-room, where the sound of stamping feet was almost incessant. It seemed as though a presence wished to dominate the room and assert its ownership.

Still the vicar held out against the disturbances, comforting his wife and children as best he could. At last the three servants went to him in a body and told him they were leaving, for they too had been subject to the attentions of the invisible intruder. Dishes had dropped from their hands, the contents of saucepans had inexplicably boiled over, and the maid declared that something kept blowing down her neck and made her shiver, even when she was sweating from the heat of the kitchen range.

'I'm sorry, vicar, but none of us will stay a moment longer,' said the housekeeper. 'A fortune wouldn't make me unpack my bags.' The others nodded in agreement, and they marched out, the maid taking care to clutch her coat tightly round her neck to prevent a last icy blast.

No new servants came forward, even though the vicar pleaded from the pulpit and advertised far and wide.

Although by driving the servants away the presence had won a victory it did not relax its efforts, and soon the thumps and bumps continued from dusk to dawn with hardly a pause. The children became ill from lack of sleep. They became pale and hollow-cheeked and refused to eat; and Mrs. Graves had to take them away, leaving the vicar alone in the house.

The presence seemed delighted at this turn of events. Now it could concentrate on one person, the real object of its malice, and the vicar was never free from persecution for one minute, day or night. At first he tried to ignore the weird happenings altogether, thinking that whatever caused them might give up when it realized it was getting nowhere, but there was no diminution of their intensity. One Saturday evening the thudding followed him to every room in which he tried to find some respite so that he could finish his sermon, and at last the vicar's nerves gave way. 'I can't stand it!' he cried, putting his hands to his aching head.

He ran to the door, only to reel back before the triumphant cackling that met him there, and made for the window instead, vaulting over the sill and falling into the soft earth of the garden below. Then he ran as fast as he could to the

The presence seemed delighted at this turn of events. Now it could concentrate on one person.

nearest farmhouse where lived John Morris, an honest Dartmoor farmer, one of his churchwardens.

There the vicar found a warm welcome and was able to tell his story openly, without reservation, knowing that he would not be laughed at or regarded with pitying eyes. When he had finished he felt as if he had emerged from a smothering cocoon of worry and fear.

The farmer was nodding wisely. ''Tis indeed a strange tale you've told me, sir, but I think I can explain why you have been persecuted and who your ghost is. It's all on account of the old vicar, you see.'

'The old vicar –' Mr. Graves repeated. 'But I don't –'

'You know he died some months ago,' the farmer went on, 'at the age of a hundred and one. He'd outlived all his family and had lived in the vicarage for nearly seventy years. He was a grumpy old fellow and the parish saw very little of him for many a year before he died. Used to spend most of his time in a dressing-gown drowsing over the fire in the sitting-room you've had altered, or he'd stand at the window looking over the moors. The thing is, he couldn't abide anything new, and I reckon you've upset him good and proper, adding bits here and there and making that poky little place into a house fit to live in and bring up a family.'

'But why should he be so spiteful?' Mr. Graves said.

'Maybe he doesn't think he's being spiteful – he's just showing how stubborn he can be, clinging on to what he considers is his own. But he's had his day – more than a hundred years of days – and 'tis only right and just that you should have yours. His ghost must be laid and laid for good. Now, vicar, this is what you must do. Go away after evensong tomorrow. Join your wife and the little ones, and leave our noisy old friend to me. I'll see to him. I know what'll cook his goose!'

So the vicar left the village the following evening and the

farmer set about fulfilling his promise. He spent a whole day travelling about the countryside until he had persuaded seven clergymen to meet together in the haunted vicarage. When they were all in the sitting-room, gazing about them with slightly nervous interest, the farmer produced seven tall candles and handed one to each of the clergymen. 'Now you know what you have to do, gentlemen,' he said.

The seven men nodded. Each in turn stood up, lighted his candle and spoke the words of the formula that was in common use for the laying of ghosts. If it was to be successful the ghost would be forced to blow out the candle and then disappear. But when six of the seven candles were still stubbornly burning at the end of the spell the clergymen and the farmer looked at each other in dismay. It was not going to work!

The farmer scratched his head thoughtfully. 'Reckon I know what's gone wrong,' he said after a long pause. 'The old parson knew you all, and he's defying you. He's playing a trick, forcing himself not to blow out your candle. No doubt he's chuckling away, telling himself that you couldn't get the better of him while he was alive, and now he's not going to allow you to lay his ghost. He was always cunning as well as stubborn!'

A quiet voice suddenly spoke. 'But he doesn't know *me*.' It was the seventh clergyman, a young man fresh from Oxford and a stranger to the district. 'It's my turn now,' he went on. 'Let us see what I can accomplish. It seems to be our last chance.' He lifted his candle high and began the words of the formula. The candle flame began to waver. By the time he had finished the light had dimmed to a faint flicker, and on the last word it went out altogether with a protesting splutter.

'He's laid!' the farmer cried excitedly, 'and now we must make sure that he stays laid! And I know the very thing that will do the trick!' He hurried from the room and returned a few minutes later bearing a large beer barrel on his strong shoulders. 'It was in the cellar,' he explained. 'The old fellow was fond of a mug of ale. Now, sir, will you do the necessary?'

The young clergyman relit his candle and again spoke the words of exorcism. Immediately the candle went out and into the barrel went the ghost. As quick as a flash the farmer pushed the bung into the hole. . . .

The eight men looked at the barrel and then at each other. The young clergyman gave expression to the thought that was in all their minds. 'What do we do with it now?'

'It certainly is a problem,' one of the others said. 'We must think of a place to put it so that it is safe from any curious intruder who might by chance open it and set its occupant free.'

'It had better stay in this house,' the farmer said, 'for I'm sure Mr. Graves won't ever be tempted to let the old man out – he's had enough of him! But where's the safest place, I wonder?'

After much discussion they decided what to do. The barrel was dragged to a corner of the room, and the clergymen guarded it while the farmer went to fetch the stonemason. When the man had finished his work the barrel was securely hidden behind a barrier of stones and mortar, and the corner of the room had been completely cut off.

The mason surveyed the results of his work and looked dubious. 'Seems queer, don't you think, gentlemen, one corner being sealed off like that? Sends the room all out of shape.'

There was a murmur of agreement from the clergymen.

'How would it be,' the mason went on, 'if I were to wall up the other three corners?'

'A fine idea!' the farmer declared. 'Not only would it even things off, but only we here would know which corner is concealing the barrel. I promise that I will never tell.'

'Nor I,' the others chorused.

'I'll start then, gentlemen,' the mason said and began to mix his mortar while the clergymen and the farmer went their several ways, well pleased with their night's work.

When Mr. Graves and his family returned to the vicarage the once elegant sitting-room was smaller than it had been, and was a very inconvenient shape, but the vicar thought it was a small price to pay for the peace that was to reign in the household for many years to come.

Ghost in the Schoolroom

JOHN DANIEL WAS NOT POPULAR with the other boys in the village of Beaminster in Dorset. There was something very odd and disturbing about him. Perhaps it was due to his appearance, his pale, sullen face under a shock of red hair, the icy stare from his blue eyes, his small, secretive mouth, and his heavy, dragging limbs. Perhaps it was his manner, abrupt and unfriendly. He went his own way and nobody knew or cared what he felt.

John Daniel was fourteen years old in the year 1728, when one day in May, a day of heavy purple clouds and frequent storms, he left the village school, which was held in a gallery of the parish church. At the end of the afternoon he made his solitary way to the cottage in which he lived with his widowed mother on the outskirts of the village. He was never seen alive again. The next day his body, sodden and muddy, was found in a field a few hundred metres from where he lived, by a farm labourer out with his dog.

June that year was hot and dry. The schoolroom in the gallery was airless, and both boys and master gasped with the heat. All were relieved one morning when the church clock struck twelve and morning school was over. The master, sweating in thick, dark clothes, left for his midday meal, and most of the boys went home too, walking slowly, unbuttoning their coats and loosening their collars. Only twelve boys stayed behind to eat their dinners in a shady spot in the churchyard, either because they lived in the next village or because both parents were working in the fields. They untied their large handkerchiefs and munched bread and cheese, boiled bacon or meat pasties.

The sun blazed down. It was too hot to play games, and after their meal they decided that they would spend the rest of the dinner hour practising their writing, which had received severe criticism from the master during the morning, with a threat of punishment if there was no improvement. Four of the boys volunteered to fetch quill pens, inkstands and paper from the schoolroom, and got up from the grass and went into the church.

One of the four closed the heavy oak door behind them and they moved towards the steps leading to the gallery. Suddenly they all stopped, as though caught at an invisible barrier. The leader turned his head sharply, looking questioningly at the others. A strange booming sound had filled the church, an eerie, echoing noise like a great brass gong being beaten by a giant hand. The clanging swelled, then gradually faded away to a last trembling whisper.

'What was that?' one of the boys asked, his voice cracking in an attempt to sound unafraid.

'There is no bell here that would make a sound like that,' whispered another.

Tom Mellish, the leader, shook his head impatiently. 'A trick,' he declared. 'Somebody is playing a trick on us.' He began to walk confidently forward.

Then footsteps started in the gallery above them, heavy dragging sounds as though whoever was making them was pulling himself along with difficulty. Backwards and forwards they went, several paces, a pause, then more slow thuds.

With one accord the four boys turned and flew to the door. Tom Mellish pulled it open and they staggered out from the gloom into strong sunlight.

They stood for a moment, wiping the sweat from their faces, neither speaking nor looking at each other. Slowly they returned to the other boys lying sprawled under the elm tree.

'Where are the pens?' called James Goodwin as he saw them approach empty-handed.

The ordinariness of the remark and the sight of their comrades' familiar faces broke the spell. Tom Mellish settled himself down on the grass and said hesitantly, 'We didn't get them. There was somebody in the schoolroom. . . .'

'But there couldn't have been,' James Goodwin objected. 'It was empty when we left and we would have seen anybody going into the church.'

'There *was* somebody up there,' Tom insisted. 'He was walking about, and in a most queer way.'

'And we heard a banging,' added Arthur Snell. 'Such a sound as I've never heard before, like a great bell being hit with a hammer.'

James gave a laugh. 'You must be joking. We would have heard it out here, and we heard no such thing. Did we?' he appealed to the others.

They shook their heads and murmured their agreement. Tom and his companions began to insist that they were not joking, and described again the sounds that had scared them. Voices were raised and tempers became high. The peace of the afternoon was stabbed with anger and accusations. At last James Goodwin stood up, brushing the grass from his clothes. 'We'd better settle it before the master comes back,' he said. 'I'm going to see for myself. Who's coming with me?'

His invitation was met with sudden coughs and downcast eyes.

'Then I'll go by myself.'

'Don't, James!' Tom Mellish said urgently.

'Rubbish!' James moved away from the suddenly silent group and swaggered towards the church.

Inside the church there was silence – no brassy banging, no dragging footsteps. James glanced round him as he approached the gallery steps. He saw a grey emptiness, broken only by shafts of sunlight streaming through the high windows. Slowly he began to climb the steps.

Behind him a muttering arose. He swung round. There was nothing. He began to pant, his eyes widened with fright. The muttering grew and he recognized the words of a prayer he heard every Sunday at the morning service. It died away and was replaced by the slow solemn notes of an organ. The voices of an invisible congregation rose in a psalm. The music filled his ears, his head seemed as though it would burst with it. Then all at once it had gone, and only one voice remained, the voice of the minister, drily intoning words from the Old Testament.

James gave a swift glance towards the lectern. There was no one there. Neither was there anyone in the pulpit. The choirstalls were empty, so were the pews. He was the only person in that great old grey church. But he *had* heard the voices and the music.

He felt his heart knocking in his chest. What should he do? Where should he go? Back through the church, peopled with unseen presences, or up to the schoolroom? He chose to go up, he did not know why. He took the last few steps at a run, feeling as though he were being pushed into the schoolroom.

His hand trembled as he opened the door. . . .

He gave a sudden wild howl, hurtled down the stairs, through the church, and fell white-faced and sobbing on the grass at the feet of his friends.

'I seen it,' he babbled. 'I seen it . . . I seen him too . . . sitting there . . . and his face all horrible. . . .'

'Seen what? Seen who?' The others crowded round him, by now frightened themselves.

'John Daniel . . . I seen him sitting there by the side of his coffin . . . in the schoolroom . . . he was sitting there all quiet . . . and he looked at me. . . .' His voice faltered.

'Yes, go on,' Tom Mellish whispered.

'His face was all white . . . an' his tongue hung out like he was making a funny face . . . but there was nothing funny about it . . . it give me the shivers. . . .'

'And what about the coffin?'

'It were open, the lid was propped up against the side. John Daniel had got out of it – he was dressed just as he used to be – with his brown jacket and moleskin breeches and his white shirt –'

A stern voice suddenly cut across his stammering. 'What is all this? What nonsense are you talking?'

The boys turned round, startled. They had not heard anyone coming across the grass. Their master stood over them, like a crow in his dark clothes. A beaky nose jutted out from beneath black brows and his mouth was a thin line. 'What is all this?'

The boys got up slowly and ranged themselves before him. They all looked at James Goodwin.

James found difficulty in speaking. 'Sir,' he began, 'I went up to the schoolroom and I seen the ghost of John Daniel –'

He went reeling as the master's hand caught him on the ear. 'Take that for your impudence, you young rogue,' the master hissed. 'Ghost indeed! You may try to frighten your stupid companions, but you should know better than to try such tricks on me. Now follow me, all of you. It is time for our afternoon lessons.'

Fear of their dreaded teacher overcame the boys' reluctance to venture into the church with its unknown terrors awaiting them, and they moved off after him, with sidelong glances at each other.

The church was as empty as before. The only sound they heard was the wind howling in the corners and beating

'Ghost indeed! You may try to frighten your stupid companions.
but you should know better than to try such tricks on me.'

against the walls. The boys looked at each other with renewed apprehension. Wind?

But there *was* no wind. Outside the air was placid and still, not a leaf nor a blade of grass was stirring. How could there be a wind?

'Sir,' began Tom Mellish.

The master seemed to hear neither him nor the dismal wailing around them. His tread up the steps was firm and reassuring. He flung open the schoolroom door.

John Daniel raised his head and looked straight at the master, a look that held no recognition or meaning, the look of a blind person.

All blood had drained away from the master's face, leaving it a mask of grey parchment. He licked his lips once, then was still, a lean black bird frozen in its tracks. The boys peered from behind his back and over his shoulder. One or two of them made small whimpering sounds. James Goodwin struggled to utter a few words. 'What did I tell you? That's John Daniel – and he's dead!'

John Daniel turned his face towards James Goodwin, glaring with sightless eyes. He stood up. By his side the open coffin gaped. Lifting his hands like a blind man he took a step forward.

That broke the spell. The boys cowered back. The master gave a sharp gasp. James Goodwin, seized by an almost overwhelming desire to run away, turned and saw, out of the corner of his eye, a heavy book lying on the end of a bench near the door. He took a step sideways, picked the book up, and flung it as hard as he could towards the figure of John Daniel.

The figure disappeared. Suddenly there was no John Daniel, no coffin, nothing in the room but desks and benches, the blackboard, the globe, everyday things connected with school . . . but all enveloped in a curious grey cloud, as though the church had been plunged into darkness.

Gradually the light returned. The master wiped beads of perspiration from his brow with a quivering hand. Dragging up his authoritative manner from the ragbag of his fear, he issued his orders. But his eyes, usually coldly compelling, did not meet those of his pupils. 'Sit down at your desks,' he ordered, 'and get out your copybooks. You will say nothing to anybody about what has happened. You will forget the whole thing completely.'

The master was optimistic. By evening the story was over the whole village. Men working in their gardens or drinking in the inn, women gossiping at their gates, children playing hopscotch in the lanes, all had heard of the appearance of the ghost of John Daniel. James Goodwin and the other boys were besieged for details and began to enjoy their parts as principal actors in the drama. The master was not approached for his version. Disliked in school by his pupils, he was avoided by the villagers because of his sharp tongue and uncertain temper. He stalked through the streets with straight back, his black cloak wrapped round him even though the evening was hot, looking neither to left nor to right.

In the next two days rumour had taken charge, and the real story was lost in an embroidery of fantastication. People were seeing John Daniel all over the place – with two heads or none, in his coffin and out. He was supposed to have foretold the deaths of babies and old people and the end of the world. No one dared go to bed without peering in every dark corner, and no one would walk alone through deserted parts of the village. His name was on everybody's lips. His presence hung over the village like a black storm cloud.

Why had John Daniel come back from the dead? What did he want? What message was he trying to convey? Those were the questions. And the answers were not long in coming. His death must have been foul play. He had appeared to accuse his murderer. But who *was* his murderer? Why should anybody want to murder a lonely eccentric boy? So the tongues prattled and the whispers were heard in corners.

Colonel Broadrep, the village squire, was one of the last to hear of the commotion among his tenants, but when he did he acted immediately. He called up the schoolmaster and the twelve boys to his study and questioned them closely.

The master declared that nothing had really happened, that they had been deceived by a trick of the light, that the whole thing was an overblown bubble. He blamed the boys for spreading false stories, and James Goodwin in particular for starting the scare. 'Don't forget,' he said, 'that this boy was on his own when he pretended to see John Daniel. He put the others into the mood to see something, and they did. That's all.'

'But did *you* see anything?' the colonel asked.

The schoolmaster hesitated, licking his thin lips. 'For a moment I thought –' he began. Then his brow clouded angrily. 'A trick of the light – that's all it was. How could it have been anything else? An intelligent man does not believe in ghosts.'

The Colonel allowed him to go. When he and the boys were alone he told them to sit down and made them feel at ease. They told their story clearly and simply, without exaggeration. They described John Daniel and the coffin, even to the kind of hinges it had. Colonel Broadrep was impressed, especially so when it turned out that Sam Cree, who had given a vivid description of John Daniel's red hair and strange blue eyes, had not even known or seen him when he was alive. Sam had only been at the school a few days, being an orphan who had just come to live with his aunt and uncle in the village. Sam's evidence made it clear to the colonel that the matter would have to be formally investigated.

'Before you go,' he said to the boys, 'is there any little detail about the – the apparition that you have forgotten to tell me? Think hard, it may be important.'

The boys screwed up their faces. Then Arthur Snell said, 'The only thing I can think of, sir, is that he had a sort of white cloth round one of his hands.'

Tom Mellish nodded. 'Yes, I remember that too, like a bandage it was, sir.'

Further questioning did not produce any new information, and the boys were dismissed. When they had gone, Colonel Broadrep went to see the woman who had prepared John Daniel's corpse for burial. He asked her to describe anything strange she had noticed.

'The only thing I remember,' she said, 'is that he had a bandage on one hand. I took it off before he was put in his coffin, poor lad. I think he had hurt his hand a few days before he died.'

Colonel Broadrep thanked the woman for her help and returned home. There is no doubt, he thought, that the boys did see some sort of apparition, and that it was John Daniel they believed they saw. The evidence was too direct, too unassailable. But why did the schoolmaster pretend that he had seen nothing? He must have had a reason for trying to make light of the whole episode. I think I'd better have another meeting with that gentleman, the colonel decided.

But the meeting never took place. The colonel's messenger returned from the schoolmaster's lodgings with the news that he was no longer there. He had left the village in great haste, bag in hand, black cloak flapping round him – never to be seen or heard of in Beaminster again.

Nor was the ghost of John Daniel ever seen again. 'He's done his work and scared off his murderer,' was the opinion of the village people, 'and his spirit is at rest.'

Ghost of the Coach-road

ONE AUTUMN EVENING, towards the end of the 18th century, Peter Jackson clambered up to the box-seat of the stagecoach as it sat in the coachyard of the *Black Swan* at Pickering in Yorkshire. He had business in Scotland, but he was travelling only as far as York where he intended to spend the night before going on the next day.

He settled himself next to the coachman, wrapping a rug round his legs for the night was chilly. Ben Priestley, the coachman, then made preparations to start, turning up the collar of his voluminous coat before arranging the sets of reins in his hands.

'Tha'll be as thankful as I am 'tis a fine night,' he remarked to his passenger, and Peter Jackson smiled.

'Yes, indeed,' he replied. 'I have a long journey ahead of me, and the finer the weather the better it will suit me.'

'There's no chance of rain,' said Ben, ''nobbut a little wind and that'll not harm thee.'

The ostler and stable lads had seen to it that all was ready for departure, and Ben called out in a stentorian voice, 'Sit fast, ladies and gentlemen!'

He took up his reins and slowly the coach began to clatter over the cobbles of the inn yard. As it travelled along at a steady pace Peter Jackson settled down to enjoy the journey. The bright moonlight brought a gentle softness to the countryside and lit up the road like a silver ribbon. Thank goodness, he thought, the coachman is not inclined to chatter. Ben drove the horses with perfect control, lost in his own thoughts.

They passed through Malton and continued along the road to York. Then suddenly, without any warning, the horses seemed to shy and swerve. Ben Priestley immediately pulled on the reins and the coach stopped with such abruptness that it almost overturned. Peter Jackson and the other outsiders were nearly thrown into the road.

Peter Jackson turned to Ben to ask him what had happened and was startled to see his expression. His face was white in the moonlight, his eyes staring and his mouth set. He looked almost hypnotized, as a rabbit is by a stoat. The situation only lasted a few seconds because the silence was broken by panicky shouts from the other passengers. 'What's amiss?' 'Is it an accident?' ''Tis a hold-up – help, help!' The passengers inside, who had been dozing, leaned out of the windows and added their questions and cries.

The coachman handed the reins to Peter Jackson and jumped down from the box. He walked round the coach and examined the springs and the bodywork. In a business-like fashion he announced to all the passengers, 'Sorry, ladies and gentlemen, but I'm not 'appy about the springs. We'll 'ave to turn back and get Herbert Grier, the blacksmith at Malton, to try to fix 'em.'

There were groans and mutterings from the passengers but Ben ignored them. He hauled himself up on to the box but before he could turn the coach Peter Jackson, who had felt vaguely troubled by the incident, remarked, 'That young woman was very fortunate! Another few yards and you would have run her down.'

Ben Priestley turned to him swiftly. 'What young woman?' he asked, an odd quiver in his voice.

'The one in the road, of course,' Peter Jackson answered. 'What became of her? She'd disappeared by the time you'd finished your inspection.'

Ben's furrowed brow showed his concern. '*You* saw her then?'

'Surely everyone saw her!' Peter Jackson exclaimed, with a touch of irritation.

'No,' said one of the passengers, 'I saw nobody.'

'Nor I,' said another. One by one the passengers denied having seen a soul. Peter Jackson began to think he had had a hallucination until a young lady, the only woman travelling outside, declared, 'There most certainly was a young woman there. I saw her too. It looked as though she were signalling the coachman to stop.'

Her remark seemed to galvanize Ben Priestley into action, for with an air of finality he said, 'The lady is right. There was someone in the road – the spirit of a young woman – and it was me she wanted. That's all I can tell you, so sit fast and we'll get back to Malton to find the blacksmith.'

His face set grimly, he turned the coach round.

When the coach pulled up in the yard of the *Black Horse* at Malton a crowd of locals appeared, eager to know what had caused its return so soon after passing through the town. Herbert Grier, the blacksmith, was one of the group. The situation was soon explained and the passengers went into the bar to wait in front of the roaring fire.

Peter Jackson noticed Ben Priestley and the blacksmith going towards the harness-room, their heads together in conversation, and then he realized that he could not hear any sounds from the yard suggesting that the blacksmith was at work. Deciding to find out what was happening, he was about to leave the inn when Ben Priestley appeared outside the porch. Herbert Grier, out of sight behind him, spoke. 'Now don't tha worry. I'll have a few chaps here inside five minutes, all of 'em willing enough to put up a fight if needs be. They'll not turn down the chance of a highwayman reward, dead or alive.'

'Thanks, Herbert, I'll go and tell the passengers.'

Peter Jackson slipped back into the bar just ahead of Ben, who, as soon as he came in, made his announcement. 'It's not safe enough, ladies and gentlemen. The springs might go any moment and the blacksmith don't reckon he can do much to 'em tonight. I'll take her into York and get new springs tomorrow.'

'Can we not take a risk and come with you?' asked one of the passengers.

'I don't advise it,' Ben told him firmly. 'You'd best stay here and go in the Malton coach in the morning. I'll have to go right slow, and if any of you have anything of worth with you, you'd be better off waiting,' he added ominously.

'Sounds as if you're expecting a visit from the Road Inspectors,' said Peter Jackson, using the well-known term for highwaymen.

Ben Priestley looked at him gravely. 'I can't say for sure, sir, but there's odd things going on tonight. What they mean I can't say, but they don't mean anything good, that I will say.'

All the passengers agreed that it would be better to stay in Malton, except a young and well-dressed man who stepped forward from his place at the bar. 'What the others do is no concern of mine,' he said, 'but I intend to accompany you, however slowly you may crawl, and whatever may be in store. I mean to be in York tonight,' and he walked arrogantly out of the room to cut short any further argument.

'Do you now, me hearty?' Ben Priestley muttered, and added to the company, 'If tha wants to see summat as'll give you a laugh, gentlemen, come outside.' He went into the yard and, their curiosity aroused, Peter Jackson and one or two others followed him.

'So tha intends to be in York this night, eh?' he said to the arrogant young stranger.

'I do, my good man,' was the reply, 'so will you ask the guard to set the steps?'

'Well now,' said Ben Priestley, 'I'm sure it'll be safer for you to ride inside. The guard will surely permit that. Besides, these new passengers will help you should we meet up with any trouble.'

New passengers, thought Peter Jackson, that's strange! He looked at the coach and saw that there were indeed some men inside he had not seen before. The young man, with a flash of irritation, ignored the open door. 'I shall ride outside. Out of my way and let me climb aboard.'

Ben Priestley barred his way. 'If tha travel with this coach you'll ride *inside*, sir.'

The man made no move to enter the coach, and Ben slammed the door and mounted the box. 'Let 'em go,' he shouted to the stable lad, and with a low rumbling the coach moved out of the yard. The would-be passenger stared after it, livid with rage.

Shortly afterwards, Peter Jackson and two of the men left behind were sitting in the bar talking over the night's events. The landlord kept them well supplied with ale and the atmosphere was so cosy that none of them felt like going to bed.

'I was complimenting myself on my good fortune in having such a speedy journey,' Peter Jackson said to the landlord, who had joined them, 'and then things began to go amiss. It all started when we nearly ran down that unfortunate girl. I wonder who she was.'

'I could tell thee,' the landlord said, a mysterious smile on his face, 'but you may not thank me if I do.'

'Why not?' asked a passenger.

'Because she wasn't a girl. She was a ghost. . . .'

'A ghost?' Peter Jackson queried, with a nervous laugh.

'Come now, landlord, you cannot expect us to believe in your country superstitions!'

'Superstitions or no, sir,' said the landlord, 'what you saw was a spirit come to warn Ben of danger ahead. I know it because he whispered to me when he got here, "Nance has been to warn me. There's trouble afoot." 'Tis not the first time Ben has had the warning and he knows better than to ignore it.'

'This is incredible,' said Peter Jackson. 'Ghosts! Warning spirits! Someone is having sport with Ben, if you ask me.'

''Tis the truth, I swear it. But I'll tell thee the story and then you can judge for yourselves.

'It all started many years ago. Tom Priestley, the grandfather of Ben, used to work on a farm in these parts. He was a good worker and popular with everyone in the village. The time came when Tom fell in love with the daughter of a neighbouring farmer. Nance was a lively girl and a good match for Tom. They began to make plans for their wedding day and there was great excitement.

'Shortly before the wedding a young and handsome stranger arrived in the village, and wealthy too, judging by the way he threw his money around. "He's a real gentleman," people said. Then he began making up to Nance and she was flattered by his attentions. The villagers hated to see the way he was slowly winning her away from Tom. "You should let the girl alone," they said, "for she is betrothed to another man." But the newcomer declared scornfully that all was fair in love and war and the best man was bound to win. He made fun of Tom's country ways and told Nance that she should wear beautiful clothes and live the life of a fine lady. "It's not Tom who can give you these things," he reminded her.

'Nance began to see herself in a new light. She started to put on airs and to treat her family and friends as though they

246

Shortly before the wedding a young and handsome stranger arrived in the village.

were beneath her. Tom pleaded with her to stop seeing the other man and marry him. It was no use. She told him she could no longer be happy as the wife of a poor man. "You'd best forget me," she told him, "and marry someone else."

'Tom was heartbroken, but even so his first concern was Nance's happiness. "Happen you won't have me, Nance," he said, "and it's plain who you're going to wed. Will you promise me one thing – that you'll wait till I've found out more about him?"

'Nance agreed, but as soon as she heard that Tom had left the village to make his enquiries she married the stranger and went away with him, telling nobody where they were going.

'When Tom returned home and learned what had happened he changed completely from the bright and happy lad of former days. He mooned about the place, speaking to nobody. His master told him as kindly as possible that he must buck his ideas up, but the village was too full of memories for Tom and he decided that he would break altogether with farming. He had always been interested in driving and he felt that the life of a coachman would help him to forget his sorrow.

'Eventually he got work as a coachman driving between York and Hull, and everything went well for about a year. Then one summer night he noticed a young woman with a baby in her lap sitting by the side of the road. Just as the coach was about to pass her she got up, raised her hand and shouted for him to stop. Tom brought the horses to a sudden jolting halt, and was about to shout at her for getting in the way of the vehicle when he saw who it was. "Nance!" he shouted. Telling the guard to hold the leaders he was off the box in a flash, just in time to save the poor dishevelled Nance from falling senseless to the ground.

'Tom held her in his arms. "Nance, my poor Nance! Whatever is wrong?" She opened her eyes and smiled faintly.

"You're good, Tom, too good for me. I betrayed you once, and now I want to ask your forgiveness before I die." She closed her eyes again. Tom, choking with emotion, stroked her hair. "You'll not die, lass. Be brave and we'll get help."

'He carried her to the coach. There were only two ladies inside and they made no fuss when Tom asked if they would permit Nance to ride with them as far as York. He saw that Nance and the baby were comfortably settled, closed the door, jumped up on the box and set off hell-bent for York.

'When they got there Tom left her with the landlady of the *York Tavern*. Nance stayed there for some weeks, gradually growing weaker. But she was able, bit by bit, to tell the story of what had happened to her since the day she had fled from the village with her new husband. He turned out to be the ne'er-do-well son of a good family who had squandered his inheritance. He had resorted to stealing and in the end had become a highwayman. Worst of all, Nance had discovered that he was already married.

'When her baby arrived Nance decided that she could stay no longer with her rascally husband. She ran away. She worked when she could and begged when there was no work. She did not dare return to the village, but when she found that Tom was driving a coach that travelled along the York road she made up her mind to wait there until he came.

'The last time Tom saw her she could not talk above a whisper. "I've something to ask you, Tom," she said to him.

"I'll do anything for thee, lass," he answered, his heart heavy to see her so low.

"When I'm dead, look after my baby."

"That I will," he assured her, "just as if he were my own boy."

"Thank you, Tom. Now will you kiss me before you go because we'll not see each other this side of death."

'He kissed her gently. "If my spirit can return," Nance

249

went on, "I promise to warn you and your children and your children's children of any danger that threatens them. That I promise, Tom. Goodbye. . . ." And with those words she died.'

There was silence in the bar when the landlord had finished. Then Peter Jackson spoke. "'And your children's children" – that means Ben Priestley, and it was Nance he saw tonight!'

'Aye,' said the landlord, 'it was Nance coming to warn him, just as she has come before, and mark this, she's never been wrong. Do you blame him for turning back?'

'No,' said Peter Jackson. 'But I wonder what she was warning him against. I thought it strange that Ben refused to carry the young passenger outside – was his return connected with him in some way?'

The landlord chuckled. 'You are not far wrong – it was very much connected with him. Do you know where that young chap is now? He's lying in a loose-box with a very sore head and his leg chained to the wall. That's where he'll stay too, till the morning.'

'Why? What has he done?'

'Nothing! It's what he meant to do. Ben was a bit suspicious of our young friend when he boarded the coach at Pickering; then, as soon as Nance pointed him out he knew that something was afoot. He told me that if the fellow refused to travel inside with the armed men he would not take him, but like as not he'd contrive to follow the coach on horseback. That's exactly what happened. After the coach had gone I found him in the stables about to take a horse.'

The landlord smiled. 'My lads soon fixed him. He'll have plenty of time to cool down where he is and repent his sins!'

'But surely he didn't intend to rob the coach by himself?'

'Oh, no, sir. His task was to give the signal to his rascally cronies who were waiting to waylay the coach. He would have had his pistol at Ben's head as soon as his friends came on the scene. But they reckoned without our Nance!'

The following morning the travellers continued their journey and arrived at York without further mishap. In the cool light of day the events of the previous night seemed improbable. The landlord had told a good story, but as for warning ghosts, and the rigmarole about the young highwayman and his signals – why, they were only for the easily fooled. The travellers chatted among themselves in this strain and agreed that they had been completely taken in.

As their coach pulled up in the coachyard at York the first sight to meet their eyes was Ben Priestley standing with a group of men which included Herbert Grier, the Malton blacksmith. As Peter Jackson climbed down from his seat he called out, 'Good day to you, sir. I can see you've had a good ride. You missed a merry party last night, didn't he, lads?'

'Aye,' cried the others, 'that he did!'

'What happened?' Peter Jackson asked.

'Near Barton Corner we were stopped. Three of 'em, there was, with masks covering their ugly faces. We were ready for 'em, though, and we got the three. Herbert and his friends here, who drove off with me last night, forced them into the coach and we delivered the lot to the authorities at York. We've just shared out the reward!'

'Excellent,' Peter Jackson smiled. 'So Nance was right!'

Ben Priestley gave him a searching look, 'So you know. . . .? Aye, she's never wrong, is Nance!'

Invitation to a Ghost

IVAN AND ALEXEI had grown up together in the same village in Russia. They had played together as small children, gone to school together, and when they became young men they always went together to the *besyedas*, the evening gatherings where young people met to talk and sing and dance.

The two friends were also good-natured rivals. Sometimes Ivan would be the first to do a thing; at other times Alexei would score over his friend, but in the long run they were evenly matched in their accomplishments.

One day Ivan and Alexei were talking about their future, and the subject of marriage was naturally mentioned. They knew that they would not be able to see as much of each other when each of them had a wife to keep, but they made a solemn pact that whichever married first would invite the other to the wedding. Then followed more friendly rivalry. Who would be the bridegroom and who would be the wedding guest?

'If I marry first,' said Ivan, 'I'll invite you to the wedding whether you're alive or dead!'

'That goes for me too,' said Alexei solemnly.

Some months passed, during which the young men worked and played together, and then Alexei was suddenly stricken by a mysterious disease, and died after several weeks of illness. Ivan was very sad at losing his friend, and for a time felt lost and lonely. He recovered his high spirits, however, when he fell in love with one of the village girls, and when she agreed to marry him he was overjoyed.

On the wedding day Ivan and his family set off in a horse-drawn carriage to fetch his bride-to-be. On the way they laughed and sang, but as the procession neared the graveyard where Alexei was buried Ivan fell silent, suddenly remembering the pact he had made with his friend all those months before.

'Stop the horses!' he cried suddenly. 'I must go to Alexei's grave!'

The driver pulled on the reins and the carriage stopped. Ivan leaped to the ground. 'What are you going to do?' his father asked.

'I'm going to invite Alexei to the wedding,' Ivan called, making his way to the graveyard. 'He was my best friend, and I want him to take part in the rejoicing.'

'But he's dead!' Ivan's mother wailed. 'How can he be a wedding guest?'

'We made a pact, and I'm going to keep it.' Ivan refused to listen to his family's protests. 'I shan't be long,' they heard him say before he disappeared into the darkness of the graveyard. The tombstones soon hid him from view.

Ivan stood before Alexei's grave. 'Dear friend,' he said, 'I hope you can hear me because I've brought you an invitation to my wedding. I haven't forgotten my promise, you see.'

A bitter wind blew across the desolate graveyard. Alexei's grave slowly opened and from the black cavity arose the pale, wasted figure of the dead man. 'Thank you, friend, for remembering our pact,' it said in a low, toneless voice. 'I shall be glad to come to your wedding, but first let us drink together to celebrate the happy occasion. Step down with me into my abode.'

Ivan hesitated, reluctant to admit to himself that he was frightened. 'I would come with you, Alexei, but the carriage is waiting for me on the road outside the graveyard. I told my parents to stay until I had summoned you.'

'Come, Ivan,' Alexei pleaded. 'It need not take us long to drink a glass in memory of the happy times we used to have. The carriage can surely wait a minute or two.'

Ivan decided that he could not disappoint the ghost of his friend. He squared his shoulders and jumped into the open grave. The dead man poured out a cup of wine and handed it to Ivan. He raised it ceremoniously and drank, not realizing that, being in the domain of the dead, he was also in the time of the dead, and as he drank, time went by. . . .

'Another cup of wine,' said the ghost of Alexei. Ivan began to protest, but the ghost took his cup, filled it and pressed it back in his hand, and Ivan was forced to drink again. As he drank, time went by. . . .

'Now I must join my family,' said Ivan, eager to be out of the dark cavern. But the ghost of Alexei restrained him.

'A third cup, I beg of you, and then go to your marriage. I shall not come with you – I do not think the other guests would welcome me. Drink this last cup in memory of our friendship, before we say farewell.' The ghost poured wine into Ivan's cup, and as he drank, time went by. . . .

'Farewell, my friend!' The words came faintly as the ghost sank back into the grave and the lid of the coffin closed after him. Then there was silence.

With the wine singing in his head Ivan clambered out of the grave and looked about him. To his amazement the landscape seemed to have changed in the few minutes he had been drinking with his friend. The grave itself had disappeared under a tangle of weeds and overgrown bushes. The graveyard had changed into a stretch of wasteland. There was no sign of a road, and where the carriage had been waiting for him patches of tall nettles grew.

Ivan stared at the unfamiliar scene, panic gradually rising

in him. Then he began to run back to the village he had set out from earlier in such high spirits. Surely he would find everything normal there! Surely he would find an explanation of this strange happening!

But more surprises awaited him in the village. It was nothing like the place in which he had been born and had grown up. The houses were built in a different style, the roads went in different directions. All the people were strangers. Instead of recognizing every single person, he could not see a single face he knew.

Only the church seemed familiar, though he could not remember it being so broken-down; it was almost a ruin. He could not trust himself to speak to any of the strange people walking about the streets. He would not have known what to say to them. But perhaps the priest could help him, and tell him what had happened to the world he had known. Father Vishnoff was old, and wise, and kind. He would make everything come right. . . .

But it was not Father Vishnoff who opened the door of the church to Ivan's frantic knocking. It was a younger man, with dark hair and a brisk, businesslike manner. 'What can I do for you, young man?' he said, looking at the wild-eyed Ivan curiously.

Ivan's story came out jerkily. The priest listened, his expression unchanging. 'What has happened?' Ivan finished, spreading out his hands imploringly. 'You must help me – I'm so confused!'

The priest frowned and shook his head, thinking that this agitated young man was out of his mind. He uttered a few soothing words and prepared to step back into the church, closing the door behind him. But Ivan followed. He clutched the priest's arm, crying, 'Please help me! Why has everything changed? Where am I? What has happened?'

The priest looked searchingly at him, then came to a

decision. 'Tell me your story again,' he commanded, and led Ivan to a seat in the church.

When Ivan came to the end of the second telling the priest looked very thoughtful. Then he grunted, 'Come with me.' He took Ivan into a room full of dusty, leather-covered books, and pulled one of them down from a shelf. 'These are the church records going back for many, many years,' he said. 'Sit down, and we will go through them.'

For hours they read through books and documents, going backwards in time, searching for any mention of Ivan and Alexei and the village people that Ivan had spoken about. They grew tired and red-eyed. The room grew dim. At last the priest gasped and pointed a shaking finger at a yellowing page.

'Read!' he ordered.

Ivan focussed his blurred gaze on the faded writing. Slowly, unbelievingly, he read the story of a bridegroom who had gone into the graveyard on his wedding day, had disappeared and had never been seen or heard of since. His family had waited for him to return, then had hunted for him high and low. When they had been unable to find any trace of him they decided that he had been carried off by demons. The waiting bride-to-be had collapsed with shock. She had been ill for a long time afterwards, then had recovered and eventually married another man. . . .

Ivan turned an incredulous face to the priest. 'But how can that be?' he asked. 'Here I am now – ready to go with my family and be married at once.'

The priest looked at him sadly. 'The date, my son, did you not notice the date? The account you have just read was written three hundred years ago. You drank with the ghost of your friend. You are now a ghost yourself. . . .'